PRAISE FOR GERALD EVERETT JONES

For *Preacher Finds a Corpse: An Evan Wycliff Mystery*

This is literature masquerading as a mystery. Carefully yet powerfully, Gerald Jones creates a small, stunning world in a tiny midwestern town, infusing each character with not just life but wit, charm and occasionally menace. This is the kind of writing one expects from John Irving or Jane Smiley.

— MARVIN J. WOLF, AUTHOR OF THE RABBI BEN
MYSTERIES, INCLUDING *A SCRIBE DIES IN BROOKLYN*

For *Bonfire of the Vanderbilts*

Mysteries hidden in plain sight in a grand painting. A fascinating adventure in the world of art and artists. Amateurs of the works of Robertson Davies will love it.

— CATHERINE DELORS, AUTHOR OF *MISTRESS OF
THE REVOLUTION* AND *FOR THE KING*

For *Choke Hold: An Eli Wolff Thriller*

A top recommendation for those who like police and legal procedural mysteries tempered by a healthy dose of social inspection and a light dash of wry humor throughout.

— D. DONOVAN, SENIOR REVIEWER, *MIDWEST
BOOK REVIEW*

CLIFFORD'S SPIRAL

A NOVEL

GERALD EVERETT JONES

LaPuerta
Books and Media
www.lapuerta.tv

LaPuerta Books and Media www.lapuerta.tv Email: bookstore@lapuerta.tv

Trade paperback ISBN: 978-1-7332684-0-0

Kindle ASIN: B07TQ8HQNM

EPUB ISBN: 978-1-7332684-2-4

Library of Congress Control Number: 2019909129

Cover and interior design by La Puerta Productions

LaPuerta is an imprint of La Puerta Productions www.lapuerta.tv

Cover photo by konstantynov © 123RF.com

Cover and interior design by La Puerta Productions

Editors: Roberta Edgar, John Rachel

Author photo by Gabriella Muttone Photography, Hollywood

Quoted verse Exodus 20:12 (the Fifth Commandment), *Holy Bible,* King James Version [PD].

Quoted lyrics from *Out of the Ivory Palaces* by Henry Barraclough [PD 1915] based on Psalm 45:8.

For My Father

1

Clifford was sufficiently aware to know he was lying on his back. He felt woozy. Although there was light all around him, he couldn't see anything. He didn't know whether his eyes were open or closed. His visual field was pinkish-orange, with bright yellow at the center. No shapes or images. Just a happy glow.

He could feel a cold compress on the back of his neck. He was grateful for the sensation, but it was making him feel chilly all over.

He felt them lift him onto a stretcher. They must have covered him with a blanket because he felt warmer.

He guessed they were carrying him into an ambulance. It would be effortless to die now, to just slip away. But he was pretty sure he wasn't going to die. Not now. He was in good hands, capable hands. They would take care of him, whatever needed to be done. Perhaps this feeling of confidence was from something they'd injected into him? If so, it was good stuff.

"I've got Brady," he heard a man with a commanding voice say.

"Bee pee ninety-two over fifty-four," a woman said, as if in response.

Moments later, the guy repeated, "I've got Brady."

If Brady is on the phone, why don't they take the call?

Clifford couldn't remember anyone named Brady in their group at the restaurant. Last he knew, he was getting up from the table at his friend Gabe's eightieth birthday party. He'd had too much to drink and a lot to eat. He was a sucker for Italian food, and, the icing on the cake, Bea had insisted on paying for everyone, and not just the cake. Eleanor wasn't there. She was already off on one of her juggernauts.

"I've got Brady," the paramedic said again.

Had he taken this fellow Brady down in his fall? Clutched at the waiter and upended his tray? Maybe poor Brady was injured, with a broken arm or something, and required more urgent attention.

Okay, okay. By all means, take care of Brady! But who's got me?

"Mr. Klovis, can you hear me?"

Clifford opened his eyes. He was flat on his back in a bed with side rails. An IV bag was connected to his left forearm through a plastic tube, and an oxygen mask covered his nose and mouth. The oxygen was delicious.

He was wearing a hospital gown, the kind that fastened in the back. He could feel the cool clamminess of the bedsheets against his backside. He hoped no one would ask him to stand up. At his age, there were divots of cellulite on his ass.

He couldn't read the information on his wristband. Stenciled on his sheets was "Rush UMC" and the medical caduceus symbol. He felt privileged, as though his case were sufficiently urgent to deserve priority treatment, the acronym perhaps meaning *Urgent Medical Condition,* when he realized the linen service had simply used a proprietary identifying logo for Rush University Medical Center, a Chicago institution he knew quite well, but till now, only from the outside.

Towering over Clifford with his hairy hands on the bedrail on the right side was a burly man in mint-colored surgical scrubs. The obligatory stethoscope hung from his neck like a decoration of honor.

"I am Dr. Garabedian. Mr. Klovis, you've had a hemorrhagic episode in the left frontal lobe of your brain. A significant stroke. How do you feel? Are you feeling dizzy?"

Clifford didn't answer.

"If you can understand me," the doctor said, "blink twice."

Clifford just stared at him.

"I see," he said. "You fainted at the restaurant. When the paramedics arrived, you had symptoms of bradycardia, that's abnormally low heart rate, and low blood pressure. You're in the hospital now, and we've stabilized you with medication. Your faculties may improve over time. For now, on the chance you can hear me, you should know that your friends gave us contact information for next of kin. We understand your wife is traveling. We'll get word to her. We've notified your son Jeremy, who will be flying in from Los Angeles to make decisions about your care — if by that time you can't express yourself. Your Medicare card was in your wallet, so Uncle Sam has your back. Any questions?"

Clifford saw no need to respond. He wondered how long his generous uncle would stand behind him.

The doctor walked away and was met by a colleague, presumably a nurse, a few paces away from the foot of the bed.

They spoke in low tones. Clifford thought he heard "cognitive workup" and "assisted living."

On the wall, Clifford noticed a poster with the headline "Let Us Know About Your Pain." There was a bubble chart with a scale from one to ten, designating each increased gradation of discomfort with a more anguished emoticon. Clifford thought this considerate but odd.

There is no negative scale! Zero pain must be the ideal. Where is the index for joy? If they shoot you up with morphine, how happy can you get? Maybe there's a law against surpassing minus ten?

As a marketing pro, he was well versed in the one-to-ten scale of the Net Promoter's Score: "How likely would you be to refer us to a friend?" As an insider, he knew the dirty secret behind these scores. The score tends to go up the more often you ask the question. So, the value of a corporate brand is more likely to increase if you continue to spend more on asking marketing questions than actually improving the quality of your product or your customer service. Where this hospital was concerned, the practice would be doubly problematic. Many of the people who have "unsuccessful" outcomes and would therefore be less likely to recommend, won't be able to vote. They're dead!

He was feeling drowsy when the often-retouched face of Gabe's wife Bea appeared beside his IV bag. She clutched the left rail. Maybe that's what those railings were for — to steady the visitors lest they be thrown by high seas or emotional turmoil.

She could barely get the words out.

Maybe they should give her *a cognitive workup.*

"Clifford, darling. You gave us all such a scare." She was sobbing. "Everything's going to be fine now."

The choppy sea must have been too much for her. She let go of the railing and hurried away.

Darling?

Too late, Clifford realized he should have said something to her. With that *darling,* maybe the two of them had a history, and he couldn't remember any of it, just now.

He told himself he *could* speak if he wanted to. But he saw no need.

2

After the episode, Clifford Klovis experienced brief moments of stark clarity. He had a collection of puzzle pieces, each of them in sharp focus, with vibrant colors and shapes. Those elements should, in combination with others, become complex forms and scenes, around which he might be able to impart some meaning. He was still, at some level, in possession of his faculties. More like beads than puzzle pieces, these snippets were the glittering jewels of his past. It was just, at this moment, he was having difficulty stringing them together. Did *this* come before *that?* The answers made a difference.

The Insiders have not spoken to me since I was hospitalized. The gap in communication affords some relief. Their intentions always seem beneficent and their manner of expression gentle, but the news they give me is distressing. Why should I even pay attention to them? Facing the truth can be uncomfortable, at best. Maybe they bring wisdom, but at what price? This situation feels like a punishment. Perhaps they will tell me what I did to deserve this, how to earn my way out. Am I supposed to wait for a message?

Meanwhile, Clifford would commit himself to his personal struggle for survival — with as much clarity as he could achieve. After all, with what else did he have to occupy his days? There was sunlight on his face in the mornings. There were three meals served by the clock, the keen anticipation of which came fully an hour before the appointed time. The ingredients were indifferent. The soup, no doubt, came from a can. The meat had been boiled to grayish-ness, the vegetables cooked to mush. There was always coffee, as if anyone would care for instant crystals dissolved in lukewarm water with cornstarch cream-substitute and, if he was lucky, a packet or two of real sugar instead of some nameless sweetener. But, even then, the taste of food was spectacular, a feast to be perpetually craved. It was definitely something to live for. He had dim memories of wine, but such delights were in a paradise perhaps not to be revisited. That other, invisible people labored mightily over steaming kettles to deliver the riches of the here and now to him, with no special instructions from him, made him profoundly thankful. He must try to get their names someday and send them — what? — an enormous basket of fresh fruit? Cash tips would be the thing, especially during the holidays, but how would he get it? He had no idea where his money was. But he was confident of its existence. Something or someone was paying for all this professional, institutional treatment.

They don't bother with people who can't pay. Not these days.

He was wearing a wristband on his left forearm. It showed his name, followed by "Willoway Manor," a number, and three two-letter alphabetic codes. He figured that was the name of this place, which would be neither a hospital nor a luxury hotel, and the number was the personal identifier of himself and his clinical file. The two-letter alpha codes must be medic-alert flags for conditions such as diabetes, high blood pressure, or drug allergies. He had no idea what his could mean. He just hoped none of those cryptographic messages meant "arrogant prick," "charity case," or "clueless idiot."

As with Rush Hospital, Willoway Manor was a place he knew about but had never been inside. He'd only seen it as a name on an architectural sign on a high security wall along Busse Highway in Elk Grove Village, out in the northwest suburbs of Chicago. Rush was closer to downtown. It must have been the nearest emergency room to the restaurant where they'd had Gabe's party. He didn't know much about Elk Grove Village, which was miles away from his home in Evanston. The town did have a literal elk grove, a public park where a few of those wild, horned animals still grazed. The park was a bubble of nature in the midst of the sprawling metropolis.

He still thought of himself as an Angelino, which he'd been ever since he and Tessa had moved the family from Cleveland decades ago. But in the last year, he and Eleanor had moved back to the Midwest to supervise her mother Lillian's hospice care. Clifford detested the weather — his blood had thinned in the perpetual Mediterranean climate of Southern California — but he didn't miss driving on the freeway, and he enjoyed taking the CTA "L" train whenever he felt like going into the city.

That's where else I've seen Willoway — on a brochure in a file folder Eleanor had. It was one of the places we'd considered for her mother — before her health went downhill fast. Eleanor must have told Jeremy about it. Yeah, it's not a hospital. But it's not exactly a resort, either. Lillian's insurance wouldn't have covered it. I doubt if Uncle Sam will be so generous. Did they do the math on my prognosis? Expected lifespan days ahead times reasonable and necessary daily maintenance fee is greater than, equal to, or less than maximum benefit cap?

MYRA WALKED IN. She was a vision.

I'm guessing her heritage is East Indian, perhaps Pakistani. I really can't tell the difference. Her skin is the color of mocha, and I swear she smells of lavender. Her uniform is immaculate and brilliantly white. She is tall and plus-sized, but well proportioned — my Wonder Woman.

An angel, my angel.

Her touch was a delight. As she bent over him, her breath was tinged with mint, which might have been merely the flavor of her toothpaste. Humans can be marvelous creatures, especially to other humans. He remembered sex could be more, far more, than simple copulation.

If he chose to speak to anyone, it would be to her. But he hadn't uttered more than a grunt since his admission. They'd given him all kinds of tests — including direct questions, pinpricks, and nefarious electronic scans — but he hadn't given them the satisfaction of answers. Physical observation, as well as the scans, let them know his reflexes were working. A technician could ask him a question, and a region of his brain would light up. But there was no way for them to assess the degree of his understanding. When asked to blink an eye or twitch a finger, which he could easily do at other times, he hadn't signaled his perception of any of their commands. Eventually, they concluded he couldn't.

It's not that I can't. I won't.

He *wanted* them to think he couldn't communicate. Doing so gave him a new sense of power, of control, in a place where, in all other respects, he was entirely under the control of others.

For example, even though he preferred strong, black tea to coffee, he refused to fill out the slip with his food choices for the day. He needed to make them think they were in control. Therein lay his freedom.

They know I'm not helpless. I can pull on my sweatpants in the morning. I can get up and find my way to the toilet. I can lift the fork to my mouth. I can stir the sugar into my coffee. They see me do these things, but if they ask me a question, if they poke or prod me, I don't — I won't — give them the satisfaction. For all those years, I avoided the sugar. First it was aspartame, then Eleanor got me onto stevia. But what am I trying to prevent now? Unsightly weight gain? A bad case of the sugar blues? What's good for me is whatever lights up my brain. So give me the caffeine and the refined carbs! They have all kinds of good drugs here, even morphine for people at death's door. But there could be a problem with my program of noncooperation — how will they know if I'm in pain? I guess at that point I should give it up, fill my lungs with air, and just scream.

In refusing to cooperate, Clifford had thus spared himself the burden and the stress of making decisions like food choices. In his opinion, this achievement was a milestone, a further step toward clarity. In the temperature-controlled, perpetually sanitized room of this efficient institution, he'd locked himself inside his own mind, where he was content to stay for however long he had left.

Yes, when necessary, he could get up, walk to the toilet, slip off his sweatpants, sit down, and do his business. (Standing up required better aim than he could manage.) No reason to signal those needs. They'd made the task harder for him by setting out diapers with his clothes. He was tempted to leave them off, but he knew it would invite confrontation. His noncooperation did not go thus far. They were just waiting for him to mess himself, and the thought distressed him. He could say, "I don't need those," but by breaking his silence, he'd be inviting all kinds of other discomforts.

Myra's touch today sent ripples of pleasure through his nervous system, and he dozed off. When he roused a few moments (hours?) later, she had left. Although she often talked to him despite his cluelessness, she hadn't said a word during this visit. What had she done? Had she dressed his private parts? Scrubbed the stink off his languid body? He admired her for doing what she'd come to do, whatever that was. Like those busy people in the kitchen, she did her job and took satisfaction in its usefulness, despite its inherent imperfection, its mundane lack of transcendent artistry. The cooks were not chefs, and she was no etheric angel, despite his wish to see her so. As one of his old mentors used to say, there is no need in this life for perfection, nor are there sufficient resources or time to achieve it. How much more so when Clifford suspected he might not have much time left.

He fell back to sleep.

HIS DREAMS WERE vivid and colorful. He was in a cafeteria. The steam tables were fully stocked with food. Except they were closing, and he wasn't permitted to have any.

I dream about food because they don't feed me enough or the right things or the things I want.

He was in the airport, having urged the cabbie to arrive in haste. He was bound for New York. There was a flight in five minutes, but he had to exchange his ticket. He raced from here to there and couldn't find the right counter.

New York, the place where reputations are made, where the rulers of the planet live. I fear I will never get there, and I probably won't.

He was back in Cleveland. He boarded the bus for downtown, not sure of the route but confident it would drop him close enough to work so he could walk the rest of the way. But the driver took off in the wrong direction and would not stop. Eventually, Clifford had to disembark at the end of the line and had no idea where he was.

Cleveland, a town where I went to work and made money. It's a world I can't begin to navigate now.

He was six and invited to a friend's birthday party. They played games, and he won every prize. It had not occurred to him to share, since he'd never won anything before. They must have chosen games that favored wits over luck. The boy's mother stared at him coldly as he took up his winnings to leave. He was not invited back.

I always tried to think of myself as a generous person. I tried to stay sensitive to what people around me were feeling, and, if they were upset, whether I'd done anything to cause it. But as I think about my current situation and as I anticipate how much more debilitated I may become, how much more I might need to depend on these people and their ministrations, I begin to think like a survivor. I get in touch with that part of my brain, which I know still works as it was designed, the semiconscious computer that obsesses only about my body's needs, from one breath to the next.

The house was a fixer, but it was perched on a sylvan hill in a sunlit glade that looked like the near side of paradise. He would mend the roof and staunch the water leakage. It would be a palace, but by that time, he would be forced to sell.

I've owned three houses, two of them fixers requiring major renova-

*tions and tender loving care. What do I have now for my investment
and effort? An extremely expensive rented room.*

He entered the familiar office space, which had been redecorated
since he'd been there last, several years ago. It was on the eleventh
floor of a gray building downtown. It was the same company
he'd known, with the same faces. He'd been gone for all those
years, but there was his desk in the same corner, and no one
seemed to know he'd been gone. He knew he'd been cheating
because he'd been collecting regular paychecks all during his
absence. Should he tell them, or just sit down and pretend to
work as if he'd never left?

*If I were to somehow recover miraculously, I wouldn't know what to
do, wouldn't even know where to begin. There isn't a way back to
where I came from.*

He boarded the Metro in Paris, not far from his old digs. He
took it to the north end of town, where there were narrow streets
with bistros and nightclubs and sumptuous marvels everywhere
you looked. He walked into a movie theater that ran only classic
films. He climbed up to the dusty mezzanine, and there on the
screen was a message just for him.

He wished he could remember what it said.

*Am I waiting for God to give me a message? Perhaps the Insiders
have an urgent message for me. Is there anywhere for me to go from
here? If so, is it even on this planet?*

～

HE WOKE to the smell of fresh flowers. Jasmine? Magnolias?
Who had bothered to send them? What a blessing, and such a
shame that he could not guess the name of the sender.

He had a visitor. Her name was Charlayne. He remembered they'd called her Cherry and made jokes about wanting to enjoy her as some after-dinner drink.

"I DON'T RESENT what you did to me," she said, almost too softly to be heard.

"What did I do to you?" was the obvious question, and he thought he'd said it out loud. He realized he'd just broken his first rule by responding. But then, he wasn't quite clear about the reality of her visitation. Was there a real woman — his old almost-girlfriend from way back — sitting there? No, she appeared to be in her mid-thirties, the same age she'd been when he'd known her almost fifty years ago. He relaxed when he decided not only was she a phantasm, but also his responses were only in his head. His vow of silence was unbroken.

Nevertheless, he was thrilled to have a visitor, doubly pleased because he could at last have an intelligent conversation with someone he recognized. It was all so unreal, and yet this apparition was a realistic fulfillment of his fondest wishes. Part of his remembering was, after all, to rewrite history, perhaps to remember it in terms more favorable to his opinion of himself.

"It was the Christmas season. In Cleveland," she said. "They drink like fish there, as you know. *We* did."

"I know," he replied, remembering. "We used to take customers to the strip bars on Lorain Avenue."

"That's where we were," she said, "at one of those supper clubs. You and me and our boss Ron and his pal Zig. And we'd all had a lot to drink. We hadn't even begun to think about dinner. So, three, four drinks in, Ron ordered Perfect Manhattans — a jigger of sweet vermouth, a jigger of dry, and a jigger of whiskey. He wanted them with a twist. Zig drank the same but with two anchovy olives. Sweet and sour. When Ron ordered, he called for a 'Perfect Man.' The wait staff in the place always knew what he meant, and he tipped them extra for knowing what he wanted and agreeing with a smile. That man had an ego the size of a Mack truck."

"Okay," Cliff said. "We must've had a good time."

"Oh, we did," she said. "Way too good."

"I don't understand. Did you enjoy yourself or not? Why are we having this conversation?"

Or, are we having a conversation at all? Is it against the rules for you to tell me?

"I was wearing pants with an elastic band and an angora sweater. Tight, so it emphasized my boobs. I knew I looked hot. That was the idea. As I say, it was Christmas, and everybody was in a party mood."

"As I remember," he said, "you did look hot. I wanted you. Yes, I admit, there was lust in my heart."

"So, we get a few drinks in, you were feeling no pain, and in front of those guys, you shoved your hand down the back of my pants."

"Wow," he said. "That took some nerve."

"You had no idea at the time. I bet you didn't even think they'd know. Stupid, yes. That's how drunk you were — *we* were. Ron and Zig, *they* were all eyes. But me, I have to tell you, I was thrilled. I'd been waiting for you to pay attention to me for months. You were so tight-assed, so worried about appearances, it took the alcohol to help you do what you — and I — had wanted you to do all along. Just without the company. Yeah, you could say it was crude. I was too smashed to be embarrassed. Like I say, I'd been waiting for you to do something for a long time."

"It sounds gross. Disgusting, even," he said.

"Like I say, it's what we'd both wanted. It just wasn't exactly what you'd call correct under the circumstances. I'd kept waiting for you to make the first move, and here you go and do it in that bar in front of *those* guys. Might as well be in Macy's window with the whole world watching! That was the stupid part. But we were both really getting high off being stupid at the time."

"And are you saying it was all okay?" he asked.

"I thought so. After dinner, I drove you in your car back to the parking lot at the office. I'd had less than you, but not a whole lot less. When we parked, we made out and you groped me for half an hour. Long enough, I hoped, for you to sober up. And I told you, nobody kissed me like that before. And I was serious. It's the kind of moment you wish would last forever, but it never does. And it should never have happened, and the next day it seemed so stupid."

"Are you trying to flatter me? It doesn't sound like I should have been proud of myself."

"Sure, but at the time I thought I loved you. I mean, as much as anybody can when they don't really know each other. Love is a relative kind of thing. It was a time in my life when having hots for longer than a day or two meant the same thing. Who was serious? But what chance for me was there? You were married and my guy had left me and I had a kid at home. You'd be a lunatic to take me on, even if your wife got hit by a truck, which, believe me, I prayed for more than once."

"But then, word got around."

"It did," she said. "I swear, not because of me."

"I'm listening," he said. "But, remember, I'm memory impaired. I get to deny. It's my show."

"I didn't snitch, but apparently Zig told his pal Mike, and Mike told anyone who would listen. 'You were all over her like some octopus!' Zig said, as if it was some kind of nature show. And somehow it got back to the office. And there was our senior manager, Millicent. Ugh. She'd just come off a divorce. For her, all men were poison. She claimed to take my side. If it was nowadays, she'd push me into filing a lawsuit. But all we could manage then was a prank payback."

"Payback? How could you buy into that?"

"How could I not?" she asked. "Once it had all come out, was I supposed to admit to the girls I wanted you to shove your hand down my pants?"

"I remember another office party. You were seated beside me. You kept trying to put your hand on my knee, then on my thigh. But you were embarrassed. You didn't want to do it, but it seemed like they encouraged you. The women at the table, and especially Millie, were egging you on. You seemed really reluctant, but you went ahead. Me, I was clueless, but you did it anyway. Somehow, I remembered it was *before* the hands-down-your-pants episode."

"No," she said. "It was right after. They made me do it. Payback, they said."

"Makes perfect sense," he said. "But that's not how I remember it."

As I remember it, I always thought she'd groped me first. Funny how confusing the order of incidents jumbles the notion of cause-and-effect. And my real or imagined guilt.

What I'd done, from the perspective of today's morality, wasn't just rude, it was probably a crime. From a legal standpoint, it might not matter whether I had her agreement or cooperation. If instead I'd shot her, it would be no defense that she'd asked for it.

I always thought Ron was a class-A jerk. He was the head of our division and my immediate supervisor. I didn't think he had earned or deserved the position, but I didn't have the guts to push him out of it. (I didn't know how. Maybe I wasn't capable of thinking on his level of betrayal or dirty tricks.) We'd go to lunch together almost every day — just the two of us, he gave me no option. We'd have drinks before and after, run up quite a tab, and I'd pay. He would tell me which customer's name to put on my expense report. There's another crime, even though it was a common executive perk in those days.

We first met Cherry at one of those restaurants. She was the hostess. Ron always memorized the names of wait staff and would soon talk himself into a regular table and whatever special treatment they could send his way. Cherry was pretty, poised, and personable. And since marketing was our game, Ron was a perpetual talent scout for "sales assistants."

So, when we needed to add a warm body for an assistant job, he hired her. Hostess for customer meetings? Pretty talking head for trade shows? But the morning she reported for work, she looked careworn and downright disheveled, as if she'd slept in her car. Ron pulled me aside and said, "Don't tell anybody we knew her —

before." From her look and his evasiveness, I assumed he'd taken full advantage of her the previous night as a condition of employment. But from then on, in the three years I was with the firm, neither of them gave me the slightest hint they ever had a thing going. Not suspecting an affair between those two made me resent him even more, as though he was cold enough to exact a price but not look back. So I asked her —

"Since we're being so honest — and maybe since this is all in my mind anyway — can I ask you a difficult question?"

"I'm all yours. Hey, better late than never."

"Okay, to get the job, did Ron make you put out for him?"

"He was the type, for sure. I could tell the day I met you guys, he was the hustler and you were his straight-arrow wingman. And I think, after he glanced at my lame resume, he'd intended to do me and do me good."

"You say it as if he didn't."

"After I'd been working for you guys a while, I heard stories. His thing was to pick up women in bars, not pros but underpaid ladder-climbing career girls, and end up getting a blowjob in the back seat of his Town Car. He was married, as you know, and Catholic. Somewhere he thought he'd read the fine print that oral sex isn't cheating."

"Whoa. He had his own ways of bending the rules, for sure."

"The night before I started work, he asked me to meet him for drinks. I was on my guard, but I didn't want to say no. I thought I could finesse it. Worst case, if he forced himself on me, I'd wriggle out of it and there'd be no new job. (I hadn't actually given notice to the restaurant, but he didn't know.) So we both had a couple of cocktails. I was feeling no pain, but I was far from drunk. One of the things you probably knew about him, he was a good talker. And an even better listener. I don't know, did he take courses in salesmanship or was he born a con man? He asked a lot of questions, and I started telling him the story of my life: A boyfriend who was totally hot but beat me when I was way too young and totally dumb, a husband who gave me a kid and then disappeared, a shoplifting conviction that didn't exactly put me on top of the pile as a job seeker — the whole disaster."

"Did he tell you anything about himself?"

"Not much. Not much at all. The guy should have gone into psychotherapy — you know, as a shrink who never lets you know what he's thinking."

"What happened? You were in no shape when you showed up the next morning."

"He took me home. To *my* home. I'd sent Robby to a friend's for a sleepover. Don't ask me why, maybe I was just suckered by Ron's sympathy ploy, but I invited him in." Then she added, "And, okay, maybe I'm thinking the guy isn't so bad. Luxury car, nice clothes. He's got money. So even if he doesn't leave his wife — I was smart enough to know that almost never happens — maybe he sets me up in a new apartment? Maybe he lays enough bonus money on me so I can send Robby to a better school? I wasn't going to get either of those things pushing fancy drinks and extra desserts at the restaurant."

"And he did have his way with you?"

"Nope. We curled up, and I literally cried on his shoulder. He took off his jacket and tie, and those were the only clothes on the floor when he picked them up to go home before the sun was up. As he left, he swore my secrets were safe with him, he'd be a good boss, and anytime I needed an ear I should go to his office and close the door. All we'd done was some serious cuddling, and he never laid a hand on me after that night."

"So you figured he was a good guy at heart? You still think so today?"

"I think he was a slick, silver-tongued devil who knew how to make a deal. And also how to keep his word."

"And what about me?"

"Like I said, straight-arrow wingman. Was Ron square with you?"

"Come to think of it, he was."

Clifford didn't see Cherry go. The window of his room looked out on the parking lot, and he couldn't help glancing out to follow a shiny, new Jaguar as it pulled into a space.

I always wanted one of those.

When he looked back at the guest chair, she was gone.

PERHAPS VISITATIONS from old girlfriends were part of a subconscious plan to achieve clarity. Life review. Shove your nose in what you did. Had Cherry really been here with him, staring at his reclining figure as the crotch slit in his pajamas gaped open? She was remarkably calm about it all. Perhaps it was just his version of Cherry, the Cherry he'd hoped for. He'd been visited by the Cherry he remembered, an eternally vibrant and voluptuous being, not the husk he supposed she'd become, not a senile throwaway like him. Her visit made him think of himself now as he'd been back then.

Do the people in heaven (or hell) look like they did the day they died? Surely God's favored ones are just as lucky as movie stars — whose images taken at their prime survive the generations.

If someone checked in with Cherry today, would she even remember Clifford?

Unless a child was at issue, what was the point? And where did he get off thinking about children all of a sudden? All they'd shared was sweat and saliva.

He was sure there was no question of a child. Had they been lovers, it would be a lot to forget. You'd think it would be indelible.

Was I all wrong about Ron, or am I just now giving him way more than the benefit of the doubt?

Cherry seemed to know it was Ron's pal Zig who spread the rumor about the groping incident. But the prank-as-revenge must have been Millie's idea. Had she also made a helpful call to Tessa? Told her about my nasty misdeeds?

Clifford had gotten the incidents reversed, the cause and effect all wrong. The groping had been at Christmas and the payback prank at New Year's, not the other way around. (He'd never thought of his groping Cherry as payback for anything she'd done to him.) But not long afterward, he now recalled another incident, which he'd assumed was unrelated, on Valentine's Day. As a joke gift, Tessa hired a stripper to call on him at the office and perform her routine. His wife must have warned the office group, because someone had also arranged for Arnie, the staff photographer, to capture Clifford's embarrassment. Everyone seemed to be in on it, and Arnie had instructions to send Tessa a set of prints. In her usual passive-aggressive manner, Tessa did not attend but must have been amused as she pulled the strings from home and imagined her husband's chagrin.

He'd been blindsided. Millie had called a meeting in the conference room. Eight other staff members took their seats. Clifford should have suspected it wasn't routine when she beckoned him to sit at the head of the table as if he were the guest of honor. He and Millie were on the same managerial level, and normally she would never have deferred to him. Ron and Zig weren't there. They were taking a long lunch, as usual.

Maybe their absence gave them deniability? If it ever came out, Ron would have to pretend to his boss that he knew nothing about the crime — or the punishment.

It wasn't a striptease but a bellydance. Even though the Arab community was growing fast in the area back then, the dancer was the wrong ethnicity. Possibly of Polish or some other Slavic ancestry, she was pallid white, and her stomach was more than ample in proportion to her plus-sized body. Her long hair was curly and artificially red. An excess of eyeshadow and kohl liner was intended to give her an exotic look, but as she perspired her face looked soot-smeared. She made a show of puckering her large lips, which were so thick that when she smiled you could only see the edges of her yellowed teeth.

Arnie's motor-drive Nikon kept up a constant *whir-click-whir-click* as he followed her belabored moves. Her dance moves were neither practiced nor sensuous, with a predictable emphasis on cushiony shapes her belly could achieve.

Millie, who was ample herself, seemed to think it was all hysterical. Clifford thought her attitude hypocritical, considering how this young dancer was allowing herself to be exploited. But perhaps Millie's entertainment was entirely from Clifford's acute embarrassment. Cherry, too, looked embarrassed, and he should have taken more notice at the time and asked himself why.

The nameless dancer finished by plopping down on Clifford's lap, loosening his necktie, and unfastening the top button of his dress shirt. Perhaps not everyone there shared his relief that her suggestive undressing of him stopped there.

Whir-click-whir-click!

With a peck on his cheek, she grabbed her discount-store fake-fur overcoat and made straight for her battered car in the slushy parking lot. At the door, she turned and chortled, "Happy Valentine's from Tessa!"

The dancer hadn't lingered for a tip, which Clifford wouldn't have been inclined to give anyway.

Would it have been more or less embarrassing if she had been more attractive? I suppose I should have been as embarrassed for her as I was for myself.

At the time, I'd thought it was a joke and in bad taste, but Tessa always had a weird sense of humor. Now I'm wondering about our decision to pull up stakes and move to California. I'd thought Tessa's motivation for encouraging the move was all about my career decisions. Not only was the company about to go under, but also I'd lost all enthusiasm for the job. We thought of California as a place to start over, to make a shift in professions I'd been thinking about for years.

Thinking she had my heart's desires at heart, I gave Tessa credit for both generosity and guts.

But what if all Tessa was trying to do was get me away from Cherry?

3

C lifford Klovis had undertaken two careers, one after the other. The two vocations were strikingly different. It was as if there were two people named Clifford Olmstead Klovis, one an advertising copywriter and marketing manager, and the other a professor of ancient history.

Clifford's career in advertising began in New York City. In yet another family migration during Clifford's junior year of college, the Klovises had moved from Greenwich, Connecticut to Des Plaines, Illinois, a suburb of the Second City, so that Franklin could undertake a new contract with the Chicago Transit Authority renovating old train stations. Clifford had hoped he could pursue acting after graduation, so he was more than ready to call himself a New Yorker.

But I was pretty sure my father wouldn't go along with that plan.

Indeed, Franklin Klovis informed Clifford that, upon graduation, he'd either have to find a paying job quickly or come live with the family in Chicago until he did. Choosing advertising as a career was Clifford's great compromise, but staying in New York City was his non-negotiable price. Rather than acknowledge his acceptance of the ultimatum, Franklin just resumed his usual practice of ignoring his son until his next letter asking for money.

In New York just a week after graduation, Clifford interviewed at Doyle Dane Bernbach and J. Walter Thompson. It was a recession year in 1971, and no one was hiring newbies. The cigar-chomping ad manager at F. W. Woolworth's headquarters had said, "Come back in two years, after you've forgotten everything you learned in school."

The experience at J. Walter Thompson had been instructive, but only in retrospect. "How do you know Wilson Marquand?" came the question from the hiring manager. Clifford was gratified to be informed his interviewer was a vice president. This was before he learned that vice presidential titles were almost as common in advertising as in the banking industry — an honorific intended to impress customers but not necessarily indicative of senior-management authority.

"We went to the same school," Clifford said. He had gotten the referral from the alumni relations office at college. He assumed it was a shoo-in to the Good Ole Boy network and that just one such invitation would suffice.

"Here's a set of guidelines," the guy said. "Write some sample copy and come back in two weeks."

Clifford did as instructed. He was sure his samples were not only clever but also solidly commercial. He wrote thirty-second TV spots for automobile tires, breath spray, and yogurt. He had a print ad for beauty supplies and a radio jingle for a department-store holiday sale.

"That's fine," the manager said, glancing at the portfolio on Clifford's return. "Now you have some samples, and good luck on your job search."

The guy could have said at the outset that they didn't have any openings. And on accepting the homework assignment, Clifford could have asked enough questions to save himself the grief. But he hadn't. If he did what was asked, he'd assumed he would be given a chance to do what was required. And be rewarded for it.

It took perhaps a month, but he went door-to-door. At each agency, he asked a pretty receptionist to see the creative director. He was turned down nine times out of ten, but he kept going. Eventually, he found himself across the desk from Lionel Bennett, the *executive* vice president at what he would later learn to call a *boutique* agency.

Bennett had cut his teeth at an industrial film studio, which occupied a converted warehouse in Queens. He had no job to offer, but he called over there and was connected with an account executive named Isabelle.

Listening to just his side of the phone conversation, I got the strong feeling he'd had a history with her, that they'd been lovers.

Isabelle got Clifford an interview. When after a ten-minute conversation the creative director offered Clifford a job, he was less thrilled than worried. He'd already put money down on a walkup apartment in the West Village, and he had no intention of moving closer.

At the film studio, walking past Stage One and the chief chargeman's office (the guy who managed the entire inventory of gear, including cameras, audio recorders, lights, and miles of cable) Clifford climbed the stairs above the edit bay to the writers' loft. There were several cubes with black, World-War-II vintage black telephones and Remington manual typewriters on gray-painted, sheet-metal stands. Besides his gray desk and a metal chair, there was nothing else. Here he would make a home and pretend to do The Man's bidding. The click-clack of his typing would be testimony to his diligent efforts. The salary was a generous $150 per week. The one-bedroom apartment he'd found on Christopher Street cost $265 per month, so he hoped the math was working in his favor.

The work in the writers' loft was more than tolerable. The creative director, Steve Tamura, was an outwardly meek, passive-aggressive type who just wanted to get by. He had a wife and a family and a savings account and a vested pension. He smiled a lot. It was clear, although Clifford was too green to notice: Steve was a survivor and intended to remain that way.

Clifford wrote ad copy and scripts for milk, lithographic press printing services, and something called the *unit train,* which was a dedicated string of railroad hopper cars that delivered coal from mines in rural Illinois to steel mills in the Rust Belt. He got good at it — good enough for Steve to give him first look at assignments, even though there were several other green copywriters tucked away in various cubes on the floor.

Clifford assumed his fellows would also be wannabes, young tyros just starting out. But not true. Some were bottle men of yesteryear who were trying to make a comeback. Someone on high had taken pity on these downcast drudges — or perhaps they had dirt on such person — and they were being given the proverbial second chance. One such was Bob Douchet, who installed himself in the cube opposite Clifford about three weeks in. Bob had a slogan: "To sell good, you gotta smell good." He wore a suit and tie every day. The ties were yesteryear, some with grease spots, and the suits had shiny patches at the elbows. But

Bob thought he was dressed for success. He smelled of Irish Spring and English Leather.

He smelled so good you wanted to leave the room.

Bob took long lunches. No one seemed to care. He was much more jocular in the afternoon, his face flushed from the Bombay gin in his dry martinis, but he didn't always bother to show up after lunch. And when it came four o'clock, he'd be napping at his desk with his hands folded over his ample gut.

Clifford worked diligently, and he was always happy to collect his paycheck, which he was handed in a windowed envelope every Friday. Life was good. This was a start.

And then there was that day. The kind of event I dreamt about, the impossible thing I'd hoped would happen but never does.

But it had.

It was a Saturday morning. Clifford had not had his coffee yet. Having abjured coffee for his entire college career, in a short time in the world of work he'd become addicted. His dose of morning caffeine set up his business day as well as his bowel movements, and from here on he'd been hooked for the rest of his life (until in his seventh decade he switched to tea).

But she'd showed up before coffee.

There was a knock on his door. Loud enough to summon him, but not so loud as to seem rude.

It was Ruth Gold from the art department. "I was thinking you could help me search for an apartment," she said quietly.

"Sure," he said. "Least I can do." He didn't think it the least bit unusual that, like him, she insisted on living in lower Manhattan instead of close to the studio.

She was sweet and nice looking, with sincere, bright eyes. She was Jewish, dark, sultry, and smart. He hadn't yet targeted Ruth as a potential conquest, but she was already on his radar. And here she was, looking for guidance and trailing her coat. A guy could get lucky.

In La Bohême, When Mimi showed up at the boys' place, what was she asking for? A cup of sugar? Money for her rent in exchange for a blowjob? Help with the Find My iPhone app? (Ridiculous. She was too poor to have both a phone and a computer.) Rodolfo probably didn't have a phone. He'd have hocked it for firewood. They'd just burned the only copy of his play. Hey, maybe the play was the thing Puccini ripped off to make the opera? Neat way to destroy the evidence of plagiarism! They kept singing about how convenient it was to be neighbors. Or did vicina *in the Italian slang back then mean* friend with benefits?

Clifford and Ruth did a thorough job of walking the neighborhood and investigating for-rent signs. Mid-afternoon, she actually found a place and put down a deposit on it. They'd done a good, diligent day's work. She would be a neighbor, and maybe the benefits would follow.

It was getting toward six, and the winter light was fading. They were in Gristedes foraging for dinner supplies because there was nothing in his cupboard.

She reached for a carton of eggs. "We'll need these for breakfast," she said.

At first, he thought he'd heard wrong. Then he decided to just shut up and pay.

And that's how it started.

∾

HE ASKED her how she made bacon so perfectly, a Jewess who knew how to fry pork to just this side of crisp without burning it. It was a new age. She explained that you stand over it, you keep turning it. Nothing special. You just pay attention, close attention. You have patience.

It was years before Eleanor convinced me to stop eating pigs. I did stop, not for religious reasons but for the practical, sustainable facts: they are intelligent beings and don't deserve to be killed, they produce enormous pond-loads of stinking shit that fouls the countryside, and their meat is laced with heart-attack-inducing fat. Never mind that, if we didn't eat them, there would be no economic reason for them to exist, at least not in the numbers they do now. Christians in Spain mocked their Jewish brethren by hanging joints of cured pork above the counters in bars, a tradition that persists to this day. One way of knowing an infidel was by his acceptance or his abhorrence of the ubiquitous, suspended haunches of slaughtered pigs. Leave it to the cold-blooded, gloomy Spaniards to turn a tavern into a charnel house as well as a place to test blasphemers on a drunken dare.

Ruth was more of a humanist than a reformed Jew, which was her family background. Religion wasn't a big thing for her. She was an intellectual because of the scholarly tradition in which she was raised, although even in the reformed shul it was the boys who were favored as would-be scholars. Nevertheless, Ruth was individualistic and self-directed in her personal philosophy. She respected Judaism, but she didn't seem to give her heritage much thought. Clifford's Christianity was nothing to brag about, and he didn't. If you judged on attendance, he hardly deserved to be counted among the faithful anymore. But she was someone who could marry a Christian and not fret too much about it. The education of the children, if there were any, would be a cause for debate, perhaps a spirited one. Reformed or not, by tradition, the children of a Jewish mother would be deemed Jewish. In deciding on whether to continue with Ruth, Clifford flashed on the idea that he might someday be attending his own son's bar mitzvah.

Practical question: Would we invite my parents?

Despite these uncertainties, Clifford had it figured out, he thought. No reason it couldn't happen with Ruth, but he was in no rush. And he didn't think she was either.

He liked to think he was giving the whole question of religious practice serious consideration. Would marrying Ruth create a rift in his personal life? Would his parents tolerate her? Would he care? Liberal as she seemed to be, was he willing to recreate his own identity in new ways? Would they celebrate Passover? (He later found out that Passover was enormously popular with gentiles, to the bewilderment of some observant Jews.) Would they be an unashamed modern couple? As unashamed as black and white? What would be the consequences?

After Ruth had been installed in her new, separate apartment for several weeks, their shared work life had become a matter of routine. Rather than taking the subway and then two public buses in an hour-long succession of transfers to the film studio, he'd wait for her at his place. She'd pull up at the curb promptly at seven each morning in her stinking VW Bug. Stinking because there was a leak somewhere in the exhaust system, and the passenger cabin was filled with gasoline fumes. But it was a tolerable ride to the studio, a half-hour on a good day with no standing around in the drizzle between buses. Besides, he didn't have the budget to offer to pay for her to get the contraption fixed. They just opened the windows, even if it was freezing outside. It was still a whole lot better than enduring the inconveniences of public transportation.

A girl he'd met in his junior year of college, Miriam Levy, had been Clifford's first adult relationship. Now Ruth was his second. Miriam was also Jewish and from a family that included both professionals and scholars. But he'd never given any thought to marrying her.

What was it about Jewish women that attracted me so?

If, as his story might have unfolded, he'd have already lost his virginity with Natalie, he could have become a more sensitive lover before he'd met Ruth. He and Miriam had used each other, pleasantly, but during most of their intimate moments together, they were listening to Beatles records and smoking grass. As a result, Clifford's foreplay technique was brief and lacked imagination. It was as though, having attained the elusive goal of penetration he'd thought about obsessively all through high school, he felt he no longer had to work for it. Now he was greedy for screwing, which never lasted very long and no doubt frustrated and baffled his partners.

But Ruth possessed an abundance of patience. She accepted him for the tyro he was and the mensch he might yet be. Their relationship became quickly comfortable, some would say boring. They maintained separate apartments — it was too early to think about combining households — but they spent most of their nonworking hours with each other. They'd stay at one place or the other all through the weekend, and sometimes the sleepover would extend through the workweek and into the next weekend. Chores like collecting the mail or doing laundry would sooner or later demand attention, necessitating brief retreats to their separate addresses.

Ruth made no demands of him, nor did he of her. And she didn't pose hypotheticals about the future.

She wasn't demanding as a lover, either. When he'd go off too soon, as often happened, she'd just say, "Stimulate me some more." He'd say, "Sure." But she wouldn't coach him as to how. Like him, she didn't seem to care about how she got there, as long as she did.

Maybe we were both narcissistic masturbators?

He didn't mistake the comfort they felt with each other for mere convenience. With Miriam, they'd both understood it wasn't for keeps. Although they never spoke of it that way, they were both experimenting with giving and receiving affection. But, this time for Clifford, the simple fact of Ruth's companionship was a comfort and a delight in itself. Their relationship was growing deeper just as the winter temperatures were descending to their lowest. Choices for evening activities were either to bundle up at home or to make a short trip to the smoky and overheated corner bar, there to hang out with neighbors, as though in a communal living room. They'd economize by sipping their beers slowly, and occasionally they'd cast glances at the game or the news playing on the TV. At one or another apartment, he would read and she would sketch. She had devoted a corner of her place as an art studio with a large easel and a full kit of supplies. She didn't paint when they were together because he was bothered by the smell of turpentine, and she agreed that only the artist should have to suffer the fumes (notwithstanding the condition of her car). Even then, she considered switching to water-based acrylics, for both of their sakes, but for now she was hooked on the rich suppleness of the oils and the magical layering of translucent coats of paint. Most of her paintings were still-life with floral themes, which Clifford thought was an appropriate choice in midwinter.

When they were at work at the film studio, they were careful to be perceived as no more than carpool buddies and friends. His cube in the writers' loft was at the other end of the building from her workstation in the art department, so their chance meetings weren't often. When they did meet, by chance or at staff functions, they'd stick to chit-chat and pretend to be unaware of each other's circumstances.

Clifford's two fellow writers — the other staff members having been reduced after a series of layoffs to a reclusive intern named Jake and the nonproductive Bob — were notoriously bad about tending their coffeemaker, keeping the area around it even passably clean, or washing their cruddy personal mugs. It might have been a right-brain thing, but for whatever reason, the graphic artists were meticulous in those habits and could be counted on to always have a fresh pot brewed. There was even a ceramic teapot with a knitted wool cozy.

One Monday morning when he found only a burnt sludge in the bottom of the writers' coffee pot, Clifford hiked over to fill his cup in the art department. He walked in on Marv Ottinger, the head of graphics, and Liam Nash, the senior illustrator. They were both hunched over their workstations. The stool where Ruth sat between them was empty. This didn't surprise Clifford, because last Friday she'd said her car would be in the shop and he'd need to take the bus to work, which he sometimes did when she had appointments. They hadn't spent the weekend together because the weather was expected to be mild, and they agreed it was the perfect time for her to catch up on her endless list of errands. (Doing laundry together was pointless togetherness and needlessly took twice as long.)

Feigning ignorance of her personal life, Clifford asked Liam, "Ruth out today?" The crusty fellow was pushing retirement and possessor of sagging jowls with a perpetual bulldog grimace. But he got a young pup's glint in his eye every time he saw Ruth.

"Out?" he harrumphed. "Out for the duration!" And he winked at Marv, who was an oafish, thirty-something geek. The guy chuckled and snorted as he shoved his heavy spectacles back up on the bridge of his nose.

"I believe she said she was having her car worked on," Clifford said.

"Bodywork, more like," Liam cracked, which drew a guffaw from Marv.

"Wuddya mean?" asked Clifford as he sipped his coffee.

"You didn't get the memo? She's getting married!" Liam shouted.

"Huh?"

"Who knew she had a steady poke from high school on the back burner all this time," Liam explained. "He calls her up, pops the question, and she snaps back up there — *zing!* — on a rubber band. He's studying library science at Stony Brook, so I guess she's gonna try for an instructor job."

"When did you find all this out?"

"Well, she was talking about it all last week," Marv offered. "You mean you didn't get any of the gossip? You writers over there really are in a world by yourselves."

Clifford felt he'd been punched in the gut, but he resolved to put in a full day at work. Before the close of business, two more milestone events occurred. After a lunch hour which he was too upset to take, the receiving department phoned his desk to say they had several packages addressed to him. He knew what they were. His first discretionary purchase since furnishing his apartment was a hi-fi stereo system. He'd bought it mail order. The shipment had been delayed so long he'd intended to write to demand his money back. He decided to pick it up on his way out of the building later. He wondered whether he should spring for the extra expense and take a cab home. He couldn't imagine how he'd get it all on the bus.

The second eventuality would have been the kicker had not Ruth's news already devastated him. Steve called him into his office and informed him curtly that he was being laid off.

"How come?" was all Clifford could think to say.

"Welcome to the friendly world of advertising," Steve said without looking up. He was filling out some kind of form.

Do I need discharge papers? Is it honorable?

"Every slowdown, we lay off," his new ex-boss explained. "The other guys we let go, they couldn't cut it. This time, it's seasonal. We might have you back to freelance, but don't count on it. You've got a real portfolio now. When business picks up, you can go out and get a real job. We don't give raises here, which is why nobody stays even if we don't let them go. If you do come back, it's because nobody wants you. God forbid, you don't want to be Bob." Then he looked up and said, without changing his dour expression, "Nice knowing you. I think you've got what it takes. You'll do okay."

Again with the portfolio! As if it were a magic ticket to the dance!

Jake the intern was staying because he wasn't being paid. Who knew why they kept Bob on? Maybe he had something on the Big Boss.

~

IT WAS ONLY FOUR O'CLOCK, but Clifford saw no reason to stay. The only personal item he had in his desk was a never-used fountain pen he'd gotten as a graduation gift from his Uncle Roy. He didn't even have a coffee mug he could call his own. He collected the four large boxes containing his precious new electronics — one each for a pair of speakers, a turntable, and a stereo receiver. He struggled to the street corner with it all, making several trips in the slush. Reentering through the lobby each time, he gave Lucinda, the pretty receptionist, a weak smile. From the weak one she gave him in return, he expected she already knew he was a dead man. Perhaps she even knew, as maybe the whole place did, that he was also a freshly jilted lover. Feeling he now had no other cause but music in which to invest his earthly treasure, he hailed a taxi and spent the cash he'd intended to use for lunch to pay for the ride home.

He stayed in all weekend, too nauseous to eat. He busied himself with setting up the hi-fi. He tested and retested the optimum separation distance between the speakers and the gram weight of the turntable stylus. He fiddled with the tone and volume controls on the receiver. He owned two LPs — *Music from Big Pink* by The Band and *Schumann's Piano Concerto in A Minor* with Van Cliburn and the Chicago Symphony under Fritz Reiner. Throughout the weekend, he played them back-to-back, almost continuously, except for bathroom breaks and more fussy tweaks of the audio.

I tried to recall some clue Ruth might have given me about her intentions to leave. I came up with nothing. She had been steady-as-she-goes, unflappable, inscrutable. She hadn't seemed the least bit moody, and I couldn't remember our ever having the slightest disagreement.

He mulled the possible reasons. His lack of skill at sex, which he attributed to an excusable lack of experience, was at the top of the list. But Ruth hadn't complained once, and until late last week, she had still been just as eager as he was to jump into bed.

Their deciding to maintain separate apartments might have been a factor. But their relationship had been going for only three months. They'd acknowledged it was too soon to think about moving into one place or the other. And hadn't they met because Ruth had wanted a place to call her own? To set up her oil paints were roommates wouldn't complain about the mess or the fumes?

The day we went looking, I knew her hardly at all. What was I supposed to say? 'Why look for your own place when you can move in with me?'

His ordering the hi-fi had predated his knowing her. It had been a kind of Christmas present to himself, a reward for his reluctantly joining consumer culture. He'd already stocked his place with serviceable but not at all stylish secondhand furniture. The exception was the bed mattress, which he'd bought new, fearing the bodily fluids or bugs or worms that must live in one that's been previously used.

One cloudless Saturday in what seemed like an early spring, he and Ruth were strolling along 6th Avenue when they passed a furniture resale shop. She told him she needed to pop in to see if they had an elbow lamp she wanted for her home studio. None of their lamps met her expectations, but he was drawn to an old, walnut-stained sideboard, vintage nineteen-twenties. It was fully six feet long, with lathe-turned legs that had big, knobby bulges. There were filigreed cabinet doors on each end and a trio of wide pull-out drawers in the middle. The thing was hideous in its way, but Clifford realized it would be immensely practical as a hi-fi cabinet. The albums he didn't have yet would fit neatly behind the cabinet doors, and he could store bed linens or dish towels or whatever else in those handy drawers.

He didn't share his reasons with Ruth. Instead, he ran his hand along its shiny top and asked, "What do you think of it?" She looked at him, then appraisingly at the behemoth piece of furniture, then back up at him.

She said, "Apropos of what? It's a sideboard for a formal dining room."

"Well, I know it's ugly, but I'm going to need a hi-fi cabinet. I mean, it's just fifteen bucks. It's a monster, but the sign out front says free delivery."

"You're right, it *is* ugly. But I can see why you'd want it," she said.

At this moment, he wasn't sure about the your-place versus my-place rules. They were hardly shopping for a trousseau, but mightn't it be presumptuous to continue stocking his bachelor lair with more stuff? So he asked her, "Would you want it for *your* place?"

She gave him one of her half-smiles, which could have meant *no* or *maybe*. He wasn't planning on buying it for her, but if she wanted it, he didn't want to be snatching it away.

When he realized no further answer was coming, he asked her, "Do you mind if I buy it?" He didn't add *for my place.*

"Go ahead," she said breezily. "Just make sure they mean what they say and won't charge more than it's worth to deliver it." As he found the salesclerk and paid, she browsed the rest of the store again but with no apparent interest.

Was this a test? Had she seen in me then a person who was too self-absorbed to deserve her love?

They'd never said anything more about this or any other piece of furniture, and now the knobby sideboard was the place of honor for his hi-fi.

One other possible reason came to mind. They'd shopped for groceries together and cooked many of their meals together. When they did dine out, it was never lavish, but they had some favorite places. One of his was a retro-trendy soup kitchen on Hudson called *Le Pain Poulain*. The simple menu was a limited selection of daily-made soups and fresh-baked bread. The soups were typically navy bean with ham hock, beef stew, or clam chowder (alternately red or white). The breads were San Francisco sourdough, Russian black, and French rustic. As welcome winter fare, the food was hot, hearty, and filling. And the price was right — a flat six bucks per person, which meant they could split a three-buck carafe of the house red to wash it all down.

The weekend before Ruth's disappearance, on Saturday night Clifford had suggested, "What say we go out?"

To which she shot him a stare and replied, *"Anyplace* but that Pullin' Pan."

So, to selfish *in my list of vices, add* hopelessly cheap.

Could a relationship turn on the choice of a restaurant? Was Ruth picturing a life of thin cabbage soup and stale, worm-eaten bread, as if we were dissidents sentenced to some gulag?

During this tortuous weekend of self-examination, Clifford had a recurring thought, which he rejected, but the suspicion persisted. From that first night, before she'd made him bacon and eggs, she'd said she was on the pill. The common STDs back then were syphilis and gonorrhea, both of which were readily curable with antibiotics. (There was the health department rule about naming names, but Clifford didn't know anyone who'd ever contracted a disease, and his own list would be embarrassingly short.) Both of them seemed just as happy for him not to use a prophylactic.

Had she forgotten to take a pill? Or had she lied about taking them at all? A hurried marriage to an old boyfriend? Was she pregnant? Was it really mine and not his but she told him it was his? Maybe the guy is Jewish. Nobody need ever know she messed around with a backsliding Southern Baptist who took her for granted and demanded she cook pork for him. All she'd have to do when she went back to him was fuck him without protection at the earliest opportunity. She could sucker him, especially if he was as much in love with her as I was.

Clifford didn't know how to reach Ruth. She never tried to contact him. And, for most of his life, he never learned anything more about her.

4

Clifford didn't want to dwell on guilty thoughts about his first marriage, which occurred fully five years after Ruth deserted him. In the interim, he'd experimented in various unsuccessful relationships, about which he would reflect much more during his institutionalization.

Why he should feel guilty about Tessa, he realized only later in life, was a matter of karmic arithmetic. The summation was complete after Tessa, too, left him, seven years after they were wed. She was still calling herself Tessa Merrihew Dunham, the Merrihew from a second marriage and the Dunham from a third. Her clutching onto surnames made Clifford wonder whether any of her divorces had been official. Not ever having met Tessa's parents or siblings, what her maiden name was he never rightly knew, until, years later, he and she applied for passports and the name Smith appeared for the first time on a birth certificate she resurrected from a silver keepsake box.

Tessa's first marriage, as she admitted during pillow talk years later, was over almost before it began. She was pregnant and in

Florida. The groom was an unnamed fellow she called The Podiatrist, and she put up with him and aggressive mosquitos the size of dragonflies for almost three months. Even as she walked down the aisle (which must have been a short trip in the private ceremony), she suspected he was taking her on out of charity (the baby wasn't his) but would eventually exact his price.

The foot doctor demanded routinely administered oral sex and an office assistant, and she performed both roles for a time. When in a matter of weeks her pregnancy ended in miscarriage, she was out of there and, like a heat-seeking missile, she flew straight into banker Merrihew's hot tailpipe. That fellow, it turned out, was cold as cash, and their marriage didn't last a year. Third husband Milton Dunham gave her children Timothy and Sarah, and only then did she realize that even the sobering responsibilities of fatherhood would not change his habits as a philanderer and a heartless batterer.

Damaged goods? Y'think?

I was, at my core, the obedient son of dutiful Southern Baptists. It was my job — my mission — to save whatever and whoever needed saving, including Tessa and her two fatherless children.

That's where the karma comes in.

Clifford worked doggedly at being an adman, first in New York and then in Cleveland (where the regrettable episode with Cherry took place). Especially after taking Tessa and her children in tow, his primary goal was making money. They'd even pulled up roots and moved to Cleveland because the New York ad world was still in recession. President Carter's new fuel-economy standards had revived the auto industry and given Rust-Belt cities like Cleveland a new boomtown economy. Clifford had followed the money, morphing from adman to marketing executive.

They'd stuck it out in Cleveland, nestled in the comfy suburb of Shaker Heights, until the car business again went bust (as it did from time to time). The year was 1983. He was unhappy in his work, as he had been for a long while. The agency he was working for looked shaky because of the resurgent car-biz recession, and Tessa was urging him to follow his dreams and move to Los Angeles. They'd sell the old house they'd renovated so meticulously, and they'd make a new life in the sun, away from the gloomy gray skies and the snow.

I didn't appreciate at the time that Tessa was far from selfless in her motivations. She just wanted to get me away from Cherry. Cause and effect. Effect and cause. Connect the dots, which I never thought to do at the time!

After Tessa — and that's skipping over a lot, for now, including Timothy's premature death — it was only a year and a half before he hooked up with Eleanor. Clifford knew — as told to him by the character of a psychiatrist acted by director Paul Mazursky in his movie *Blume in Love* — divorced people, especially men, were entitled to a forgivable period of "sport fucking." After Tessa, and partly as revenge, Clifford intended to claim his due. But before he could get himself on the roster, he met Eleanor in an evening extension course, after which she jumped on him eagerly and continued to ride, and he never had energy leftover for anyone else.

Tim left the planet before I had a chance to get to know him, much less begin to understand him. I grieve his loss more than I am sorry for my parents' passing — but, to my regret, not as much as if it had been Jeremy. Although I judge myself for not caring enough, the genes cry out, and I suppose that's just the biology of survival asserting itself from the reptile brain.

Whereas Tessa had been a lapsed-Catholic agnostic, Eleanor was more of a grounded, New Age spiritualist. Admittedly, although she brought her own load of baggage, hers was a relative sea of calm after navigating the storms of Tessa's emotional life and her distress over why her children were not behaving like the perfect angels she'd wanted them to be. Even after several years, those children regarded their new father with indifference, which didn't promote the necessary fusion in their nuclear family.

Among the life changes that Eleanor had encouraged, even before they were married, was his career change. Tessa had understood that Clifford wanted to write — novels, not product brochures. He'd wanted to live in California ever since he'd experienced it for the first time when Franklin and Dot took the family on vacation there in his teens. As the behaviorists might say, Tessa's suggestion to move was more of an *away-from* than a *toward* motivation (away from Cherry rather than toward a new chapter in his personal development). What Eleanor understood and Tessa didn't was that Clifford's penchant for storytelling went along with a fascination with history. Eleanor convinced him to go back to school and earn his doctorate so he could teach. He drifted into ancient history, and his thesis advisor steered him toward Hellenic Egypt, mainly because no one else in the department was concentrating on the area.

By now, daughter Sarah was in her mid-teens, living alone with Clifford, and rebellious as a novice witch. She was carrying on with Travis, a scrawny drummer in a rock band, misbehavior which her father felt powerless to stop, guilty as he felt for the breakup of the family, which he judged was not so much his doing as ultimately his fault. Before long, Sarah would leave to go live with her mother, which Clifford thought was not in the girl's best interest, but he didn't put up a fight.

Although Tessa hadn't demanded alimony and Clifford didn't owe child support for a stepdaughter, he sent them checks anyway. And even though Sarah's wardrobe of jeans and T-shirts wouldn't break the bank, the decision to send her to private school to keep her out of trouble (or at least on its fringes) was costly. And the rock drummer had lots of plans and places for them to go, but no way to pay. Money in any amount just burned holes in Sarah's pockets. Clifford hoped she either didn't want drugs or couldn't afford them. He tried to keep the lines of communication open, but neither Tessa nor Sarah was inclined to share the events of their new personal lives with him.

Around this time, Clifford flew to Chicago to see his father, Franklin Lewiston Klovis. He thought of the trip as a prince might pay obeisance to a king. His mother was still alive then and he'd be seeing both parents. But far from being a strong-willed queen, Dot kept herself perpetually in the background. As she aged, she became even more withdrawn than the submissive housewife she'd been when Clifford was growing up. These days, she didn't express her own opinions, and whenever Clifford phoned and she answered, she'd pass the handset to Franklin almost immediately. She'd never been expressive to her son either verbally or physically, but now she was downright uncommunicative. When she died the next year of undiagnosed leukemia, her husband's response was stoic, just as inscrutable as her own silence had been.

Franklin died suddenly from a devastating stroke two years after she did, three years after this last meeting with Clifford. Coping with his mother's death as he tried pointlessly to comfort his father, Clifford felt an absence, a hollowness of heart. He had the strong sense that some force, like a magnetic pull, had been withdrawn from his life. But later, after the initial shock of his father's passing, missing the old man was more of a relief. The event became a mile marker in his mental landscape, a signpost showing the way to his new life, a life in a new place on the Left Coast where he couldn't be second-guessed or lectured to, where he would fully own all his decisions.

For both funerals, Clifford's sister Kathleen had handled the arrangements. She was living in suburban Chicago, just a few minutes' drive from their parents' apartment, and, because she was an Illinois resident and Clifford was now in faraway California, Franklin had named Kathleen executor of his will. What's more, she'd become a no-nonsense social worker, and she knew the paperwork routine in such matters. Except to exchange signatures via fax, she and Clifford communicated almost not at all.

Why did I decide to visit my father just then? It wasn't like I looked forward to it. I had always thought it was to let him know it was over between Tessa and me. I needed to tell him I was getting serious about Eleanor. I also wanted to say I'd given up the ad biz and wanted to go back to school so I could teach history. Did he know I'd gone to L.A. without hope of a job? Did I also go to him to ask for money? I certainly needed it, and I don't know whether I asked, but I came away with a check.

Cause and effect. Chronology matters.

Clifford and Franklin were having tea and biscuits in the kitchen dining area. They were looking through the picture window at squirrels who had come to fetch the leavings Clifford's mother had set on a sawn-off tree stump. She somehow knew the critters liked peanut butter.

"God is all that there is," Clifford said.

"You mean rocks, all the rest?" Franklin was incredulous.

"Sure," he said. "Think of the Big Bang. There's nothing. Then the Big Guy says, 'Let there be light.' How could the created be separate from the Creator?"

"I'll have to think about that one," his father said.

At this point in his life, Clifford did not believe fervently that God was the stuff of which everything is made. He'd picked up the notion from a New Age lecture he'd heard on the teachings of theologian Ernest Holmes. Clifford had offered the idea, not because he sincerely wanted to argue theology, but because he knew it ran counter to his father's fundamentalist beliefs and was sure to annoy him.

In serious moments on his own, Clifford was curious about these things. There was disagreement, even among today's astrophysicists, about the Big Bang, about dark matter. The origin and the purpose of everything might turn on the value of a variable in some equation, but did the theorists care? What was in vogue today would be deprecated tomorrow. In one version, you are eternal but undergoing constant reinvention. In another, you are the shit on God's shoes — as undeserving, as the New Testament says, as filthy rags. How should we humans think about the universe in all its myriad combinations and with its unimaginable extent? Was it created for the likes of filthy rags to appreciate? You might as well say the Sistine Chapel was built for the cockroaches that live in its crannies.

For whom, then?

On that day watching the squirrels, Clifford and his father agreed to disagree. His father had been a Sunday School teacher, and never once in all the years he'd done it had he faced such a challenging and difficult question.

"Rocks?" he asked. "How is God a rock?"

"How is She not?" was Clifford's reply. His father was furious with the answer but wouldn't let on. They spent the rest of their teatime talking about football, a sport which disgusted Clifford but that his father followed — religiously.

CLIFFORD REMEMBERED the Bible verse from Exodus, the fifth of the Ten Commandments:

> Honor thy father and thy mother that thy days may be long upon the land which the Lord thy God giveth thee.

Maybe it's why I've been struck down. What I gave my father was resentment — and to my mother, indifference.

Dot Klovis had been a chronic depressive, taciturn at the best of times. Communicating with her about almost anything but the weather had been difficult. So, Clifford's attitude toward her was understandable, if not forgivable.

By contrast, Franklin Klovis had been both opinionated and expressive. His primary approach to parenting was intimidation. When he was upset with either Clifford or Kathleen, he'd go quiet — a noticeable shift of mood because he was otherwise talkative. His silent message to his children in such cases (and a punishment he sometimes visited even on Dot) was:

I'm angry with you. You should be able to guess why.

Also, not the mark of a skilled communicator.

Is it any wonder I felt so misunderstood?

Before children reach puberty, they commonly hold their parents in respect, if not outright admiration. The young ones naturally assume the adults know better — mostly because mother and father are always doling out corrective instructions or advice. Some children no doubt think their parents are perfect.

As children enter their preteens, they begin to look for flaws. From a psychological standpoint, this change in perspective occurs because the child needs to pull away from the emotional control of its parents to form a separate, mature personality — to become an individual. During this phase of life, children are always on the lookout for evidence their parents are not perfect.

Over the years as he was growing up, Clifford heard stories about his father from his cousins. Because Franklin was the oldest of his siblings, those kids were all younger than Clifford. They were not yet mature enough to be careful about sharing family secrets.

Clifford remembered several of these stories vividly. The lesson from all of them did not so much prove his father's imperfection as it did his victimhood, rooted in unfortunate experiences that may have shaped (or bent) his character. And although Clifford regarded his own upbringing as strict, he guessed his grandparents' household was severe. They were also Southern Baptists, but conservative in ways one associated with austere sects such as the Amish. Paired-off dancing and attending movies were discouraged, if not forbidden. Not only was alcohol prohibited but also tipping up a bottle of any kind, including soft drinks, was thought to lead to derelict habits.

But Dad never prevented me or Kathleen from doing any of those things.

Generations of Klovises had been farmers. Franklin was the first to go to college, the first to practice any kind of profession (engineer). His brother Roy and sister Tina never made the transition to the big city. When Clifford was ten, on a visit to Roy's farm near Sedalia, he bunked with his cousins, Randy, who was seven, and Lester, who was six. There being a shortage of bedrooms and the boys having no sisters, Kathleen slept on a cot in their parents' room.

The boys were put to bed soon after it was dark. Roy Klovis was abstemious about the use of electricity, and Randy and Lester were expected to literally be up with the chickens to do their chores. But this didn't prevent Randy from staying up to tell tales after lights out.

"I bet you didn't know when he was our age your father was a real brat," Randy said in a hush. "God punished him, though."

Clifford didn't say anything. He had trouble imagining his father had been punished, especially by God, since he was still alive and seemed to be thriving.

"The kids were all fishing in the Smithfield pond. You get catfish and smallmouth bass there. So they were all bait-casting, but your father says there's this other way called fly fishing. He waves his pole around, and wouldn't you know it, he hooks his cousin Clifford in the eye. Clifford, did you ever meet Uncle Clifford?"

"No," Clifford said. "Never did."

The unfortunate fellow was his father's second cousin, Clifford later learned.

"Well, to this day, he's got one glass eye, and it's all your father's fault," Randy announced.

Clifford wasn't sure this information was reliable, but he didn't know enough to deny the story. And even though those boys were younger than he was, there were two of them, and he feared they had scrappy talents with their fists he didn't possess.

"That's not all," Randy said, believing from the silence he'd stunned his cousin as intended. "Did you see my dad's hand?"

Clifford admitted that he had. At dinner, Clifford couldn't help noticing the shriveled index finger of Roy's left hand as he hefted his glass of milk.

"It was a shotgun accident, but your dad was horsing around. I think they were older than us, but not much. Hunting for squirrel with four-ten shotguns. You're supposed to keep the safety on. They were climbing through some fence or maybe over some gate, and your dad's gun went off. No safety. My dad always tells people he did it by mistake to himself, but he told us different."

Clifford let it all sink in, then asked quietly, "You said God got him? My dad?"

"Yeah," Roy said. "When Franklin was older, maybe fourteen. They were riding horses in the back pasture. Galloping, which we're not allowed to do. The horse threw him. He hit the ground hard, mashed his shoulder."

Clifford's father did indeed complain of a chronically stiff right arm. He often took painkillers for it. He told anyone who was rude enough to ask that it was a war wound.

Upsetting as these stories might have been to Clifford, he didn't give them much thought after his family's visit to Roy's farm. It was only later — much later after his stroke — that he thought back, when he was playing with the puzzle pieces of his life. He began to appreciate that, for perhaps these but also for more significant reasons, his father carried a hefty load of guilt, much of it undeserved.

Two stories — which his father had told on himself to Clifford — underscored the fragility of his own ego and self-doubts he'd carried around since his own childhood.

In the first story, Franklin described how, when he was just six, he'd have to babysit Roy and Tina. Roy was a wayward four and Tina was just a toddler. They'd be left in Franklin's care in the farmhouse twice a week — once during Sunday-evening services when there was no Sunday school for them as during the morning service, and once on Wednesday nights, when the adults of the congregation gathered for prayer meetings. There would be times, Franklin explained, when he knew his parents were overdue getting home. And since he'd heard about prophecies in Sunday-school lessons, he feared the Rapture had occurred, his parents had been borne up with the faithful, and his unworthy self was left here on Earth to care for his brother and his sister for the rest of their natural lives.

The second story was even more chilling. Also at that time in Franklin's childhood, his maternal grandfather, Ernst Augsburger, came to live with them. Grandfather Augsburger was a stern Prussian who spoke only broken English, but enough to conduct his business as a salesman of cattle-slaughter equipment. Franklin's mother Ludmilla was of the opinion that her husband Wilfried, a mild-mannered and kindly Christian, was not sufficiently strict with the children. Therefore, when she thought either Franklin or Roy deserved punishment, she sent them upstairs to Ernst's room, where he administered what he thought was the appropriate number of blows to their backsides with his cane.

Grandmother Millie, as they called her, told some tales of her own, but they were bedtime stories for Clifford and Kathleen. Their favorite was the story of Sparky, the wayward but beloved dog of two children — Klaus and Mindy — who were exactly the same ages as the Klovis children. One day, poor Sparky got locked by accident in the back of a moving van, which transported him far, far away. After frantic searches, promises to improve their behavior, and their fervent prayers, Sparky miraculously made his way home to them.

Millie, you dyspeptic old prune! Your Sparky story is a lesson of Christian redemption, the kind of fable that sticks in your subconscious and influences your decisions and behavior long after you think you've forgotten it. There was love your heart after all, but it took a child's eyes to see it.

And then there was the story Dad told me himself about how I would never have been born if it hadn't been for President Truman's decision to drop the A-bomb and incinerate all those Japanese children.

~

ON HIS RETURN trip from visiting Franklin and Dot, a milestone incident occurred when Clifford was at O'Hare waiting to board the plane back to L.A. He decided to treat himself to a substantial meal. He asked to be seated in one of the few restaurants with table service, and he had time to enjoy his lunch. He relaxed so much he lost track of time. Having endured the meeting with his father, he was becoming more comfortable with the decisions he'd made. He wouldn't chase after Tessa, even if there was a chance of winning her back, which there wasn't. Eleanor was a comforting spirit who grounded him. She'd support his new ambitions and help him discover whatever came next.

When he finally glanced at his watch, he realized they'd be closing the doors on his flight in just minutes. He signaled for his check and paid hurriedly with a credit card.

When he plopped into his Economy aisle seat panting from his sprint to the gate, it dawned on him he didn't have his wallet — which held his father's uncharacteristically generous check. There was no time to disembark, and this was an era before cell phones. His stomach churned all through the four-hour flight, and he went straight to a pay phone on landing. He phoned the restaurant, talked to the manager, and explained he was pretty sure he'd left his wallet on the table. The manager explained that she was responsible for several eating places in the airport, and her office wasn't in the restaurant where Clifford had been served. She said she couldn't look into it right away. She did promise to call over there, then investigate in person as soon as she could get away from her desk.

Even though it would have been prudent to call his father immediately and tell him to void the check, Clifford held off. Here he was a grown man who should be entirely responsible for his affairs, and he'd pulled a dumb stunt worthy of a teenage screwup. He just couldn't bring himself to admit to Franklin that he'd lost the check.

He wasn't yet living with Eleanor, and Sarah had already left home to be with Tessa. Clifford spent a fitful night in his own bed in his apartment, so worried about the check that he hadn't even bothered to report the loss of his credit card to the bank.

In the early light of morning, Clifford concluded he was being childish about withholding the information. The safe thing to do would be for Franklin to merely phone his bank and stop payment on the check. There'd be the risk he'd be so irked he wouldn't write Clifford another one, but it would be far worse if the money went to the wrong person.

It was 5 a.m. in Los Angeles, which would be two hours later Chicago time, and Clifford figured his early-riser parents would already be awake. When his mother answered the phone, Clifford blurted out, "Mom, craziest thing. I didn't realize until I went to put my pants on this morning my wallet wasn't in the hip pocket. I was dead tired when I got back. Dad's check was in there, so you'd better tell him to stop payment."

"I'll tell him," she said. "He's not up yet. He wasn't making any sense last night. Kept asking me whether I think God is a rock. Did you put that in his head?"

"We talked about it, yes. But I didn't think he'd take it seriously."

"About the check, don't fret. Could happen to anybody. And do call us and let us know how things are going. You know, all the things."

"Sure, Mom" was all Clifford said before he ended the call. Saying "I love you," even as a matter of routine at the end of conversations, was not a Klovis family habit.

Minutes afterward, the restaurant manager called to say she had Clifford's wallet locked safely in her desk. She said the waiter had returned it to his supervisor promptly the previous evening. Clifford asked her about its contents, and she confirmed that his driver's license, credit card, cash, and the personal check were all in there. She wrote down his apartment address and promised to ship the wallet to him air express later that day. Clifford thanked her profusely, and he asked for her office mailing address so he could send the waiter a reward and a letter of commendation for his personnel file. The manager insisted it wasn't necessary but thanked him all the same.

Clifford called his mother back right away and gave her the good news, along with the surprising story about the manager's helpfulness and the waiter's honesty. He asked whether his father was up yet and whether she'd told him. He wasn't and she hadn't. Clifford hoped she might decide not to tell him at all, but he dared not ask her to keep secrets from him because he knew she wouldn't.

Greatly relieved now, Clifford took a leisurely, hot shower and dressed. Not having any food in the house, he settled for a cup of coffee. Since he was without ready cash and his credit card, he couldn't go out for a quick breakfast. He'd have to take his checkbook to the bank, where he was desperately low on funds, but perhaps he had enough for groceries. Then he had the idea of calling Eleanor, sharing the story of his adventure with her, and asking if she might take a break from work and treat him to lunch.

He was about to call her when his phone rang. It was his father.

"I've just been to our local police station," Franklin Klovis announced.

Ohmigod, thought Clifford. *Didn't he get the news?*

"I'm getting the wallet back," insisted Clifford. "And the check. I'm sorry if I caused you any trouble."

"I went to the police," Franklin explained, as if to a child, "to ask them what you *should do* if such a thing were to happen *again.*"

"You shouldn't have gone to the trouble."

Ignoring Clifford's protest, Franklin continued, "They *said,* you'd get a quicker response and a better chance of recovery if you'd phoned the airport police and reported the wallet *stolen.*"

"Thank you for that" was all Clifford could think to say, and there was a gap while neither of them could offer anything more.

Then Franklin said, "Here's your mother. I'll say goodbye for now. I need to run downstairs for a paper."

It took several moments for the phone handover to take place on their end. Then Clifford could hear their front door closing as Franklin left on his errand.

"Mom? What was *that* all about? Is Dad upset? All's well that ends well, you know? Didn't you tell him I'm getting everything back?"

"I sure did," she said.

"I'm really sorry to put him to so much trouble."

There was a long pause during which she sighed deeply while she considered what to say next.

Finally, she said. "It gave him something to do."

And they never mentioned it again.

I blamed him at the time, not only for being a cynic but also for lecturing me for no reason. As if I still needed his life lessons, as if I could never do anything right. But if I'd handled it his way — if I'd filed a police report — maybe instead of getting the waiter a commendation I'd have thrown suspicion on him. As it was, things worked out fine for all concerned.

Thinking back, why did I leave the wallet in the restaurant? A shrink would say there are no accidents, especially about such a significant thing. The check was their approval, a ticket to the next phase of my life. Didn't I think I deserved the money? Especially from him? I don't remember asking for it. But they certainly knew enough about the poor state of my finances, what with the divorce and the career change. I never had a thought about turning it down.

I never considered that my never-demonstrative Dad would take action, however unnecessary, to show he cared. He'd never said he worried about my divorce, but his impulse in this relatively minor incident was to protect me. So, maybe that's why I lost it — to draw him out, to make him show he cared. If the wallet hadn't been recovered, he'd be forced into having second thoughts about giving me the money.

ELEANOR HAD BEEN the love of Clifford's life — judging, at least, by the length of time they'd been together. But after those first few impassioned years, had he ever actually come out and said he loved her? He couldn't remember her saying it to him. And he knew he'd never said those words to either of his parents.

Where is Eleanor, now I'm in the hospital? (Is this a hospital? It seems so.) I'm pretty sure she hasn't visited me. Is she even alive?

The gaping hole in Clifford's life after the stroke was his missing Eleanor. But she'd departed at just the wrong time — or, from the standpoint of karma and her own independence, perhaps just the right one. Seven months before the fateful incident, she'd informed him she wanted to undertake a new project in Africa. She'd met a like-minded soul at church, Marta Kosinski, who had already been to Rwanda and invested her life savings in a startup orphanage. Most of the children were offspring of victims of tribal conflict of a generation before. Attackers wielded machetes in raids on villages, which ended in mass murder. Some survivors had lost limbs, which made it difficult to care for their babies. And some of the children were abandoned or even killed by their parents for lack of food or means of support. Marta's photo postings on Facebook were both touching and pathetic. Eleanor wasn't sure what her role would be, but she knew she wanted to help Marta.

Clifford had retired from his teaching job by then. He was drawing a modest but adequate pension, and in theory he was willing to live anywhere on the planet as long as he could manage basic comforts. (He knew nothing about Rwanda, didn't even know where to find it on a map.) They'd agreed she would make a scouting trip, connect with her friend, and collect ground-truth about the logistics of making a life there. She made it easier for Clifford to agree when they decided they were willing to give her stint two years. She said she didn't intend to live there forever, and, after all, she wasn't about to abandon Jeremy.

So Eleanor was already set up in Rwanda when she got word of Clifford's stroke. When Jeremy assured her he'd take charge of his father's care, she postponed any decisions about coming home.

Yes, I miss her. I miss talking to her, but then I'd have to break my silence. She has her freedom now, and I need what's left of mine. Mostly I miss arguing with her. She'd call it spirited debate. We had what I thought I'd found with Ruth way back when. A trustful comfort. But it was far from boring.

There were so many of his friends, his intimates, who no longer existed. Herein was the profound sadness of his present circumstances. He had read, although he didn't recall where, that there was a syndrome called *survivor's guilt*. He was a survivor. He had no excuses to offer. The rest of living, breathing humanity had no business criticizing him. What was he to do but continue to use up his quota of the Earth's resources?

I have set a task to achieve clarity, and I will strive toward it. Life is

*its own imperative. I understand at least that. Shouldn't living —
survival — be its own excuse for all transgressions, past and present?*

*The medical practitioners and the ethicists debate about quality of
life, and that's as it may be. But when you've arrived in the end
stages, it's not a matter of debate. You simply will to be. You may
have signed all the directives that made perfect sense at the time.
But, in the end, you only wish to be. A rational person might anticipate otherwise. But at this stage, I refuse to be rational.*

5

The spiral was Clifford's preoccupation:

It was a problem I fretted over, that I felt was somehow mine to solve. Like other problems I puzzled over, I knew there were finer minds in the world at work on these subjects. But I didn't know any of those people. And if I did, doubtlessly they'd write me off as an amateur — a talented amateur, but I'd be ignored nevertheless.

When he'd been at what he considered to be his mental peak — in the ten years or so leading up to his stroke — he'd taken up the habit of meditating every morning. Get up, drink one-half cup of coffee, flip on the electrically ignited gas fire in the fireplace, and settle in for about fifteen minutes. Legs crossed or not. Eyes closed. On the advice of a bygone instructor, he'd started with a mantra, to be repeated silently for the duration. Problem was, it was nonsense, at least to him. Guided meditations by silken-voiced gurus in his earbuds had the opposite effect. Their words made too much sense, engaged rather than released what the enlightened ones called the *monkey mind.* But sound effects and synthesizer music were just right, as long as not too structured. Meandering tonal patterns, singing bowls, not-too-insistent drumming, and flutes — these stimuli receded neatly into the background but tended to suppress the ongoing chatter of language in his mind. The day's practical concerns swam in and out, but none of them commanded his attention.

At these times, every now and then, I'd see the spiral. It was like a sign. But like my mundane thoughts, its shifting shapes flitted by even when I tried to hold onto them.

Even now, when he felt he couldn't muster the attention for so much as a brief meditation, images of the spiral would come. These appearances occurred at the boundary between sleeping and waking, often during the afternoon, when he'd drift off easily into a quiet nap. Or late at night, when he'd plunge back quickly into a deep sleep after being startled awake by some dream. His sleep was like that these days. Fitful. But the bliss of falling asleep remained. And it was during those times the wondrous geometric visions would come.

Spiral was the wrong word. At least, it was an imprecise description of what I saw. Coil is closer, but that term implies a fixed and unchanging diameter. Helix is a synonym, but not sufficiently suggestive. A metal coil could not change in amplitude. A helix, at

*least the familiar model of DNA, the double helix, is the twisted
pairing of two signals.*

*I'd had visions of the spiral since I'd seen sine-wave diagrams in my
seventh-grade science book:*

He'd turned in a paper on Sir Isaac Newton for one of his weekly
book reports. Never mind that he wasn't reporting on a book but
just cribbing from the "Newton, Sir Isaac" entry in the *World
Book Encyclopedia* in the school library. The school did not own a
set of the *Encyclopedia Britannica*. For that, he'd have to venture
to the public library, and he hadn't yet been motivated to go so
far in his studies of electromagnetism and waveforms.

*What occurred to me immediately on seeing a sine wave was that it
is a flattened coil. And I knew how to reproduce the shape. I would
swing my yo-yo at the full length of its three-foot tether around in
front of me, keeping the end of the string at my waist — holding the
center-point of rotation steady. Then, I'd just walk forward. An
observer looking at my progress from the side would see — a sine
wave.*

He had deduced with his simplistic seventh-grade mind that the
sine wave is a two-dimensional representation of a three-dimensional phenomenon — the linear progress of a rotating object
through space.

None of his science or math books had described a sine wave this way. In his high-school trigonometry class — four years later than his "discovery" of the sine wave — he learned its complicated mathematical description. A sine function — which seemed to be an arbitrary table of numbers — had to be applied to the linear motion to generate such a wave. No one — *not one teacher or person in authority* — admitted, even parenthetically, that you could do the same thing by taking a casual walk while spinning your yo-yo.

When he got to college, he queried professors on this point, and he got blank looks. They seemed to understand, intuitively as he did, that circular motion progressing in time would indeed produce a sine wave. But they seemed to regard this correlation as almost coincidental. To Clifford, it was *essential* — it was *basic* — like understanding that the reason the sun travels across the sky is because the Earth is orbiting around it. Later, when he'd studied the history of astronomy, he saw a similarity between the epicycles of crystalline spheres proposed by pre-Keplerian theorists and the cumbersome invention of the sine function. Both were needlessly complicated explanations of an elegantly simple process.

It was only now, in his confinement and only during his occasional periods of lucidity, that Clifford guessed at the reasons the old mathematical wizardry seemed so obtuse. The problem was, ever since the beginning of recorded history, all these thinkers got their ideas from images written or printed on *flat* pages. It was only in the twentieth century that motion-picture and then computer-generated imagery and then holography could render images in three dimensions. Which is not to say that the thinkers of yesteryear couldn't *think* in three dimensions. And what of the sculptors? What was the rediscovery of perspective drawing in the Renaissance but a clever and accurate way of simulating solid objects and scenes in two dimensions? But it must have been commonplace for these thinkers to visualize in two dimensions, then extrapolate to three. Much as we can think in three but have to extrapolate to four because Herr Doktor Einstein showed time is the fourth dimension, and even a trained scientist has trouble visualizing a reality that is mathematical rather than experiential.

Liberated by the page — and imprisoned by it! Limited to two-dimensional thinking! René Descartes and his coordinate system? And the graphs statisticians have dutifully plotted against that grid? Two dimensional — capable of being extended into three, but who thinks of 3D as the basic — the essential — view? Yes, the child looking out on the world. But not the artist who is sketching it or the mathematician who is busy constructing diagrams.

Varying the amplitude of the wave would be an easy trick, too. Replace the yo-yo string with a rubber band. And varying the frequency? Speed up your walking or slow it down.

Clifford hadn't done well in trigonometry, despite what he thought was an innate understanding of shapes and motion. And it appalled him that these gurus who set themselves up as instructors seemed to understand their abstruse calculations but didn't appreciate the simplicity and elegance of the physical world they were trying to describe.

Seconds before his nose picked up the aroma of steaming food from the catering cart coming down the hall, his stomach told him it was time for lunch. Before he was in institutional care, when he was a free agent in the outside world, his mealtimes were flexible. He could even get absorbed in a project, skip lunch, and only then realize at teatime that he was hungry. But now, when his meals were brought to him on a strict schedule, his gut was an unerring timepiece. Even a five-minute delay in the delivery — which rarely happened — was excruciating.

Today's appetizer, according to the printed menu he'd received this morning, was pepperpot soup. He vaguely remembered this was a euphemism for finely chopped cow's intestines served in a spicy, tomato-based broth. Not bothering with the spoon, he upended the cup and gulped it down, then dove into the Swiss steak, which meant artificially tenderized beef swimming in gravy poured from a can.

He was sure the potatoes had been either dried or frozen in a prior state. But it's hard to ruin potatoes.

Another glorious meal!

6

C lifford's eyelids floated closed, not because he was drifting off to sleep but because he'd given into bliss. Nurse Myra was running the heel of her right thumb with deep pressure repeatedly along his inner left thigh from knee to groin, tracing the route of his femoral artery. She'd just finished working on his calf with both thumbs, after having used acupressure reflexology on the soles of his feet. He marveled at her confident skill and the strength in her hands. When she'd been working on his feet, he'd wished he'd studied some reflexology himself. If he had, the precise points where he'd felt brief, excruciating pain would have given him clues about what was going on with his internal organs. He didn't think he was sick — any more than the consequences of having had a stroke. His appetite was normal if not sometimes voracious, his digestion proceeded relentlessly, and he hadn't noted any congestion in his respiratory tract. Given this lack of symptomatology, how had Myra been able to find those nasty pain points? Was his liver going bad? Tumors growing in his colon? Kidneys about to fail? Undoubtedly, any of those conditions would present other, more ominous, symptoms.

Wouldn't they? But, come to think of it, why should I worry? A second stroke would probably finish me off, and there are undoubtedly more painful ways to go.

It's like what his internist told him about prostate cancer — yes, it's serious and potentially fatal — but it usually progresses so slowly that something else will get you first. None of his doctors had ever told him he actually *had* prostate cancer, so he wondered why this guy would have told him such a thing. These days they weren't allowed to hint, much less withhold information. If you had something, they were supposed to tell you — describing your condition in no uncertain terms even if they were sure you'd rather not know. Gone were the days of letting the patient think he'd live forever until the day he felt so sick he knew he wouldn't.

As Myra's thumb reached the top of his inner thigh, it veered away quickly before touching his scrotum. It was a deft movement, executed at just the right place to avoid exciting him sexually. Not that he wasn't already interested. But there's a difference between being interested and getting aroused. If she were a masseuse and they were at a spa, he'd think he was being teased into asking for extra favors. Now, he didn't imagine that giving him a rubdown was in Myra's formal job description as a registered nurse. Instead, he guessed it had something to do with promoting circulation in someone who didn't get much exercise. She was a thorough professional and wanted to do a good job. No one could fault her for that.

Could it be she likes me?

He was vain, but not vain enough to assume she found him attractive. More realistically, perhaps she liked him as one might be fond of a crotchety but colorful neighbor. If they weren't in this patient-and-caregiver situation in a medical institution, perhaps she'd be baking him cookies. He didn't want to go so far as to assume she was giving him extra attention out of pity. He was pretty sure there were other more pitiable cases among her charges, probably even on this floor. He doubted she'd be as diligent with them. She had too much else to do.

She finished by giving him a vigorous scalp rub, pausing at the base of his skull, then at his temples, applying just enough pressure with those marvelous thumbs. If she was doing this to everybody, not only would she have trouble finding time for her other chores, but also the muscles of her hands would certainly get sore. No, he was a special case, and he wondered why she thought he deserved special treatment.

He'd heard of women who had father fixations, although he'd never been involved with one. Back when younger women were interested in him, he'd also been more youthful, and a natural magnetism would have been at least plausible. But in his case, considering that Myra must be less than half his age, she'd need to have a grandfather or even a great-grandfather complex, and other than a little girl's adoration of Santa Claus, Clifford didn't think such things were possible.

"There," she said, ruffling what was left of the hair on top of his head. "We've brought some pink to your cheeks. I'll be back around two after you've had your lunch." Then she laughed. "But if you feel like a nap then, don't wait up. Bye for now, Mr. Klovis."

"Cwwfff," was what came out when he tried to say his name.

She shot him a startled look. "You're not supposed to be able to do that, Clifford." And she hurried out.

~

NOT LONG AFTER Myra walked out, Jesus walked in. He'd cleverly donned a lab coat over his Jos. A. Bank suit, and his badge represented him to be Dr. J. Christensen. But Clifford was not fooled. The Son of Man looked precisely as he'd been traditionally rendered in Southern Baptist portraiture. His was the slender, serene face in the spotlighted print than used to hang above the spinet piano in the Sunday School community room: wavy chestnut-brown hair not quite to shoulder-length, neatly trimmed beard, noble European aquiline nose, and golden Mediterranean skin without the slightest blemish. The high, curved brow of his forehead shone in the overhead lighting like the premium leather of a spit-shined Oxford.

Clifford had betrayed himself by breaking the rules! No doubt Myra had put him on report, and the doctor had come to find out whether Clifford was faking imbecility.

Christ's smile was not as radiant as it could have been, but his teeth were immaculately and uniformly white. No cavities, no zits — a modest genetic inheritance when you weigh it against a birthright that had required him to die prematurely in excruciating pain.

"How are you feeling today, Mr. Klovis?"

That's a disingenuous question coming from Him, Cliff thought. *Fine, but why don't you tell me?*

Given the patient's observed inability or refusal to form words vocally, the following conversation might or might not have actually occurred. Clifford heard it clearly enough in his mind, so either he fantasized all of it, or, as even a part-time believer would guess, the Son of Man's omnipotence extends to bidirectional telepathy. (What else is prayer if you don't speak it out loud?)

Clifford clearly heard the doctor say with a twinkle in his stellar gaze, "I want to hear what you think, not what I know."

"Point taken," Clifford replied. "I'm disappointed, frankly. I prayed, and there was no answer."

"What did you pray for?"

"Again, what's with Newcastle asking for coals? I seem to remember something about 'I know what you need even before you ask?'"

"What *do* you think you need? Are we talking about medication? Yes, we draw blood, a physician compiles vitals. We get a fair picture. We feel we know which courses of treatment to recommend. But then we can't force anything on you. If we think you don't concur — or if we suspect you're having trouble making any kind of decision — we have to ask someone who has responsibility for you."

"Is someone saying I'm not taking my pills?"

"I haven't heard that. Are you not taking them?"

"I'm not *not* taking them. There's nothing under my tongue, and only piss and crap in the crapper. You can have a look, cavity search, whatever makes you happy."

"Your neck vein is unobstructed, and you're not hiding anything in your rectum. But there's a portion of your cerebrum, about the size of a golf ball, that looks more like scrambled eggs than healthy brain tissue. Specifically, it's a portion of the left frontal lobe, in Broca's area. Brain cells don't regenerate, at least not without miracle-class intervention, so the question is whether there are enough comparably structured cells in the surrounding area to which skills could be reassigned. Were it possible, and it might be, the relearning would take some effort on your part. Does that answer your question, er, prayer?"

"What about the miracle? I mean, as long as you're here."

The doctor smiled. "Now that would be cheating karma, wouldn't it?"

"What about Lazarus?"

"These things go case-by-case. He didn't deserve what he got. A corrective accounting measure was applied. I don't break the rules. I enforce them."

"Are you saying I did something to deserve this?"

"Let's just say everything is as it should be in this moment."

"But you said things could change if I made an effort?"

"Yes, a strong possibility. The question is, how much do you want to speak? What do you have left to say? And, how much do you want to go on living? Do you have any more to contribute?"

"I'm getting that this is a test."

"Test? Challenge? Sometimes the English language is so limited. How's this — do you have a reason to want to wake up in the morning?"

Dr. Christensen used his gleaming gold stylus to make a note on the screen of his tablet. Then, flashing a radiant smile this time, he turned abruptly and strode out.

Clifford's stomach told him dinner would be on its way. Perhaps he'd think more clearly after dinner and a nap. He'd hoped there would be potatoes and gravy. He could wish until the cows came home for a glass of wine with it, but they'd probably bring milk. *Feh.*

What do I have to contribute?

And what did I do to deserve this?

MYRA HAD NOT YET SHARED her suspicions with anyone about Clifford's degree of awareness. But she'd been thinking about it, both from the standpoint of how her disclosure might affect his treatment plan, as well as what protocol her professional ethics should demand. She eventually decided she had an obligation to tell Dr. Christensen. His office was over in the ambulatory wing of Willoway Manor, where residents occupied private suites that looked much like the accommodations designed for traveling businesspeople in upscale motels.

The doctor's office was at the end of one such hallway. Its outer door looked like all the rest, except those of the residents had little shelves by the doorknobs. On those shelves they had permission to place memorabilia, such as stuffed animals and framed family photos on easel stands. Some still-ambitious types changed their displays with the seasons — like the window dressings in the department stores they'd patronized all their lives.

On the other side of the hallway, across from the doctor's office, was a nursing station, also behind a nondescript door. Both of these enclosed cubes were designed to look more like administrative offices than clinical workstations. Each had a desk, a desktop computer setup, and file racks behind plain cabinet doors. From the furnishings of his workspace, you'd think the doctor was some kind of travel agent for the residents (which, from a spiritual standpoint, perhaps he was).

Myra had chosen to venture over there right before her lunch break. Not finding Christensen at his desk, she passed down the hallway toward the floor's dining area.

Some of the doors were open as cleaning staff did their chores. Myra knew the layout. All the resident rooms, or *apartments* as everyone was instructed to call them, were virtually identical. Each suite had a sitting room, a bedroom, and a full bathroom. The sitting rooms were furnished with a loveseat upholstered in a discreet brocade, two matching guest chairs, a small coffee table, and a writing desk with office-style, ergonomic swivel chair. The bathrooms had walk-in showers (there were no tubs to waste hot water or invite slip-and-fall accidents). Beside each toilet was a pull-cord attached to an emergency medic-alert switch. Off the sitting room was an alcove with a kitchen counter and pantry doors, a compact-sized fridge, a coffeemaker, and a microwave.

The decorations were also identical, not only as to colors and fabrics but also right down to the pictures on the walls, which included one Audubon bird engraving featuring a duckling-less pair of Mallards and two Georgia O'Keefe floral prints of the kind that postmodern critics said were meant to suggest vaginas. (Most of the residents were widowed women.)

At the end of the floor opposite the clinical offices was a common dining room, decorated elegantly with walnut-stained, highly polished individual tables and chairs, heavy white table linens, ersatz-Oriental carpeting, walnut-panel wainscoting with molding, and rose-colored, watered-silk wallpaper. The effect was to suggest the refectory of a private club rather than a hospital cafeteria.

Set into the center-back wall of the dining area was an impressive stone-façade fireplace where a gas fire licked a set of ceramic fire logs that would never be consumed. Over the mantle of the fireplace was a print of Da Vinci's *The Last Supper* in an elegant gilt frame.

The irony was probably lost on the room's patrons.

With this arrangement, meals were just a short walk away for any resident on the floor. (To be housed in this ambulatory wing, these patients had to be able to traverse the distance down the hall to their meals, even if assisted by a cane or walker. Many could just manage that much.) Mealtimes were flexible within a range of hours. Catering staff dressed in restaurant-style uniforms took food orders from their guests, who were given menus with exactly two choices for each course — three if you counted the soup of the day. Even though the residents on the floor knew each other well — on a first-name basis as well as their medical histories and names of their visiting relatives — most of them, by personal preference rather than administrative policy, dined alone. However, in exceptional situations, a coffee-klatch group would form around a table spontaneously, often growing in size through the mealtime so that staff would need to shove several tables together. Such situations coincided with gossip-worthy events, including the death or worsening illness of one of their own, or juicy news, typically brought by a visitor from the outside world.

Myra found Christensen seated at a private table in the dining room and enjoying his lunch. When he looked up and saw her, he invited her to sit.

"Chicken à la King or beef bourguignon," he announced with his mouth full. "The chicken is predictably rubbery, but they pressure-cook the chuck, so the beef is reliable."

"I'm a vegan," she said.

He grinned as he kept focused on his plate and speared another forkful of his beef. "In that case, your choices are salad or salad, and don't forget to take your B vitamins."

The doctor didn't look up. A waiter approached, but Myra waved him off.

Then she asked Christensen, "How much do you think Mr. Klovis understands?"

"Did you read the notes of my last visit in his chart?"

"Yes, I did."

Christensen didn't look up as he continued to eat. "Then you know the answer. Nobody home. Mr. Klovis has left the building."

"And what makes you so sure?"

He finally looked up. "I tried to have a very basic conversation with him. In simple terms. I explained his condition, essentials of the prognosis. No recognition. None." And he returned his attention to his food.

"Just because he doesn't acknowledge you doesn't mean he doesn't understand. I mean, for the most part, he doesn't need assistance. He can dress, make it to the toilet, and eat his food. And he does seem to enjoy his food."

"Which could suggest his taste buds are impaired as well!" Christensen chuckled. When he saw she didn't appreciate his humor, he put on his serious, professional face, looked her in the eye, and said, "You're talking about rote behaviors. It would be possible to train a monkey or even a dog to do as much. That doesn't mean the animal can reflect on the meanings of those tasks or has an opinion about their environment or their emotional state. Rote behavior is no indication of consciousness

— of *human* consciousness." In another lame attempt at humor, he cracked, "We don't yet have the technology to read minds, and I'm not sure I'd want to."

"He seems to watch the TV with interest," she suggested.

"So does my girlfriend's cat! Does he *read*? Has he asked for a newspaper, a magazine, a *comic book* for Chrissake?"

"No," she said. "But he could be thinking all kinds of things!" she protested. "Why should he care about *this* environment? If you had to be confined here twenty-four-seven, wouldn't you rather be in some alternate universe?"

For a moment, Christensen seemed genuinely interested. "Has he said something to you? Written a note on a napkin? Expressed himself in some way I haven't heard about?"

She took a moment to consider her answer before she replied, "No. No, he hasn't."

The doctor cast an annoyed glance at his watch, then mopped up the rest of the beef gravy with a dinner roll. As he popped the greasy wad into his mouth and chewed hurriedly, he asked her, "So what's your interest in this patient?"

As she got up and pushed her chair back in, she said, "There's something in his eyes."

The anger in her rose so suddenly it brought a flush to her brow. If she hadn't been afraid of being drowsy through the rest of her shift, she'd have taken her lunch at the corner bar and grill, starting with two vodka martinis.

7

The Gatsky grandkid was playing in the middle of the freeway. This wasn't necessarily dangerous. Although their drivers might be near-blind or almost deaf or both, the electric wheelchairs moved slowly. The boy would be agile enough to dodge them. The pace of the few ambulatory dodderers wobbling their way on walkers was glacial and likewise posed no threat except to themselves should the little brat miscalculate in his trajectory. If he progressed as far as the nurse's station, which the residents referred to as *downtown,* the situation would become more perilous. There the freeway merged and widened into a busy, lushly carpeted interchange, patterned improbably with palm fronds and royal crests. Past that nexus, the carpet extended over the enclosed pedestrian overpass to the Mauna Loa Room, where the nightly buffet had a Hawaiian theme on Fridays, presumably in anticipation of the weekend, which staff saw as no vacation at all since hordes of loved ones and their brats would be descending on the apprehensive residents. That's when the traffic would be loud and confusing, even to the residents who navigated the route to their food with regularity.

Mauna Loa was where the residents dined who were not either housed in Clifford's assisted-living wing or residing in the hotel-like environment of the "ambulatory apartments."

The electric wheelchairs were equipped with warning horns, which in such situations created a chorus of honks not unlike a gaggle of taxis at rush hour in Manhattan.

Clifford had not dined in the Mauna Loa. But he knew he wouldn't have missed anything. There are only so many entrees that can be improved by a garnish of pineapple. He did wish he could partake in the amiable buzz of conversation amid the clanking of silverware on china that filled the room from the early-bird hour starting at five until the last of the dawdlers was served at eight. He would delight in the occasional sit-down chinwag with a resident he hardly knew who was in a talkative mood. Despite his proclivity for women who managed to retain their ladylike bearing and took time to care how they dressed, painted their faces, and applied enticing scents, for conversation he preferred the company of other men. They'd talk politics or about world destinations they'd visited. The women wanted to talk about their families, especially about their grand- and great-grandbrats. Those stories had a boring consistency, at least to Clifford. He could participate in the same drama without the pain of its real-world consequences by tuning in to any soap opera on the TV. The men were usually wise enough to know they had little time left to solve the problems of the world. But they still had strong opinions about how to fix things, and Clifford would find their passionate rants inspiring.

It was the middle of the afternoon on a weekday (he wasn't sure which day), and the hallway outside Clifford's room was deserted except for the kid with the yo-yo. He looked to be about seven, the age when they ask all kinds of embarrassing questions with equal curiosity whether inquiring about colostomy bags or vaginas.

Dressed in his pajamas because he had no reason to change, Clifford stood in his doorway with his weight propped against the jamb. He monitored the boy's progress in a straight line from the far end at the floor-length window toward the nurse's station. As the boy walked briskly, he swung the yo-yo in a continuous series of 'Round the Worlds. As the translucent yo-yo freewheeled at the end of its string, an internal microcircuit inside it generated enough current to light its flashing LED. Whether it was the side effect of a drug in Clifford's regimen or a temporary artifact from lack of sleep, he marveled that the luminous arc of the yo-yo's travel described persistent shapes in his vision.

So, as the boy approached him almost head-on, Clifford saw a brilliant circle:

As the heedless boy passed him, the yo-yo's path described a sine wave:

And as the boy retreated toward downtown, over a longer duration than his brief approach, the radius of the yo-yo's path appeared to diminish, describing a narrowing spiral:

(Never mind that the boy's legs interrupted the form. Clifford was clever enough to interpolate and piece it all together.)

I remember! I remember the yo-yo!

Although young Gatsky was as reckless as a skateboarder barreling down a busy sidewalk, this demonstration would brighten the rest of Clifford's day. It would even have him thinking into the night. The boy was a one-person Fourth of July parade!

The festivities were halted abruptly when a staff member finally looked up and called out, "Can't do that in here, son. Take it outside. Where's your mother?" The boy didn't protest, didn't sulk, but pocketed the yo-yo promptly, spun around, and ran back past Clifford to Glo Gatsky's room. Clifford suspected both the old woman and her visiting daughter Crystal were catching naps, probably from exhaustion induced by coping with this kid's ceaseless energy.

As a result of the Epiphany of the Yo-Yo, Clifford now had a compelling reason to speak. On the heels of Dr. Christensen's departure just last evening, he'd been blessed with not only a powerful motivation to talk but also to *expound.*

Clifford had to tell someone of his revelation and was inspired to dress. Although he could buzz for help, he managed to do so himself if he took it slowly. And he wasn't about to tell a staff member, despite his needing someone with more critical intelligence to help him work through the implications of what he'd seen. He would have tried to find a way to confide in Myra, but he hadn't seen her this morning and guessed it was her day off.

I thought I had nothing less than a solution to a fundamental mystery of the universe. If only I could speak to Einstein!

Clifford dutifully washed his pits and asshole with a soapy cloth at the sink, followed by a spritz of deodorant. He didn't want to offend should he find a listener who was willing to sit close. He wet a comb and ran it through his thinning hair. His eyes looked puffy in the mirror, which was nothing new.

No sooner had he dressed in reasonably clean sweatpants and pullover than Hypatia of Alexandria and René Descartes strode in, cleverly disguised as social workers.

"I⊤'s all about circles and arrows!" Clifford informed them as he sat back smugly in his propped-up bed.

The Frenchman looked over at the lady as if to say, *Why are we wasting our time with this idiot?*

They were seated comfortably in guest chairs. Hypatia's indulgent smile suggested she was prepared to stay for a while and listen. "What do you mean by that?" she asked. "And why have you summoned *us?*"

Her language was Greek and Descartes' was French, but Clifford had no problem understanding them. Perhaps it was a telepathic exchange. Perhaps they understood that Clifford would have difficulty enough expressing technical concepts in English — if, indeed, the musculature of his mouth could form words. Somehow, communication occurred. After all, Clifford had already had engaging conversations with a babe named Cherry and with Jesus. Anything was possible.

"I mean to say, you've had it wrong," Clifford said (or thought he said). "All of you deep thinkers have boxed yourselves into a corner — at least all of you since you started writing things down. Mathematics is fundamentally flawed because its original viewpoint — its fundamental mindset — is needlessly limited. Not limited in inspiration but in expression and description. It's been limited in its ability to both model and communicate."

"Monsieur," Descartes began, delicately as if he were addressing a hostile diplomat, "no doubt you believe fervently whatever you are about to share with us. But your own expression fails to communicate your thesis — at least, so far."

Clifford insisted, "The very act of writing something down — and then asking someone else to read it and understand it by scanning the surface of a page — limits perception to two dimensions."

Descartes sniffed and replied, "Mathematics — arithmetic, algebra, geometry, trigonometry, calculus — these tools are quite successful at describing the world in three dimensions — in fact, in any number of dimensions. Even though Hypatia did not have all these techniques in her time, I'm sure she will readily agree."

Hypatia nodded.

"I have a simple proof," Clifford said, and he took his writing pad from his bedside tray and drew this:

He handed it to Hypatia, who was seated closest to him. She glanced at it impassively and then gave it to Descartes.

"What is that?" Clifford asked him.

The Frenchman shrugged. "A squiggle?"

"What's the technical term?" Clifford asked him.

"A corkscrew?" Hypatia asked. (It surprised Clifford that she knew the term, considering such devices must have been invented centuries later than her era in fifth-century Egypt.)

"The sine function?" Descartes guessed. "Did you intend to draw a sine wave?"

"What you hold in your hand," Clifford said, "is my rendering of a three-dimensional form *flattened* so as to depict it on a page. The picture you hold there should have always been called a *coil.*"

"True enough, a coil would be one of the form's manifestations as would the wave," Hypatia agreed. "But how would thinking of the sine function in this way change anything?"

"I'm no expert," Clifford admitted. "I'm embarrassed to be telling you this, frankly. I wanted to tell someone because I sense it's important. From what I remember of sine waves in trigonometry, it was all about measuring the waveform with two-dimensional triangles. The underlying math was so complicated there were tables and tables of the numeric results of the trigonometric functions. There were tables because the calculations were elaborate and tedious. It was all so messy. I propose a simpler point of view, an elegant mindset: It all comes down to circles and arrows — orbit and direction, spinning and time. Every shape — every motion — you can think of can be generated in this way."

"I'm not sure you can generalize so much," Descartes shrugged.

"Ah, yes," Clifford added gleefully. "You're right. We must also allow for *amplitude* — excitation and entropy — especially entropy. In looking at this example I gave you, the amplitude of this sequence of points — this stream of particles, if you will — is constant over time. I show the line progressing from left to right, as we do by convention, thanks to you, René. We could go right to left, but then we'd be Arabs or Hebrews. But what we know about entropy is that a system, if undisturbed, must lose energy over time. Everything deteriorates. We all rot. What will happen to the coil if its amplitude — the diameter of its orbit — diminishes steadily as it progresses? What would be the resulting shape?"

"Why, a spiral," Hypatia answered.

Clifford was delighted to have an appreciative audience. "A ray of light propagating through space. A sluice of water spinning down the drain. A galaxy collapsing into a black hole. All spirals!"

"I still fail to see where you're going with all this," Descartes said.

"I told you, I don't know," Clifford said. "I don't know all the implications. I just know that mathematics and especially physics would be a whole lot simpler if you had been thinking of spirals from the beginning."

Hypatia gave Clifford another beatific smile and said, "Well, Mr. Klovis, you've given us a lot to think about."

"Think of it this way," Clifford suggested. "Sir Isaac Newton's math was rooted in two dimensions to describe motion in three. Albert Einstein came along and said Newton should have been thinking in four. And yet they both persisted in using a mathematical language invented to capture reality using just two dimensions, despite its ability to suggest — but not show — any number of dimensions. I don't know what the math would be. I just bet it would be simpler, more elegant."

"Unfortunately," Hypatia said delicately, "René and I have both spiraled into nonexistence. And so shall you, my friend. And relatively soon, in the scheme of things. I know you know this."

The exertion of pressing his argument had made Clifford drowsy. As his eyelids closed, he thought, *I had to tell somebody.*

8

Clifford often had difficulty sleeping. He could fall asleep readily enough, as he did without effort when he'd had little more to say to Hypatia and René. He'd wake, too soon, from active REM sleep after just a few hours. He wished his dreams were more imaginative. There were frequent bathroom themes, locker rooms, and stinky stalls, and he guessed these were merely the mind's tricks to keep him sleeping when his bladder was full and he'd otherwise want to get up to go relieve himself. He wasn't surprised. In his waking life, too, bathroom urges had become more frequent and their satisfaction more logistically complicated.

Now, in the early morning, he'd been asleep for hours. The Epiphany of the Yo-Yo had taken place in the late afternoon, just as visitors, including the Gatsky kid and his mother, had over-stayed their welcome. Hypatia and Descartes had arrived just after dinner, and then Clifford had dozed off. So here he was, wide awake, and it would be four or five hours before the sky would begin to brighten and the sun would rise again.

This gray area between sleeping and waking was a magical space. He'd see faces of people he'd never met. At least, he thought he didn't know them. He'd have inklings of ghostly figures standing by his bed. They weren't threatening, but their presence was hardly warm. They were just *there*. Perhaps they were Insiders — or sent by Insiders.

And memories would bubble up. Tonight it was a flood of recollections about Sissy Sidley, one of his teenage sweethearts.

During his high-school years, the Klovises made their home in Catonsville, Maryland. Franklin was working for the city of Baltimore on several large-scale civil-engineering projects.

The improbable thing was, Sissy was a foot taller than Clifford was at that age. (Myra was similarly proportioned, he realized.) Sissy had ample breasts for a woman of any age, eyes as blue as ice, and a smile that would melt the coldest of hearts. She was a babe, a hottie, and just seventeen. There are indeed such spectacular beings on the planet, but their physical goddess powers, like their fertility, lasts only a portion of their gorgeous lifetimes.

Sissy was not a complicated person. She did her homework, she spoke frankly, and she wasn't a ditz. But she lacked the cleverness and the malice to be a witch. (Or so Clifford thought until her actions gave him cause for worry.) She liked boys, she liked openmouthed kissing, and she loved rock 'n' roll. She was therefore the ideal date. You could take her to the movies and neck, and she wouldn't be upset if you didn't follow the story. And she wouldn't insist on talking about it later. You could park on a back road and grope her breasts, but no further. You could take her flowers, and she'd think you were a god. Hers was a generous heart, and she didn't judge.

From Clifford's standpoint, and of crucial importance at this stage of his life, Sissy didn't expect her boyfriends to be jocks. Being excellent at anything — including algebra, in which she was struggling to keep up — was sufficient to attract her admiration. Clifford was something of a science geek. He'd done an essay on the formation of clouds in which he claimed that the presence of dust or smoke in the atmosphere was essential to cloud formation. Their science teacher, Mr. Yoshimura, disagreed. Sissy didn't know which of them was right, but her money was on Clifford, who based most of his argument on an experiment he'd seen on an educational TV program. Yoshimura was going by what he'd read in *The Book of Knowledge,* which seemed to lack any empirical proof. So in the ensuing classroom discussion, Sissy had stuck by Clifford, which was all it took to engender their romance.

Clifford's cause was also helped by Sissy's father, who was an assistant principal at a local elementary school. Robert Sidley was a pragmatist. He was a widower, and Sissy was his only child. Although a pretty daughter's teenage years can be fraught with torturous worry for any otherwise sane parent, Bob took a more reasoned view. He calculated that his dear Sissy would get knocked up sooner rather than later. Although he owned a shotgun, he wasn't about to make himself into an ogre guarding the bridge to their castle. His only requirement was that any boy she dated should be at least a barely suitable son-in-law. If he were to grade her potential suitors, all he was asking for was candidates of C-plus or above.

When Clifford pulled up on a Friday night in his father's lackluster Ford Fairlane to pick up Sissy for their date, their history together was a new thing. So far, they'd been on two dates. The first actually hadn't been a date at all but a hookup at a party. In the late phase of the evening, there had been a blackout during a spin-the-bottle game, and Clifford had been all over Sissy like a horny ape. She hadn't seemed to mind. The next weekend, he'd asked her out to see *The Fall of the Roman Empire,* and they'd missed almost all of the movie because they'd had more urgent things to do in the back row.

So here he was at her house, hoping to close on third base before the evening was over.

Bob met him at the door. "What've you kids got planned for tonight?" he asked.

"Bowling, sir," Clifford said.

"Now you cut out that *sir* stuff. Makes me feel old," Bob winked. "In my day it was duckpins. But I bet you shoot a mean eight ball."

Clifford didn't realize he was being set up. Nervous as he was in the moment, it escaped him that *eight ball* refers to billiards.

"You bet," Clifford said. "Sometimes it only takes me seven."

Bob chuckled. "When are you kids planning on getting back?"

Clifford shot Sissy a look. She shrugged. "Does she have a curfew?" he asked Bob.

"Well, you might-could get her back by eleven," he said. "Could be later. But then, I don't stay up."

"So, eleven, then?"

"As I say, I don't stay up. Yes, it would be a good idea you children get yourselves back here by eleven. Past that hour, you know, too many drunks on the road. But then, when *you* leave *here,* that would be up to Sissy. Unless your own daddy's setting his watch."

Now that the question had come up, Clifford didn't know what his father would do if he stayed out late. His own curfew was to be back at *his home* by eleven.

"We'll make it back okay, sir," Clifford assured Bob.

"See you do," Bob said as he walked back into the TV room. "And cut out that *sir* crap."

At the bowling alley, Sissy beat Clifford easily in a series of games. And she knew how to keep score in the bizarre ways of this aggravating sport (which was surprising considering her lack of talent for algebra). Clifford's technique imparted an unintentional right hook, which usually landed his ball in the gutter. At this point in the history of the sport, bowling alleys had yet to be equipped with side rails, which not only protect the fragile egos of novice bowlers but also ease tensions on coed dates.

After Clifford had conceded defeat with a shrug and a smile, they lingered in the lounge.

"Have you picked any colleges yet?" she asked as she sipped her Coke.

"Nope," he said. "I guess I have to get serious about that pretty soon."

"Do you want a local campus? Maybe so you can live at home?"

"Are you kidding? So my parents can keep clocking me in and out?"

At this age, Clifford was even worse at decoding messages from females than he was in later life. He thought it odd that she looked disappointed.

"You could probably get into Hopkins," she suggested, naming the most prestigious school in Baltimore. "You could even live in a dorm. I mean, you're a big boy. You wouldn't have to come home *every* weekend. Or, at least, not to their place."

He wasn't about to tell her, but he had been thinking about Johns Hopkins, which was known mainly for its world-class medical school. But he knew they also had an excellent English department. John Barth taught there. He was just making something of a splash with his novel *Giles Goat Boy*.

For her part, she wanted him to know she'd pretty much decided about her own plans. She went on, "With all the expenses, I have to stay here for nursing school to be possible at all. And after hearing my father complain about his daily grief at school, I certainly don't want to be a teacher." Then, without a pause to warn him she was changing topics, she asked him, "Do you want to have a family?"

"Whew! Slow down. I have trouble deciding whether my gym clothes stink enough to take home."

"So your mother does your laundry?"

He laughed. "When my father went away to college, which was hundreds of miles from home, to save money he'd mail his laundry back to his mother parcel post. That was during the Great Depression. Me, somehow I learned how to use the machines, and I can iron a shirt. Spray starch, even. I don't know whether college guys these days care about wrinkles, but either way, I'm ready. I guess maybe it depends on where you go to school. I mean, I don't think they wear ties most places. But some might. I'm really going to have to check that out."

Clifford's growing checklist already included such trivial items, as well as others he totally missed that would result in gut-wrenching freshman culture shock.

The lights in the lounge dimmed. The sounds of rolling balls and falling pins had ceased some time ago. The management was signaling closing time.

Clifford had remembered to wear a watch (he didn't always), but he'd been neglectful about looking at it. Glancing at it now, he realized it was half-past midnight. He'd never been out this late on a date before. Until now, he'd never come close to violating the eleven-o'clock rule.

"We'd better get going," he said as he pulled a bill from his wallet to pay for their sodas.

"You heard what my father said. He doesn't stay up."

"I don't think mine is still awake," Clifford said. "But I think he can tell time in his sleep."

By the time Clifford pulled the Fairlane into Sissy's driveway, it was past one o'clock. He felt he had to walk her to her door, but then he was surprised when she invited him in.

"Come on," she cooed. "If you don't want to come home weekends, you can show 'em you're a big boy now."

He dreaded the consequences when he got home, but he couldn't resist her invitation. After all, he liked her, she certainly was sexy, and, if he did end up going to Hopkins, he'd need a girlfriend so he'd be ready for the first party weekend. Maybe she wouldn't be a keeper for long, but who was to say? He refused to think so far ahead.

She closed the front door softly behind them and led him by the hand into the den. There she pulled him down onto the couch so suddenly that he literally fell on top of her. She covered his mouth with wet kisses, greasy from her generous application of hot-pink lipstick.

They rolled around for about ten minutes, all while Clifford's overheated mind was trying to formulate an exit strategy.

He was starting to say *I'd better go* when she startled him by reaching down and grabbing his crotch. She caressed him with her cupped hand, rubbing his already swollen ardor. Even when he wasn't aroused, his peg-bottom pants were a bit tight, per the boy-teen fashion of the day. Now the upward pressure on his zipper was so great Clifford feared his pants would pop open no matter how he decided to proceed. Her attentions engorged him even more, which he hadn't thought possible. No doubt his erection achieved a personal best in size that night.

Were he an adult with more experience, Clifford would have known there are alternatives to coitus in such situations. He craved relief, but he feared the consequences. He had no rubber, not having mustered the courage to ask for them at the pharmacy. And he hoped, for the sake of her reputation, that Sissy didn't have any handy. He was still a virgin, although the skill and brazen confidence of her touch made him suspect she wasn't. He assumed his choices were either going all the way with her, which she seemed to want eagerly, or leaving her with embarrassing haste. He opted for the latter, mumbling something about it being past curfew as he retreated out the door.

As he drove away, he wiped her lipstick from his face with the back of his hand. He thought about their conversation, including her wanting him nearby in the years ahead as she studied nursing, her plans for dating him, and her future intentions for mothering a squalling brood. And then there were her father's encouragements, culminating in his looking the other way regarding when he'd bring her home — or what they'd do when they got there. The chain of evidence led to a single conclusion — *his entrapment!*

He flashed on what their wedding photo might look like. There they'd be at the altar, turning back to present their happy faces to the photographer. He looked like an awkward, gray penguin in his cutaway, striped pants, and spats. Standing beside him and beaming in her victory, Sissy was in an Alençon lace-covered white dress with full train. The shocker was — she looked to be a foot taller than him! She had five inches on him *plus* the height of her heels.

Worse thought: Once their kids reached puberty, they might well tower over him. Aren't the tall genes dominant? He'd be the runt of his own litter.

Clifford's mind was so agitated by these musings that he took the left turn into his own driveway too abruptly. The three-foot-high lawn jockey on the driver's side scored a nasty scratch in the car door. The figure of a dark-skinned, gaily-uniformed fellow with its helpful proffered hand had been somehow turned to face the path to the garage rather than the street. The outstretched hand, pierced with a large ring for tying up the horses of yesteryear, had done the damage.

Clifford was not as worried about the scratch as he was about his gross breach of curfew. It was just past two in the morning.

He crept into the house as silently as he could. Amazingly, he was not greeted by lights blazing and anxious, sleepless Mom and Dad. In fact, he could hear soft snoring as he walked past the open door of their bedroom and into his.

Quickly shucking his pants as he noted the wet spot on his shorts, he slipped under the covers of his own bed. He slept the sleep of the guiltless, although his dreams were animated and their content was unfamiliar and confusing. In the morning, he wouldn't remember any of it, but creepy sensations remained.

Clifford didn't wake until 10 a.m. Saturday morning. The family often slept-in on Saturdays. It was a day for addressing his father's list of household tasks, which he insisted on calling *chores,* a reference to the agricultural habits of his forebears, who had been Missouri dirt-farmers before some of his parents' generation migrated to the big city during the Depression. Clifford was allowed to sleep late on those days, as long as he finished his chores, such as mowing the lawn and taking out the trash, before he asked permission to leave the house for other activities.

Dressed for doing chores in jeans, T-shirt, and sneakers, Clifford walked cautiously into the kitchen. He said a weak "Morning" to his father, who was seated at the table drinking coffee and pretending to read the newspaper.

"Cliff" was his father's reply. Franklin Klovis did not look up and continued to read.

His mother, the ever-dutiful Dorothy, or Dot as her husband loved to diminish her, was at the sink making a show of washing the breakfast dishes, even though she and his father must have had their scrambled eggs with sausage patties hours ago. The first sign of trouble was the presence at the table of Clifford's thirteen-year-old sister Kathleen, who wasn't eating. The little snot wasn't doing much of anything. She should have been off doing her own chores or talking on the phone to a friend or watching TV. Instead, implausibly, here she was as if waiting outside the stage door to catch a glimpse of some rock star — as she feigned disinterest.

She's here to watch the fight!

Clifford took his place at the table. In front of him were a box of cold cereal and a small pitcher of milk. This was no doubt the minimum ration for a condemned man.

"Do you want to tell me about the accident with the car?" his father asked, finally lowering his paper.

Clifford was not at all prepared for this line of questioning.

"Accident, sir?" Had a hit-and-run driver slammed the car while they'd slept?

His father did not call it a *scratch.* "The foot-long gash on the right side?"

"Oh, that," Clifford said, hoping it didn't sound as though he was trivializing the damage. He swallowed hard as he poured himself some cereal, hoping this routine action would somehow lend an innocent air to his reply. "When I pulled in last night, I took the turn too hard, and I guess I scraped the side of the car on the lawn jockey. I didn't get a good look in the dark. Really, I thought it was just a paint scratch. You know, something I could buff out?"

Franklin studied his son's face the way a cop would stare at a perp who was giving his best alibi. Then, without further comment, he got up abruptly and left the room.

Kathleen shot Clifford the slightest sneer, which said *You stupid shit.*

Clifford busied himself with pouring just the right amount of milk on his cereal, then making an effort to spoon it into his mouth with nonchalance.

Without turning around, his mother said, as though she were announcing the probability of rain in the forecast, "Honesty is always the best policy, you know."

After five minutes, his father strode back in. The consummate engineer carried a metal spooling tape measure. The tape protruded about two feet in front of his belly, like a saber.

He held his thumb on the precise point of measurement. "Twenty-four-and-a-half inches," he announced.

Clifford laid down his spoon. "The scratch is that long?"

"No," his father said as he sat. "The gash is seven-and-five-eighths. I'm talking about the distance from the ground to the gash."

"O-kay," Clifford said.

"You're telling the truth," his father said, almost resentfully, to the cold coffee in his cup.

"Sure," Clifford said, although he wasn't, not entirely.

"Distance from the ground to the lawn-jockey's finger — the same," the senior Klovis admitted. "The thing's a hazard. I'll have it taken out."

Franklin started to pick up his paper, and just when Clifford began to take a sigh of relief, his father asked him, "By the way. When did you get in last night? We drifted off during Johnny Carson. When I got up to turn off the set, I don't think you were back yet. I never heard you come in."

Clifford swallowed a mouthful of soggy cereal, then said, "Two."

"Two what?"

"Two in the morning."

"Two? *Three hours* past when you *promised* to be home?"

"Yessir, I'm afraid so. You see —"

"Were you out drinking? Is that why couldn't control the car?"

"No, not at all. Just, we were at her house. We kind of lost track of time."

"*Her* house? Doing what? May I ask."

"Talking, actually. Jane Austen. Themes in *Pride and Prejudice*. We have a big test on Monday."

Strictly speaking, there were no lies in Clifford's excuse. He and Sissy had indeed talked a lot at the bowling alley. And their general topic had been how a woman faces the challenge of snaring the right mate. It was all too true there would be an exam on that topic at school on Monday, for which Clifford was unprepared. He wondered now whether his recent practical experience with Sissy might help him if the test included an essay question.

"And what about her father?" Franklin asked. "Bob didn't object?"

"Like you, he was off in dreamland, I guess. Like I said, we lost track. I doubt if he heard me leave. I told Sissy I'd apologize to him if he gave her any grief for it. All my responsibility."

"You realize," Franklin said earnestly as if he were an attorney advising his guilty client how to testify, "Bob Sidley is a deacon of the church. In all probability, we will see him tomorrow. Sissy sings in the *choir*. You *know* they'll have to be there. And what am I supposed to say to *excuse* the fact that *my son* is so far out of line? And *two*? Two — in the *morning!* Do you know how *bad* that looks?"

It stunned Clifford that his father had no trouble believing his son was an unskilled driver but harbored no suspicion whatever that Clifford had taken carnal advantage of Sissy Sidley. Was it because Franklin thought Clifford was honorable? Naïve? Incompetent?

"I'm sorry, it won't happen again," Clifford said.

"Grounded for two weeks, my boy," Franklin pronounced, and he made a noise sipping his cold coffee.

Clifford decided not to share his conspiracy theory — namely that Sissy Sidley had laid a deliberate plan to entrap and then marry him, such plan possibly involving Clifford's putting her in a compromising position by impregnating her on the night in question.

All evidence pointed to the girl's father, Assistant Principal and Deacon Robert Sidley, colluding with her in this plan, if not being its prime architect.

Clifford knew that this truth would sound to Franklin like a ridiculous lie.

Reflecting back, the post-stroke Clifford considered these events in light of the groping incident he'd discussed with Cherry. In the episode with Sissy, he felt *he* was the offended party.

She hadn't violated me so much as she'd wanted to take away my freedom of choice!

9

I t was after Ruth and before Tessa. Clifford was dating Chloe, who worked as an administrative assistant for one of the big consulting engineering firms. Chloe's work pal was Pam, who was in a committed relationship with Larry, a Vietnam vet who was ten years her senior. Larry was news traffic manager at a local TV station, a tedious job with a graveyard shift. He had a way of making his work sound like high adventure to his barroom buddies.

Larry claimed to have had flying experience in Nam, but he was no fighter pilot. More likely he'd flown a desk, as the jet jockeys say, coordinating Air Force logistics. His job in news traffic demanded much the same skills as he dispatched and tracked helicopter crews to cover highway accidents, car chases, and big thunderstorms. Larry was proud to hold a single-engine private-aircraft license, which was how Clifford came to meet him. Their brief acquaintance added another memorable experience to Clifford's mental album — and his fear of flying.

Before dawn on a Saturday that promised to be bright and

sunny, Pam phoned Clifford's apartment, where she expected to find Chloe. Pam asked whether they'd like to have breakfast. When Chloe yawned and asked her friend if she had a place in mind, Pam had a fit of the giggles and asked, "How about — Mystic Seaport?" Larry was offering to fly them to a Connecticut resort town in a Bellanca, a luxury four-seater prop plane he planned to rent for the day.

Clifford and Chloe dressed hurriedly and took a cab to LaGuardia, which handled some private-plane traffic. There they met Pam and boarded the single-prop aircraft, where Larry was already busy conversing with the tower over the radio about his flight plan.

It was a golden, cloudless day, perfect conditions for their excursion. Larry invited Clifford to sit in the right seat, the copilot's position, and Pam and Chloe sat side-by-side behind them.

As they taxied for takeoff, Larry looked over at Clifford and cracked, "You know, if I have a heart attack, it'll be up to you to land this baby." And he laughed.

Clifford gave him a weak smile while he worried his stomach might go from queasy to vomitous, despite the lack of turbulence in the skies on this gorgeous day.

The girls were talking nonstop to each other, oblivious to the fact that they were being lofted rapidly into the air in a thin-skinned aluminum craft about the size of a Volkswagen bug with wings. They were nervous about a scene in their office the previous day. Their boss, Archie Leffler, was a senior structural engineering officer at the Shoreham Nuclear Power Plant. The facility had recently been in the news because it was undergoing an upgrade and would soon be going through potentially controversial recertification by federal safety inspectors. The reactor would be on their flight path today, partway between LaGuardia and their destination, Groton-New London Airport. The plant was located on the shores of Long Island Sound, where seawater could be piped directly into the reactor's cooling systems. Renovations were almost done, and the inspectors would soon be swarming over the site to make sure the nuke wasn't a disaster waiting to happen.

One of the concerns about the plant was whether its reactor dome could withstand the impact if a plane were to crash into it. The year was 1973, and while terrorist incidents were not unheard of back then, the main worry was about a hypothetical distressed commercial flight. The plant was miles from major airport takeoff or approach paths, including JFK's, and even in an emergency situation, a pilot might well have enough maneuverability to avoid hitting the plant, if not nearby buildings. Archie's responsibility included ensuring that the reactor dome was doubly, perhaps triply, reinforced to specification.

But an irritating investigative reporter from one of the news services had been asking questions intended to be both provocative and embarrassing to the engineers, the utility, and the county government. According to the girls, who had overheard it all, Archie had been with the fellow on the phone for much of the afternoon, and the ordinarily mild-mannered engineer had grown livid. Chloe was unusually respectful of their boss, swearing that he was honorable to a fault and that the due diligence under his supervision had been performed meticulously.

Chloe must have been having an affair with Archie, a married man with four children, when I met her. Pam was eagerly supportive of our new relationship — maybe not only because she saw no future for her friend's attraction to their boss, but also because she was probably jealous. If Chloe continued to be cozy with Archie, she'd likely be favored for any promotion. Two months later, when Chloe cried out, "Oh, Arch!" during an orgasm, I told myself I'd heard it wrong, that she'd said, "Oh, ouch!" or some such. But the revelation was the end of it for me, and I dumped her as nicely as I knew how, after a pricey dinner at our local pasta-and-Chianti joint. Another reason I wanted nothing more to do with her was because of what happened next. No way did I want Larry in my life, even as a friend of a friend.

Larry's flight plan was to take them due east from LaGuardia, along the Sound, then veer north to Groton. He and Pam said there was a funky seafood restaurant a short cab ride away in Mystic where they always laid out a lavish brunch. On this fine day, pilots of small aircraft would operate on "visual flight rules," which meant they could navigate at will in a general direction — sightseeing, in effect, as they flew way beneath the big jets — as long as they stayed within a prescribed range of altitudes. They were sure to get a good look at the power plant.

Cutting into the girls' conversation and yelling to make himself heard above the drone of the engine, Larry called out, "There she is!" as the reactor dome came into view. "They should ring the thing with antiaircraft guns. Anything gets close, blow it out of the sky! Doesn't matter who's onboard!"

"Maybe they've done that already," Clifford yelled back, wondering whether Larry's headphones would prevent his hearing.

But Larry turned to his unqualified copilot and with a devilish grin exclaimed, "Well, we're gonna find out!"

And he pushed the stick forward, putting the plane into a steep dive aimed directly at the reactor dome.

Chloe gasped. Pam hissed, "It's okay!"

But it wasn't. Larry's throttle setting was wrong or the dive was too steep or both, because the plane's engine choked to a stop. The whistle of the air rushing over the fuselage was terrifying. They had no power to defy the Earth's irresistible pull.

"Jesus!" Larry shouted. Clifford's mind flashed on the phrase *God is my co-pilot*. But that was his seat now. Maybe their guardian angel was in another time zone and wouldn't learn of their peril soon enough to rescue them.

Where are the Blue Angels? Would those guys scoop us up or just blast us out of the sky? The contents of my stomach, which was only a half-cup of morning coffee with cream, came up my esophagus, but I choked it back.

Larry was pulling back with all his might on the stick. When they were within a few hundred feet of the reactor dome, he steered hard to port, banking the plane sharply to circle the site. As their altitude leveled off, their speed slowed, and the daredevil pilot was able to restart the engine.

We'd been in trouble for less than ten seconds. I remembered what Dad had said about his time in the Navy — two years of boredom and fifteen minutes of pure terror. Some personnel on the bases, in the camps, and at home flew desks and never faced sudden death. Others dodged it daily.

Larry tried to relieve the tension with, "I guess they gave those gunners the day off!" He circumnavigated the dome twice before resuming their easterly course.

How could it be that no one on the ground paid us any attention? We continued our excursion to the airstrip at Groton and the cab ride to Mystic. It was indeed a lavish brunch, but all I could manage was a piece of cheese and a handful of grapes. Chloe, who turned out not to be a keeper but was nonetheless on my side, suggested I have a double whiskey "to settle your stomach." None of us criticized Larry. I hoped I'd never see him again. But I did. One more time.

Roughly coincident with Clifford's finding out about Chloe's affair with her boss — which could have still been going on, for all he knew — she found out something upsetting about *him*. He'd known she was older than he was, just not by how much. Clifford was twenty-three, but she must have assumed he was older. Because she'd already told him about Pam and Larry, they all knew that her boyfriend was ten years older than Pam. As it turned out, Clifford was at least ten years younger than Chloe. She never did confess her age, but during a round of drunken truth-or-dare when the couples were at a party together, Clifford had had to tell his. Chloe's face turned red, and she said she had to step out for a breath of air. Even if he'd known her age to the exact year, it wouldn't have mattered to him. He was enjoying her company for a time, and he didn't expect anything like a committed relationship. Her expectations must have been different.

I thought I was the one who told her we were done. But I never came out and accused her of being with Archie. Maybe she never knew that I knew. But because of the age thing, maybe she wanted to call it off as much as I did — and she assumed wrongly it was her age that was bothering me.

After he and Chloe had said their goodbyes, they never got back together, and neither of them tried. More than twenty years later, back in 1989, Clifford was relieved to read that the electric utility had decided to decommission the Shoreham plant.

AROUND THE TIME of the near-miss kamikaze event, Clifford

began to have flying dreams. He wasn't piloting an aircraft. He was prone with his arms stretched out to the sides.

Not like Superman. More like a horizontal Christ on the cross.

He'd fly in the dream twilight over boggy marshes, the kind you might see in the dark wood of some creepy, gothic fantasy movie. He'd be flying along well and happily, and then he'd suddenly flip over and fall to the ground — as he'd seen done in the comical crashes of derring-do would-be pilots of yesteryear in old silent movie clips before the Wright brothers got it right. But before he hit — before he'd be buried and drowned in green swamp slime — he'd wake up.

He hadn't remembered having such dreams before. But now — he thought it had occurred over a period of weeks, and after he'd said goodbye to Chloe — the etheric aviator scenarios were a recurring motif, a nocturnal experience giving rise to the oneiric thought:

I'm having that dream again!

At the time, he didn't connect his nighttime flights of fantasy with what he regarded as a near-death experience in Larry's rented Bellanca. He assumed the dream's origins were in some sense spiritual, although he hadn't been taking any courses, undertaken meditation, or started dating some metaphysically minded female. And the feeling he got while flying wasn't connected to fear, as he might have expected would occur after he'd been frightened almost to the point of upchucking as they had banked sharply over the nuke plant. No, he felt exhilaration — but then disappointment as he awoke suddenly with the thought:

I flopped again.

One night, he was flying, scudding along soundlessly like a cloud, with his outstretched arms embracing the curvature of the Earth, as a glittering carpet slipped by beneath him. This time it wasn't the swamp but the dazzling nighttime landscape of the metropolis, a sight he'd seen countless times as his passenger flight approached the airport. But this time his trajectory didn't veer downward. Instead, he suddenly corkscrewed up, going vertical, then shot straight upward, accelerating into the starry heavens. Then he woke up.

I had that dream again. I didn't flop, I ascended!

On waking, he assumed he'd had a wet dream, but he reached down to find his pajama bottoms were dry. But neither was his ascent a climactic etheric one, because here he was, still on the planet, still breathing.

Significant as this experience seemed, it didn't transform his daily routine. He was working at an ad agency, literally on Madison Avenue, having bounced back after getting booted out of the industrial film studio and several months of fevered job search. The pay was good, and his new boss, Delila Crowell, was only demanding about deadlines. He was coping and making the rent. He was reasonably content, at least for the time being, with the mundane, middle-class life of a bachelor in the big city.

The next milestone event occurred on a bitterly cold Saturday morning in January. As he remembered, it had been a week since Clifford's ascent episode, and not only had his daytime experiences been unremarkable, but also he couldn't recall anything unusual about his dream life. In fact, he couldn't remember having any dreams at all, not even the usual annoyance themes of getting lost on the subway or boarding a bus only to find he had no clothes on.

That frigid morning, he was overcome by the alternative prospects of either inhospitable weather outside or boredom if he stayed home. He had no social plans for the weekend. He wasn't seeing anyone, and after Chloe he wasn't anxious to go looking for someone else right away. After a modest breakfast of coffee and toast, he decided he'd take a long, expeditionary walk around his neighborhood. Against the cold and a nasty westerly wind, Clifford donned a woolen lumberjack shirt, flannel-lined jeans, thick boots, and a sheepskin jacket. He topped it off with a knitted fisherman's stocking cap that came down over his ears. He wrapped a long scarf around his neck and slipped on a pair of bulbous mittens that looked almost as bulky as a prizefighter's gloves.

He walked west on Christopher Street, then turned right on Bleecker. Situated several blocks east of the river, the buildings there offered a partial barrier against the biting wind blasts. Clifford was curious to explore some of the storefronts on this street. Along with the usual liquor and convenience stores, fluff-and-fold laundries, and mattress outlets, there were used furniture (not to say, antique) stores, head shops, and several bookstores. There was also an inexpensive diner where he expected to order a late breakfast when he got too tired or too cold.

Last week's dirty snow still clung to the edges of the sidewalks and the curbs. In the street, which had been liberally strewn with pellet spray from municipal salt trucks, the constant flow of the cars, city buses, and taxis liquified the ice, giving the vehicle tires contact with the pavement and traction. But on the sidewalk, even though conscientious shopkeepers spread rock-crystal salt or sand in front of their establishments, the unwary walker could slip on an icy patch and go down with a thud. For most of the hardy pedestrians, including Clifford, the danger was mitigated by their thick clothing, which afforded padding to their falls.

As luck or fate would have it, Clifford took an embarrassing tumble in front of the very bookstore he'd intended to visit. Without hesitating a moment to dress against the cold, the shop's clerk rushed out the door to his aid. She was a diminutive blond, not quite five feet tall, but she had a surprisingly firm grip, made sure her work-booted feet had purchase on the pavement, and hoisted Clifford until he was standing.

"You okay?" she asked him in a squeaky voice, spewing vapor into the air. The cheeks of her pale complexion were already flushed rosy from the chill. She had buck teeth, smoke-hazel eyes, freckles across her nose, and eyelashes so fair they were almost invisible. Her lips were oddly full for such a thin face, which right then Clifford thought gave her a kissable allure.

"I think I hurt my pride," he cracked as he straightened his jacket and gave each glove an unnecessary pull.

"Come on in," she beckoned. "I've got tea."

The name of the shop was Magickal Mysterie Tours, which made Clifford think fondly of the languorous hours he and Miriam had spent smoking dope and listening to the Beatles. Its contents were devoted to esoteric and occult subjects.

Clifford unwrapped himself and removed his coat and gloves. Without asking his preferences, the girl poured him a cup of yohimbe bark tea to which she added a generous dollop of raw honey.

He took a place on the settee in front of a circular brass coffee table. As she handed him the drink, she smiled demurely and said, "Yohimben. They say it gives massive erections, but I wouldn't know." She had made no tea for herself. She sat down next to him and announced, "My name is Celeste."

The tea tasted awful, incredibly bitter despite the sweetener. But it was hot, and her description of its benefits made its cheerful consumption mandatory under the circumstances.

"I intended to come in here anyway," he said after a few brave sips.

"Something brought you here," she said. "Do you read books on metaphysics?"

"Nope," he said, gulping more. He remembered saying, "I've been having these dreams. Flying dreams. And in one of them, the most recent one, instead of flipping over as I used to do, I shot up into the sky. Then I woke up. I was wondering whether anyone else has written about that."

"There's only one book I know of," she said as she got up and walked over to a shelf in the back. "Here it is," and she returned with a used hardcover with a tattered black-and-white dust jacket — *The Poetics of Space* by Gaston Bachelard. "Do you read French? We only have the English translation."

"I did spend some time in Paris," he said as he accepted the book. "But my reading skills are about on the level of the Metro train schedule."

She sat back down, clearly pleased with herself that she'd known the obscure answer to his question. "Bachelard called it *la chute en air* — falling upward."

"So what does he say about it?"

She smiled. "Not much, actually. He talks about it mostly as a feeling, as a sense of ecstatic joy — expansiveness. Like the sky has no limits, and you dive into it."

"That's it?"

"I'm not insisting you buy the book, but you'd find Bachelard isn't terribly specific in his descriptions. He speaks in metaphor. He was a philosopher of science — of all things — but he's not at all scientific about how he expresses himself. And I don't think, about this kind of thing, he's been too well understood. *The Poetics of Space* is mostly about the places we call home — the actual structures, the buildings and their features — and how they give rise to certain feelings, poetic feelings. For example, he talks about *intimate immensity,* how a small, enclosed space — or going within yourself during meditation — can give a sense of expansion, unlimited space."

"Sounds like he was on drugs a lot," Clifford observed.

"Whatever," she shrugged. "He wrote mainly during the Thirties and Forties, and he was taken quite seriously in Europe. He taught at the Sorbonne, and he was inducted into the Royal Academy in Belgium."

"He's dead now?"

"Unless you guess he's an ascended master," she said and laughed. "You know, oddly, the people who took his *Poetics* to heart have been architects. They regard his notions as a kind of Western *feng shui* for how to design buildings. *I* think it's all about imagery and emotion — more about what inspires poetry than how to design buildings — but what do I know?"

"I'll go ahead and buy the book," he said as he thumbed its pages in a vain show of interest. "But from what you say, I'm not so sure it's going to give me any practical advice about my dreams."

"Carl Jung wrote about falling," she said, "but in the sense of falling and then rising back up. You know, you have to make mistakes to learn, to progress. You said you flipped over in some of those dreams. That sounds like failure or fear of failure. Maybe

Jung has more to say about it, but he wasn't one to give practical advice either."

She got up again, went over to a table, and came back with a small box and a paperback book.

"If it's insight and guidance you want, maybe you should get more into symbols and their messages."

It was a deck of tarot cards and a book about ways to lay them out and interpret them.

"Wow," he said, reading the covers. "This could take a while. I mean, all the study. And even then maybe I don't have the talent or the intuition or whatever it takes. Maybe I should just go to someone who already knows."

She lightly laid a delicate hand on his. "I can give you a reading."

"I'll go ahead and buy it all anyway, no problem," he said.

As she took his hand to stand him up, she said, "We'll need some privacy and someplace where we can spread them out."

She locked the front door and hung a "Back Soon" sign in the window with clock hands indicating 2 p.m., which gave them an hour and a half. Then she led him upstairs to her apartment, a claustrophobic room not much bigger than a closet, directly above the shop. There was a mattress on the floor and a table with a hotplate — your basic hippie crash pad.

He was patient and attentive while she read the cards, spreading them out on the bed as they sat cross-legged, yoga-style, facing each other.

For the card that would represent him, she chose The Hanged Man, a fellow hanging upside-down by one ankle with the other leg bent, the foot of that leg touching his other knee and forming an inverted figure four. Years later in his scholarly studies, Clifford would learn that the tarot adherent usually picks his own card. This one symbolizes a man, who may have been victimized, a neophyte who is at the beginning of a spiritual quest. He further learned that the image of the hanged man commemorates the torture and execution of Jacques de Molay, the last Grand Master of the Knights Templar in the fourteenth century and a hero of Freemasonry, by the King of France, who owed the Templars more money than he could repay.

Whether Celeste applied what she saw in the imagery of the cards, the evidence she found in his words and behavior, her own intuition, or all these factors, Clifford never knew. Some of it seemed rather obvious, but none of it was untrue. She told him a strong authority figure intimidated and inhibited all his actions. He thought he'd failed at several relationships. He feared failure not only on the emotional level but in all efforts. Because of his fears, he mistrusted and refused to follow his heart, so unless he changed his outlook, he'd never have his heart's desire. To achieve his desire — indeed, to even discover what his true desires might be — he would need to defy the opinions of others, take risks, and accept and learn from the consequences.

At the conclusion of the reading, they undressed wordlessly and made tender love on the mattress. (The tea had no appreciable effect, but he thought he did okay.) Like the bookstore and most interiors in town these days, the room was grossly overheated. Perhaps enough, or too much, had already been said, so they dozed quietly without conversation afterward. She broke the long silence with a yawn and told him softly, "It's almost two." Then they dressed and went downstairs. She rang up his items.

He had trouble finding words. "Thank you," he said. "For everything. You are amazing."

She shrugged and smiled. "You know where to find me."

In fact, he didn't. The next day, Sunday, he woke feeling he had a flu bug, and he stayed inside at home. He thought about phoning the store, but he didn't. Whatever he had to say might sound foolish, and he hadn't begun to read the books. He thought about starting them that day, but he mostly slept.

He missed work on Monday and Tuesday, and he still didn't get around to doing any reading. Rather than phone, he decided he'd drop by the store on Wednesday evening. He was exhausted after his first day back at work, but the weather had warmed considerably, and there was no reason not to make the trip. He even thought about proposing dinner, depending on when she got off work.

Standing behind the register at Magickal Mysterie Tours, Clifford found Malcolm, a frail, fortyish fellow looking like the stereotype of a starved librarian in a cardigan sweater and thick glasses. Malcolm explained he was new, had started on Monday, and he'd never met Celeste. The store owner had been on extended vacation in Greece, and an employment agency had sent him over, telling him how to get the keys from a lockbox on the door. He had no information about the former employee to give Clifford and said he couldn't provide it even if he had.

"I don't know the inventory yet," Malcolm explained. "But until recently I worked in the gift shop at the Guggenheim, so some subjects I know pretty well."

"What happened there?" Clifford asked, to have something to say.

"They're redecorating. The store won't reopen for months."

"Well, I hope you like it here," Clifford offered.

"Sure. Maybe by that time I'll like it here so much I won't want to go back! There's so much cool stuff in here."

"Do you have contact information for the owner?"

"Alas, not," Malcolm said. Clifford didn't know whether this meant the fellow didn't know or wouldn't say.

"Did they give you the apartment upstairs?" Clifford thought to ask.

"Yeah! It's a benefit!"

"Be sure to try the tea," Clifford said on his way out.

I never saw or heard from Celeste again. I didn't even know her last name. I guess she knew mine if she paid attention to the credit card. The sex was spontaneous and unprotected, so who knows? You'd think she'd try to reach me if she needed to.

As Clifford thought back on this episode, he began to wonder about the order of events — the physical flying in the Bellanca, the dreams, the message of the tarot cards, and the generous, spontaneous sex. He thought he understood some causes and effects, but perhaps he had it all wrong.

I can peg the encounter in the bookstore because of the weather. Despite the supposedly mild Mid-Atlantic weather, New York can be brutal during January and February — particularly when it's both icy and windy. But the airplane stunt — did it occur before or after? Was I still dating Chloe? It was such a clear day, but it could have been the previous fall or the following spring. If it happened after and not before the stunt or the dreams, it could have been the manifestation rather than the cause of my fears. Maybe I attracted what I dreaded most. Looking back, all of these events seem somehow related to my parting from Chloe and my issues with my father. Did I walk into the store having had the dreams or had I just heard about falling upward, was curious, and had not yet experienced it myself? And the tarot — it seemed a summation, but it could have been a prologue. Did Celeste and I actually hook up, or did I just fantasize about what it would be like with her? I still have Bachelard's book — or did have unless somebody's already cleared out my house.

During these later reflections, he remembered something else Celeste had said. She said she'd been in psychotherapy, but she didn't say how recently. He replied saying he was afraid of it, afraid that finding out dark secrets about himself could make him more depressed than he already was.

She replied, "Maybe instead you'd find out what a beautiful person you really are."

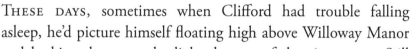

THESE DAYS, sometimes when Clifford had trouble falling asleep, he'd picture himself floating high above Willoway Manor and looking down on the lighted maze of the city streets. Still looking down, he'd rise up until he could see the shoreline of the lake and the stark blackness to the east, punctuated only by the running lights of a lonely freighter.

I haven't fallen upward. Perhaps I'm not ready.

10

I t was a warm, sunny morning after a weeklong spring thaw. The ground was freshly muddy and not yet green. The funky straw of last season's Kentucky bluegrass would be mulch for the new sprouts. The air was ripe with rot that would feed the next generation of plants and animals. It was the smell of defrosted dog shit sinking into piles of damp, moldy leaves. It was the smell of death morphing into new life.

Clifford took a deep breath and smiled. Myra had wheeled him out on the veranda and turned his wheelchair to face the glaring sun. Mind you, he didn't need a wheelchair. He was still ambulatory. He could still cross a room on his own, although unsteadily. But, to prevent injuries from falling, mandatory policy in the place was to wheel patients around when the destination was anywhere outside of their rooms.

It was glorious. The staff had only a vague notion of his quality of life. It probably came down to something like survival with the absence of pain. They used drugs in various forms — injections, drips, and pills — to deal with both. Well, he had survived, and he had no pain to speak of (that is, if he could or would speak of anything). He'd attained the next layer on a human's hierarchy of needs — namely, a comfort zone. He had shelter and warmth, a bed that was clean and dry (most of the time), recurring hot meals, and — thanks to Myra's diligence today — the sun on his face. There are exquisitely spoiled family dogs who don't get as much. Those dutiful animals no doubt fret about their jobs — or their perceived lack of a job: "Am I supposed to guard the baby or the back door? Do I alert the household of all strangers in uniform? What about those shiftless people on the sidewalk who smell bad? Is this some kind of trial period or a long-term gig? If you leave, will you return? Will I eat tonight? Tomorrow?"

As she set the brake on his wheelchair, Myra sat down stiffly in the lawn chair opposite him and leaned in very close. She spoke in a low tone, even though no one else was near enough to hear: "Clifford, I'm going to tell you something, and I want you to give me an eye blink to let me know you know I'm telling you something."

She's on to me! No use pretending!

Or, maybe she hasn't told the doctor, er, Jesus. Maybe my crude ability to communicate is still our secret.

Clifford stared at her and realized she was waiting for him to close his eyes. He managed to close the right one part-way, which he feared would look to her like a wink. He didn't want to be impertinent. He wasn't incapable of grabbing a breast when she leaned over him. But he wanted to behave himself because he feared, if he misbehaved, they'd replace her with someone ugly, or worse, nasty. Or nasty smelling.

She smiled. Signal acknowledged. Then she went on, "You didn't play nice with Dr. Christensen. Did he give you the blink test?"

Clifford didn't reply with a blink to her because the answer was no. And he daren't shake his head. His head shook uncontrollably at times, so his nodding could hardly be interpreted as deliberate.

"Here's the thing," she said. "You can't go taking off your pants anytime you want."

It's either an army of fire ants crawling up my asshole or I'm so hot the sweat is gushing from my pores. I don't know how to tell you or anyone when I'm uncomfortable. And it's pretty clear by now you can't read my mind. You're intuitive, I'll give you that. But bothering to care every time I itch is too much to expect, even for you.

God, you're beautiful!

"You've got your reasons, I'm sure. We try to keep you comfortable. You've got clean sweatpants, softer than flannel pajamas even. We make sure, no food stains or crud. But I need to tell you. If you try to take your pants off, you're sure to try to stand up out of your chair. Now, it's going to be hard to do that by yourself. You could fall. If you fall, you're going to break something, like your hip. And surgery at your age, you might not make it through. Another thing, by law, we can't restrain you. They can make you wear a seatbelt in a car, but if a stubborn old fool like you in a place like this wants to jump up out of his wheelchair, well, there's nothing we can do about it. No straitjacket, no handcuffs — and no lap belt, even if it's terrycloth. Strictly against the law."

I know all this. But nice of you to take the time to explain. And I'm not caring why you're giving me all this special attention. I like your perfume.

"Here's the thing, the point I'm trying to make." And she dropped her voice to almost a whisper. "You keep trying those things, since they can't restrain you physically, they're going to restrain you with drugs. This is what I'm telling you, and I'm not supposed to be saying anything like this at all. They will shoot you up with Thorazine or Haldol or some other nasty shit. They'll up and up the dose until you're zoned out. They'll pump you full of it until you're staring into space. Then you won't even be able to *think* about getting up. You won't be thinking *at all.*"

She tapped the side of his head gently with her finger.

"So if there's anything going on in there — and I'm guessing there is — after they do that, there won't be. You'll be a space cadet, sleeping while you're wide awake, for however many days you've got left. I don't want that to happen to you, Mr. Klovis. Behave yourself. And I mean, no rants, either. You try to speak, we'll get a speech therapist in here. But you won't get any prizes for howling like some hurt dog."

They used to say, "Keep it in your pants," and it meant you could do some serious damage if you didn't. Now all it means to me is, "Sit tight and act stupid" — or else they'll make me so stupid I can't do anything else but sit.

He wished he could think of a way to keep the magical Myra with him longer, but she just smiled, gave his knee a pat, got up, and walked off.

11

W hat Clifford didn't expect today was a visit from his son. He and Jeremy had their stark differences, just as Clifford had contended with his father. There was no getting along between the generations of male Klovises. Clifford was basking in the sun not long after Myra's exit when he heard an electric whine, followed by a voice behind him:

"Catching some rays, I think was the slang in your day," Jeremy quipped.

Jeremy was in his own wheelchair, an electric one, and Clifford thought it grossly unfair that the boy had arrived unannounced. Jeremy was hardly a boy — twenty-eight by his father's dim reckoning.

Myra should have prepared me.

"They say you can't speak," Jeremy said. "And it's a damn shame because I'm sure you've got a lecture for me all pent up in there somewhere." And he laughed.

As Myra suspected and Jeremy dared hope, he believed his father understood what was going on around him. Based on clinical tests, Christensen — and perhaps the rest of his colleagues — seemed to think Clifford was a dim bulb. But Myra sincerely wanted Clifford to comprehend her advice.

Jeremy wanted — he needed — his father to listen and understand. Over the years, their conversations had been rare, and even then mostly trivial. An introvert himself, the son didn't have any confidants. At work, his colleagues tended to be even more withdrawn than he was. He hadn't given up on finding a girlfriend who could overlook his disabilities, and he'd considered hooking up with someone who was similarly impaired, but his love life had been at a standstill for years. His mother would have been eager to give him advice and counsel on any topic he might bring to her, but, to Jeremy, mothering was smothering, and he'd had too much of Eleanor's worrying and fretting, especially after his accident. Besides, these days she was off on another continent doing a professional job of worrying and fretting about other disadvantaged children.

Jeremy went on, "I was cleaning out your place. It's not like you'll be going back there. Oh, and don't worry about your privacy. My helper was a guy from the street corner who spoke only Spanish, of which I can speak next to none. Ten bucks an hour, and we won't tell the government. I pointed and he lifted. Your secrets, if you had any, are safe.

"I can't believe the amount of junk people accumulate over their lifetimes. It's ridiculous. You go into some antique store, and that stuff is priced like it's museum artifacts. But you try to unload any of your shit yourself, and nobody wants it. *Nobody wants your glitzy stuff!* It's a life lesson, my man.

"You had that executive desk. Was it granddad's? Solid walnut, nineteen twenties, hand-carved. Big as a fucking subcompact car. Anyhow, I go looking on eBay, and I see other stuff, quite similar actually, and the replicas are going for, like, three *grand.* So, I think — *hello!* — maybe we can actually score on this one. I list it, and *no takers.* A few watchers but — no — fucking — takers. Then I relist it on auction — at a starting price of *ninety-nine bucks!* Just *one* bid, *any* bid, and it's sold for a laughable price! I'm thinking, *At least somebody's going to pay the freight to take it out of our lives.* But *no takers!* Not one! And here it is something you'll see on some movie set tomorrow because there aren't many of them — and who wants to make more? So somebody scored, and maybe they peddled it to the prop guys at the studio, but such was not our luck.

"And the rest of your old stuff? Mountains of it! Files and books and files and — *LPs?* Are you kidding me? — *junk.* I called the junk guys, and they charged me *half a grand* — half a *truckload* — to haul it all away. Best day of my life, frankly. No more old musty shit to worry about. You, I doubt you're worried, but just so you know, I did you a favor. A *big* favor."

Jeremy smiled, all generosity, the doting son. "And how is *your* day going?"

Clifford turned his head and smiled back, or he intended to.

"Yeah, right. How bad can it possibly be? Believe me, I don't mean to make light of your situation. But we make the best of what we have, don't we?"

I was not about to disagree. As if I could or would, one way or the other.

"Actually, the reason I came is interesting. I don't know if you'll think it's worth a crap, or not. I thought it was kind of a kick. I found a stack of love letters some chick wrote to you while you were studying in Paris. Natalie Bedard? We're talking late Sixties, right? I bet you didn't know you'd saved them. Apparently, she was quite taken with you."

Clifford had, indeed, spent a semester of his undergraduate studies in an exchange program with the Sorbonne in Paris. When he'd informed his father of his intention to apply for the program, Franklin's predictable response was to worry Clifford's foreign stint would end up costing more money than they'd budgeted for his education. But students who'd been through the program assured Clifford's classmates that the semester could well cost less than living stateside. Even so, Clifford spent the semester prior to his leaving for Paris earning money scrubbing pots at the college commissary. All this despite his mother's admonition not to accept a campus job "so you can concentrate on your studies."

When Jeremy hinted at having Natalie's letters, Clifford's heart sank, as if Dr. Christensen had just given him more bad news. This development was unexpected. And coming from his son, for all Clifford knew, the agenda was to torture him with his own past. And Jeremy was right — Clifford didn't remember saving those letters, although he most certainly remembered getting them. As far as he knew, he'd never replied to them. He'd felt guilty then, but it had been a deliberate decision. He'd wanted his relationship with Natalie to end. He hadn't felt as though he had the emotional strength to keep it up at a distance. He didn't want her waiting for him. And he certainly hadn't wanted to constrain his own foraging for fresh game. And there were other reasons to believe, for both of them, that falling deeper in love would have been a momentous mistake.

"There aren't many letters, actually. What was this? Over a period of months? A letter from her every couple of weeks? She was pretty good about it. Wish I had a picture of her. I bet she was a babe, knowing you. Anyhow, here goes." And he read aloud:

February 6, 1968

Dear Clifton,

Jeremy salted his reading with a running commentary: "She seems to be trying out different names for you," he said. "She rarely uses the same one twice. I'm sure she knew what she was doing, not that she couldn't get it right if she wanted to. She has an oddball sense of humor. I like that about her. Maybe you found it annoying?"

This is my fifth try at writing this letter. I've wadded up my false starts and thrown them across the room. I've decided I'm committing to this one no matter what.

"Why is she hesitating? Is there something she wants to say and she can't get it out? I'm not finding any clues in here. She's chatty but not particularly newsy, as you'll see."

I'm dashing this off to let you know exams are over, and I'm still alive. Barely. Oh, there's nothing wrong with me. Just exhausted. I'm a bit irked that Paris sounds so amazing, and I'm not thrilled that you seem so happy. It doesn't help that when I'm falling off to sleep at night I see your face with your sappy grin. I wonder if your smirk will wear off as you get older. I honestly don't know how I would feel about it. (But then I might not be around to see it. Wuddya think?)

Please don't hesitate to write again whenever the mood strikes, or even when it doesn't. What you've got here is an unrehearsed and unedited missive. I don't mind if you just let yourself go and do the same. You just might let something interesting slip.

I miss you, but it shouldn't be, needn't be, a matter of importance to you. Really. I'm not going to be making up any rules.

Over to you, Chet.

Love,

'Natch

Even though it had been more than fifty years since he'd read this letter, Clifford wasn't much surprised by it. He remembered Natalie as a gushing sweetie, lusciously curvy and cute, whose sharp tongue made her so much sexier. The nickname in her sign-off was both clever and nasty (while riffing on TV news anchors Chet Huntley and David Brinkley). She'd coined it just for this occasion. But her joke wasn't lost on him, then or now. The apostrophe hinted at the missing letter. She was his *Snatch*. The teasing in it was doubly snarky because, up to this point in their relationship, he'd never so much as seen her with her panties off.

What *did* surprise him — and refuted his lifelong memories of her — was that her letter of February 6 must not have been the first in their exchange. Through all these years, Clifford had held to the guilty belief that she'd written to him, but he'd never written back. Now, Jeremy's latter-day reading made it clear that, at the time of this writing, Natalie was already in possession of at least one letter from Clifford. Jeremy had started with this one as though it were the earliest of the several he'd found. But if in fact Clifford had saved all of the letters she'd sent to him in Paris, he must have written to her *first!*

So why had I carried a gut-wrenching, guilt-inducing lie about my own behavior and character around with me? Why had I assumed I'd been an arrogant cad to ignore her passionate, if sarcastic, expressions of affection? Such was not my self-image. I was never a lady-killer, and I could cite scores of abrupt turndowns with accompanying painful consequences of blue balls to prove it.

Or are those assumptions about myself all wrong?

Before Jeremy continued reading, Clifford resolved to listen intently to every word for new clues. He thought he'd loved Natalie, as she'd loved him. As he remembered it — and he persisted in believing — they'd parted sadly, but without bitterness.

Jeremy prefaced his reading of the second letter by warning, "Now, I'm going to read you the handful of them. When I'm done, I won't be responsible for what happens to the paper. The letters are yours, not mine. It's not like she ended up being my mother, so it's really of no concern to anybody but you. I'm not going to scan or preserve them. I was going to leave them here on your bedside table, but, much as I enjoy teasing you with them, I do believe in privacy — however little you have left — and I don't like the idea of the staff chuckling over this petty soap opera of yours. So I'll read them to you, discharge my duty, you make of them what you will, and you can consider them destroyed. Yes?"

Clifford just stared at him. Jeremy had the appalling talent of being generous and condescending in the same breath.

February 23, 1968

My Steamed Clifford,

"Why does she begin that way?" Jeremy mused. "A pun on *esteemed,* I get it. But did you come off angry in your reply to her? Pity we don't have those. Email threads would be so much more informative, but the gaps in the story are intriguing, don't you think? She certainly is one for packing it between the lines, I will say."

I'm sitting by the window basking in the warm, golden afternoon sun on a Friday. No more classes this week. I usually have coffee after lunch (I don't suppose you remember that about me), so I'm feeling softly sleepy. No bra, I just slipped on a V-neck sweater this morning. Jeans with no panties. (Maybe I'm turning into a hippie?) If you were here (and I'm not saying you should be), it would be a classy move to take your time caressing my nipples through the Angora wool and not be in your usual rush.

Hmm, do I have your attention?

Even though it's the weekend, I'm not carefree. I don't have a date (make nothing of that). I don't have to fret about my studies, but I'm way behind on my housekeeping. I guess guys can just let it all pile up, live in a stinky locker room until at the very last minute they realize late on a drunken Friday that their weekend date is going to show up on the bus in the morning. What do you do? Throw it all in a closet? If you manage to get her into the room, how are you going to get her in the mood as you roll around on those smelly, sweat-stained sheets?

"Different set of rules back then," Jeremy realized. "You at a Little Ivy school — all men. She at one of the Seven Sisters — all women. It was one of the last years before — what you would you call it — desegregation?" And he laughed.

Indeed, Clifford remembered how challenging the logistics were of trying to manage a social life at a men's college. On weekends, you either went to where the women lived (on a road trip with a posse led by some guy who had a car) or you paid for the girl's bus ticket to your campus along with a bed in an approved rooming house (which you hoped she wouldn't have a chance to use). During the week, the local female population was minuscule. There were some female graduate students, some daughters of faculty members, and the townies who worked as wait staff and clerks in the commissary. There were even some young female faculty members who were not unapproachable. (He remembered a voice coach in the music department and an instructor in French.) But at this point — during his fling with Natalie — Clifford was an incompetent sophomore. He could just manage with a date he'd met at a mixer who had about his level of experience, but he wouldn't dare bat out of his league. He didn't have the self-confidence of a senior who could aspire to put the moves on older women. And even so much as flirting with one of the faculty brats would no doubt be academic suicide.

And in New England during the winter months when black ice on the roads made transportation difficult, a campus full of more than a thousand lonely, horny, grumpy young men was not a happy place. Commiserating jokes about life in a monastery required no stretch of the imagination.

> There are piles of laundry in my own closet (mea culpa, don't start). I need to vacuum, wash and iron the curtains, and badger Parkhurst until she finally cleans up her half. At least I have a laundry bag. She just throws her stuff wherever, usually on the floor where she's taken it off, or, just as a bad, on the

chair or the table, which soon becomes unusable for its intended purpose.

"Wash and iron the curtains? Who are we kidding? This woman had seriously little to do," Jeremy observed before he went on reading.

Speaking of Parkhurst, we have a little drama going. Do you remember the little cactus Mrs. Luchese (housemother) gave me?

Clifford didn't.

I named it "Olmstead."

"Your middle name! You have a surrogate, a familiar. She's invested all kinds of emotions in this thing. You'll see," Jeremy said.

Clifford didn't remember ever having visited Natalie's dorm room, let alone having seen the plant. If he'd been consulted at its christening, he wouldn't have forgotten the event.

It was a hardy thing, lived happily on our windowsill. But then the thoughtless Parkhurst took it upon herself to water it, only hours after I had done so myself. Why she engaged herself in any chore at all is a complete mystery to me. And why she could not see that the potting soil was damp before she decided to drown poor Olmstead — that's a bafflement, too. Result — Olmstead drank it all up like a sailor on a binge, became bloated, turned white, and gave up his green ghost. (Or maybe only half of him died. Stay tuned.) Anyhow, after she screwed this up, I regarded my roommate as not just careless but mean, a murderess even.

"Now here's where it gets juicy, in my opinion," Jeremy said. Clifford's son had a bachelor's degree in psychology, but he was working on his graduate degree in mathematics while laboring at a tedious but lucrative career as a programmer. Perhaps it was his introversion that made him not only content to spend hours by himself writing code, but also eager to observe people as he applied his detached, semiprofessional practice of psychoanalysis.

"She's not just invested this prickly thing with your personality — she's also saying her roommate tried to *kill* you. Do you see what's going on here?"

Clifford couldn't see it, and if there was an insight to be gained, he was sure it was a concoction of Jeremy's.

"No further mention of the roommate in this installment. But the plot thickens, as you'll see. She goes on here to talk about the weather and her studies. It's as if she touched a nerve with the cactus murder and has to catch her breath."

> You may not be interested to know that in northern New Hampshire during 16 of the first 21 days in January, the temperature never got above zero. My mother told me that back home for a week straight it was below zero — down to minus 40 — every night!
>
> How's that for a good place to be from? (Well, you told me to tell you about the weather.)

"You *told* her to talk about the weather? Again, we have to wonder what was in your reply to her first one. But here she's pleading with you to write whenever the mood strikes — or doesn't — and you must have asked her to do the same. Her letters seem downright needy. I'm wondering about yours. Anyhow, the next part's more the kind of campus news you'd expect."

> I'm getting a lot out of my psychology course. I'm doing what they tell you not to do — applying the lectures to myself and everyone around me. However, I think I've got some insights on dealing with my medical condition, and if making some life changes makes a difference, it will be worth any amount of tuition.

Odd coincidence that both Jeremy and Natalie were into self-applied psychology. Doubly odd that their sarcastic attitudes seemed so similar. Jeremy's was a feigned cynicism, which might pass among his peers as worldliness. Natalie's was a mask to hide her vulnerabilities.

"Medical condition?" Jeremy asked. "What's she talking about? That's a whole new wrinkle."

Clifford knew exactly what it was. And its existence, its persistence, was, in his own version of the truth, the main reason Natalie had not been Jeremy's mother. (Or somebody's, depending on whether you believe the eternal soul chooses the body in which it incarnates or just comes along with the genetics.)

Clifford had no way to explain any of this to Jeremy, nor would he be inclined to do so if he could. For this reason, Clifford knew, no matter how much correspondence Jeremy studied or how much psychoanalytical skill he applied, he'd never arrive at the truth. And the truth would justify both Clifford's opinion of himself and his judgment about how things had turned out with Natalie.

"Okay," Jeremy said. "Maybe you don't know either. Then there's a mention of some mutual friend?"

> Oh, my. I've run out of news. Have you heard anything from Edwin? I just wonder what's going on with him now that the rest of you in the program took off. Are you in courses, or just sitting around smoking dope and/or getting drunk? How and where do you meet girls? Are you trying? Do they have Maalox over there, or do I need to send you some?
>
> Love,
>
> Nat
>
> P.S. By the bye, my menstrual period is all out of whack. Pregnancy is not a possibility, I assure you, but my cycles were more regular when I could look forward to your stimulating influence. So add this to my list of gripes and your to-do list on your return!
>
> P.P.S. Rereading your last letter, it seems like you're criticizing? Cut it out, or there won't be any more!!

"Menstrual period, hmm. Almost too much information there. You must have been getting it on with her pretty regularly before you departed so rudely."

No, Clifford had never gotten past second base with her. Theirs had been an old-fashioned relationship, despite its occurring in the midst of the sexual revolution of the Sixties. Oh, they rolled around, with groping and wet kisses, but their clothes never came off. They were abiding by dorm-room visiting rules and the university's stuffily named *parietal* rules, but those weren't their reasons. No, it was all because of her medical condition, or so Clifford thought. Let Jeremy think whatever he would. Without the underlying truth, he'd always be way off base.

"Criticizing? I'm really wondering what was in those letters of yours," Jeremy said. "Perhaps you complained about the brevity of her first one. Hence this long, chatty reply. Well, the next one's just as long — and written just *three days* later! We can safely assume you couldn't have replied to the cactus letter so quickly, so what we have here is kind of a long afterthought. And here she *does* really start to dish on her roommate."

My Darling Clive,

It's Sunday evening. I've already surveyed the chapter for tomorrow's crack-of-dawn psych lecture (I must pay more attention to session times when choosing courses for the Fall quarter). I'm in the room by myself, which brings on feelings of both abandonment and contentment. I have Gershwin on the hi-fi (Peter Nero and Arthur Fiedler). I drained the tea from my bone-china cup much too quickly, and I'd have to go through the chore with the heating coil and risk burning myself to make another. Judith lit out of here right after dinner, and even though she has no chance whatever to read my letters before I send them, I have the strong sense that I can now talk freely behind her back.

Barely an hour ago, she popped in, shucked her dirty, white jeans (which are still on the floor where she stepped out of them), and put on fresh clothes as if she cared for once what she looks like — a neat pair of wool slacks with a knife-edge crease and a fuzzy, hot-pink sweater. V-neck, revealing significant cleavage, and of course no bra to show off her perky, pointed udders.

She paints her face, applying both eyeliner and lipstick, and no sooner has she informed me she's off to the S.U. than she's out the door. (S.U. = Student Union — not in your past campus experience here — or was it?)

Something new is going on with that girl.

Understand, in her normal behavior in this habitat, she's a slob. She has worn the same pair of white jeans for three weeks, and when she does finally get around to washing them, she will wonder why they don't come out sparkling. Also, she will wear the same shirt for a week, a men's button-down worn untucked, wrinkled and damp with her perspiration, and not ironed in the first place. Overnight, it's flung over a chair, never on a hanger. She's owned that pair of slacks since she unpacked last fall, but I've never seen her in them. You see, she's something of a tomboy, despite her long tresses and rich-bitch airs. (She needn't work all that hard for her M.R.S. degree. She's ready for the Long Island lawn-party circuit as long as she has a houseful of servants to get her dressed and cleaned up afterward.) Judith (never Judy) is a hyperactive type who might have been a cheerleader but wouldn't have the patience to learn the drill and won't have the chance anyway because I doubt if our athletic department even owns a football, and I don't think anyone cheers for the field-hockey team. (She'd be better off in the tall corn at Iowa, but I doubt she has the chops for the Writers' Workshop.) Long story short, in her routine whirl of existence, she's probably afraid she'll bag out the knees of those slacks — or rip them as she vaults over the divan in the sitting room. Ergo, her one pair of nice pants hasn't left the closet until moments ago.

Why? I'm guessing she has her eye on a man. From Amherst? A townie? God forbid, an instructor? At what hour do the housemothers politely shoo the riffraff out of the S.U.? (I have no idea. All my weekend dates, which is mostly you, stayed just long enough after dinner to scarf down dessert before hitting the road.)

Anyhow, that's the view from here. I did get Parkhurst to neaten up the place somewhat yesterday before she went off jogging or wrestling or whatever she does for fun when she has no date, which is typical for her, despite her oh-so-casual (to the point of looking soiled) hotness as viewed by the visiting scholars. So I'm trying mightily to resist the urge when I finish this letter (which I really must do to preserve my sanity, not to mention my pride) and pick up her nasty pair of jeans and toss them in her hamper.

That's right — separate hampers. Do you think I want her cooties? The few times I was a guest in your dorm room, I seem to recall it was rather neat, as was your typical outward appearance. You did seem to take some care in how you (over)dressed!

With much affection,

Your Natty Lee

Jeremy gave a sigh of exasperation as he let the stack of letters rest in his lap. "Give me credit for going through the last one without interruption. There were so many places I had to bite my tongue, but I wanted you to get the full dramatic effect. I'm picking up jealousy all over the place — but after reading this — and I admit I've studied it a few times — I don't think what's going on here is the obvious. It's not that Judith has a social life and Natalie doesn't. Yes, for the moment, the writer is sitting by herself with nothing better to do than write to you — the boyfriend who left her so rudely to spew a trail of semen through

Europe. But on closer reading, I'm getting something else. I think she's jealous of *anyone else* hitting on Judith! And all her fussing about the girl's manners? Mother hen! Or, more likely, the dominant one in a lesbian relationship. I mean, I don't know — am I making this up?"

It had never occurred to Clifford, then or now, that Natalie was either lesbian or bisexual. She made no secret of her horniness, on paper or in person. Nevertheless, she had her issues and her boundaries. But, back then, homosexuality wasn't something anyone in their crowd discussed, much less understood. It was years after graduation, usually at alumni functions, when Clifford's gaydar was even turned on at all. Then he stopped wondering why certain members of his fraternity, including some of the handsomest, never seemed to have dates.

"Shall we press on?" Jeremy asked. "There's some dreary stuff in here, but I find a few diamonds among the shards of glass. Since you won't have another go at these, I'd better not summarize. I'm giving you the unvarnished truth, as they say."

March 9, 1968

O Sola Mio,

Wow, what did I do to deserve this? I get a letter AND a postcard in the very same week? Okay, the letter was sarcastic, and the postcard was briefer than brief, but I'm feeling the overwhelm.

I did write you those two letters back-to-back, the second one elaborating on "That Parkhurst Girl" (the soap opera). Perhaps you were a bit overwhelmed yourself and decided to reply in kind? I mean, that's being kind of literal about your responsibilities as a correspondent.

I want to tell you how I feel about spring. You Mid-Atlantic types (Maryland, as I recall?) can't appreciate it nearly enough. You don't realize I've never experienced spring as a whole season. All I ever got back home was a couple of Mud Weeks somewhere in May-June. Here it is only March and winter is almost over! Have any of you pansies even seen an April blizzard? I'm quite sure you never had the sinking feeling of seeing snow fall in May. Now, last year, I was so intimidated by the Freshman crise de nerfs that I spent most of these beautiful months indoors with my nose stuck in a book. (Meeting you was also something of a distraction.) But now, I find myself wandering around outside for no special reason but to sniff the funky air. As I walk along, I can hear water running, little streams rushing to purge all the dirty snow and ice. Water was there even during the frozen months, hundreds of feet down there where the cold can't reach, running, running, just biding its time.

When I go home for spring break (March 15), it will be winter all over again. (It was -15 ° there last week!) So if my news includes my boring reflections on the weather, you can suffer a little, bud.

Are you depressed? Your letter sounded as if you were. Depressed in Paris?! Gimme a break. Reread the above, then think about where you are. Okay, I believe what you say that it's raining all the time. April showers, May flowers. Or maybe you never got your dose of nursery rhymes.

Oh, and, just by the way, you're getting pretentious. What's with writing your 7's and 1's that way? If you come back with an accent, you will be teased out of existence. Just a warning. Putting up with Bostonians here is bad enough.

Did I really write 'Look forward to seeing you soon?' It's a cliché. Forget it. Speaking of sooner or later, what's up these days with your draft board? Honoring your student deferment, are they? Then again, LBJ might not get reelected. I certainly don't know anyone who wants him in there or who thinks being patriotic means believing it's your duty to run hellbent into a machine-gun nest armed with a single-shot rifle — for no good reason.

I'm sincerely glad you're finding yourself — although you didn't seem all that lost before. Was I serious about suggesting you really wanted to be an actor? It's possible I forget what I've said just as soon as I say (or write) it.

Clifford knew what this meant. Jeremy didn't, and he wouldn't be able to guess. "Finding himself" was a reference to Clifford's decision to apply to several summer-stock theaters in New England for a job as an apprentice actor — to commence upon his return to the States at the end of his semester in Paris. Despite her denials, Natalie had strongly encouraged him in this direction. When they'd first met (at a "tea dance" in the spring of 1967), he told her he wanted to be a novelist. But when she learned that his usual way of telling a joke or a story was to flavor it with an accent (Cockney or French — his Spanish and Italian were barely recognizable as such), she insisted he was repressing a desire to act. Even though her letters to him in Paris never repeated this coaching, his subconscious must have been listening the first time. In his solitary moments on the Left Bank, he'd decided she could be right.

Once again, our spring vacation begins March 15 for two weeks. You can write me at the igloo (the same address where you learned to dip your buttered toast in hot chocolate during Christmas break last year, right before you flew away on the wings of Icelandic). That is, if you still feel inclined to write.

Love,

N

Natalie's allusion to the time they spent together at her family's home in New Hampshire was another razor cut. It was during winter break, almost a year after they'd met. Natalie had invited him to visit her at her family's home in a small town in the northernmost region of New Hampshire, just five miles from the Canadian border. Her father was a veterinarian there, his practice mostly involving prenatal care for dairy cows and then delivering their calves — year-round in the bitter cold, when the added discomfort of a frozen parka went along with getting drenched with afterbirth.

The day after Christmas, Clifford borrowed his dad's car and drove up there from the family's new home in Connecticut (the Klovises had moved there from Maryland during his freshman year). The plan was for him to stay over a few days, meet her folks, and appreciate the quietude of rural life in the dense evergreen foothills of the White Mountains. Then he'd drive back a day or two before the drunks hit the road on New Year's. He wouldn't be going back to campus. Instead, he'd pack up for Paris, making sure he had his passport and a wad of travelers' checks, and catch a flight from New York JFK on Icelandic Airlines the second week in January. (In an era when jet airliners had all but replaced prop planes for transatlantic passenger flights, Icelandic offered cut-rate fares on Canadair CL-44 turboprops, which needed a two-hour refueling stop in Reykjavik to make it across the pond, landing in Luxembourg. To Clifford, the most vivid memory of the trip was the uncomfortable, sleepy ride in a minibus in the middle of the night from Findel Airport to Paris.)

Natalie's reference to the cocoa was fraught with subtext. At the time, he'd feared that, in her mind, the invitation to meet her parents was an invitation for him to discuss marriage, if not to actually propose. Now, in the version of events he'd carried with him all these years, they both had good reasons for avoiding the decision. They'd not yet decided being a couple was altogether hopeless, and the timing would have been opportune. He suspected she wanted some kind of avowal of his intentions before he took off. She wanted to wait for his return, but not without some commitment. Thinking back on it, Clifford wondered why they'd both made it into such a big deal. Yes, they were teenagers about to become young adults. As everyone learns, a year is an eon for a young person. And when you think about how fast and how fundamentally both the organism and the personality are developing at that age, you realize how elastic time spans are in the human psyche. But even Clifford's contemporaries who were being shipped off to Vietnam would face the prospect of much longer absences — tours of at least two years instead of a fifteen-week semester. In later life, he'd be away from his wife on business trips for that long. And anyone in a relationship with someone who took foreign assignments — a war correspondent, a wildlife photographer, or a movie director — would have to endure such extended separations.

His stay with the Bedards was mostly uneventful. The father, Jack, was mostly absent, much in demand because he was the only large-animal vet in the county. Clifford's contact with him amounted to two suppers, after which the burly, soft-spoken fellow excused himself and went straight to bed. Notably lacking in their dinner-table conversation were any of the expected fatherly questions about Clifford's college major, his career plans, his family background, or his intentions toward Natalie. Jack and his wife Madeleine did want to know about student life in Paris, on which subject the inexperienced Clifford knew almost as little as they did. Both parents were French-Canadian by birth, and neither had ever traveled back to France. Jack (who may have been born Jacques) spoke with a hint of Quebecois. Madeleine's accent was plain, flat New England. Clifford would soon learn that her personal manner was just as straightforward.

Over the first night's dinner of meatloaf, green beans with bacon bits, and mashed potatoes with gravy, Jack asked between mouthfuls, "They take dollars over there?"

"I don't know," Clifford said. "I'll have travelers' checks."

"Watch the rate," he said. "Don't get gypped. There's French going back in my family, you know. Smile to your face, stab you in the back. At least, that's what they'd say about the old-timers. Lumberjacks in Quebec. Why did they come? Ha! Probably criminals."

He went back to his meal and didn't say another word before he excused himself with a reassuring wink to Clifford and got up.

Natalie had a younger sister, Suzanne, who from her pictures was blonde and prettier. She was away at a Catholic boarding school in Boston, and other than Natalie's saying out of her parent's hearing, "*She's* a spoiled brat," there was no further mention of the cute baby sister.

That night, they put him up in Suzanne's room. He remembered the horsehair blanket on the bed was a half-inch thick and about as heavy as those lead aprons they use to shield you from X-rays at the dentist's office.

Clifford hoped Natalie would slip into the room during the

night, but it never happened. He didn't dare make the move into her room himself. Here he had these expectations of bucolic togetherness, and there wasn't even an opportunity for serious necking. If they went outside to kiss, he feared their lips might freeze together.

He planned to leave early Saturday morning to avoid the Sunday rush on the highways leading back to New York. On Friday night after dinner, Natalie proposed they take a walk.

"It must be pretty cold out there," Clifford said.

"Damn right," Natalie said. "It's forty below!"

"So you're joking about the walk, right?"

"Not at all. We'll get bundled up. Complete with mittens and wool scarves wrapped around our noses. We'll be out for maybe five minutes, but you'll be able to tell all those French sophisticates what it's like to step out on a frigid, crystal-blue night in the country, dead still. And you'll never forget the sound your boots make in the snow."

When they were both wrapped up like padded furniture, they ventured out on the stoop of the old clapboard farmhouse. As she'd said, the air was perfectly still. The frozen boards of the stairs creaked loudly as they stepped down to a snow-covered walkway.

They wore galoshes with double layers of heavy wool socks. Clifford wore a pair of Jack's, which were easily two sizes too large. When Clifford took his first step, he understood her remark about the sound. It was like the eerie noise cellophane makes when you crumple it, something like a screech and a crackle. The snow was not wet and not damp, but a kind of exotic, granular material on the surface of some other planet.

"See!" she exclaimed, all muffled.

"Wow!" he replied, and they walked on — *screech, screech, screech, screech...*

Through those scarves, there was no way for them to have a conversation, much less a wet kiss. The heart-to-heart that Clifford had both anticipated and dreaded didn't take place.

When they'd gone a short distance marveling at the sound of their footfall, Natalie took his arm to make him stop. She pointed a mitten skyward.

Clifford had never seen so many stars. The Milky Way was indeed milky here in dairy land, something you'll never see in the city or even in the exurbs. The blackest black canopy strewn with stars was another special effect, adding to the impression he'd landed on another planet.

After several minutes that seemed like an hour, they hurried back inside. After they'd unwrapped themselves and dried off their boots, Natalie said, "Now we'll have hot chocolate!"

And they did, sitting side-by-side at the kitchen table. Natalie said her mother was in her sewing room, but probably not sewing. Maybe with her favorite *Reader's Digest* or a crossword puzzle. She wouldn't be bothering them.

Natalie poised her buttered toast over her steaming cup and asked, "Mind if I dunk?"

"I guess not," Clifford said. "Doesn't the bread fall apart?"

"You never did this?"

"Never really thought about it," he said.

"Shut up and try it."

And he did. They giggled as half of his bread fell, *glop,* into the chocolate soup.

Having drained their cocoa and fished the dregs of the bread out with their fingers, they experienced one of those moments when one of them should say something significant. It was a movie moment, the opportunity for him to say he loved her and would miss her or for her to say I wish you wouldn't go but I hope you have a wonderful time.

The time for a kiss would be now.

They let the moment pass. Or *he* did, and perhaps she took some meaning from his hesitation.

She said, "Now I'm going to have a hot bath. And I mean a luxurious, steaming, soaking bath, not a shower. So I'll be in there for a while. Mom may come down, and if she does, see if you can make nice small-talk. And by all means, no religion or politics."

She got up and went upstairs. Clifford thought she hadn't seemed irked or disappointed. She had a glowing, self-satisfied look, as though she'd fulfilled a fantasy in introducing him to the crunch of the snow at forty below.

He was thinking he just might get away clean when her mother came down the stairs.

She sat down at the table, not directly across from him, and smoothed the crease in her gray slacks.

"Leaving tomorrow?"

"Driving back to Connecticut, yes. I figure about six hours. But you've got to allow for some delays."

"Oh, yes. That's wise. Back to Middletown?"

"No, I won't be going back there just now. Home to Greenwich where my folks live. Then get ready for my flight on the tenth from New York."

"Greenwich. Lotsa rich folks down there?"

"I suppose. Not us, though," he said, giving her a lame grin.

"Jack does well enough, works so hard. But these farmers have no choice. He's the only one they can call for miles around. I have some family money. That's how we can send our girls to those snob schools."

"I think Natalie likes it there, even if she does complain a little."

"A little?" And she laughed. "She liked meeting up with you, I'm sure you know."

"She's the best thing that's happened to me there," he admitted.

"You're probably wondering why a girl like me would take up with a guy like Jack just so we could hole up in this overheated house and hardly ever go out for fear of frostbite."

Clifford didn't know what to say. "You have a wonderful family. I'm sure Suzanne is —"

"She *is* a brat, but no matter. Fact is, I love Jack. I go where he goes. He wants to be needed. He's needed here. Simple as that."

"I suppose it is."

"You got yourself an opportunity." She paused, then added, "I guess you have to take it."

"Sure, yes. It's just a semester unless I decide to stay on for a couple of months in the summer. You know, hitch-hike around. I mean, as long as I'm there."

"It'll be an adjustment."

"I'm sure it will be. I'm kind of looking forward to it."

"For both of you, I mean." She got up and, on her way back up the stairs, shot him a smile and said, "Safe journeys. Pleasure meeting you."

"Likewise," he said, but she was gone.

This memory, triggered by hot cocoa, unspooled in a flash as Jeremy took a breath and continued reading from Natalie's letter:

> P.S. I tried to pry information out of a classmate who went to high school with Edwin. She's extremely close to one of his buddies. All of them are from Indy, and they do hang tight. I think if you're not absolutely bonkers for basketball, they think you are from some other country. Anyhow, no word on Edwin's fate, except that back in the day he had a thing going with a chick named Mary (if that's not a codeword), and she is nowhere nearby. She's doing agribusiness at Purdue. So, when your profs gave Edwin the blackball, perhaps he chucked it all for romance in the tall corn (there's that phrase again! I do remember some things).
>
> Did or will Edwin leave school? Will Edwin go West to marry Mary? Will Mary marry Edwin?
>
> More episodes to follow in this subplot to "That Parkhurst Girl," same time, next letter.

Clifford experienced another brain flash, triggered by *basketball* and *tall corn.* Edwin Shackleford had been Clifford's roommate when he'd met Natalie in the spring of their freshman year. Like Clifford, Ed planned to major in literature, and he'd applied for the same Sorbonne program where Clifford was enrolled at the time of these letters. The semester-long program began after winter break in the sophomore year. The primary requirement for participation was to keep up passing grades in the preceding fall quarter. Clifford had managed it, but Ed hadn't and therefore was informed by the dean he wouldn't be packing his bags for Paris. The unfortunate fellow was bright enough and already spoke passable French. But he'd been more focused on excelling at his fraternity pledge chores than finishing his essay, "Cynicism in Voltaire." (Given the implications of his theme, a one-pager probably would have sufficed.)

Clifford could not remember Natalie's meeting Edwin, but she must have. She knew the fellow was from Indianapolis, as were several of Clifford's classmates in the program. It occurred to Clifford now, as it hadn't then, that Natalie was both more curious and more knowledgeable about Edwin than would be justified by their few brief meetings in the dorm. Edwin was handsome, not exceptionally tall, and was a fair storyteller, even though he drew most of his anecdotes from his party-time at Shortridge High School. He was much too short to have been even a guard on the basketball team, but, as were all of them in the Shortridge crowd, he was a rabid fan. When Clifford was preparing to leave for Paris in January, Edwin and his cohort were still talking about the high-school tournament back home that had taken place over Thanksgiving break.

Had Natalie been interested in dating Edwin?

After Clifford had flown away, had she come down for a weekend with him and then been rejected or ignored? Her telling of "That Parkhurst Girl" episodes betrayed her as a small-town gossip, but you'd think she'd have juicier material than this academic setback of Edwin's. After all, he hadn't failed out of school, and Clifford thought he remembered hearing that Ed had forsaken the comparative lit program and undertaken American Studies. (Take that! — you dead white Europeans!) Surely he'd be able to find cynicism enough in the likes of Eugene O'Neill and John O'Hara.

The idea that Natalie was stuck on Edwin didn't fit with Jeremy's theory about her secret and proprietary lust for Judith. Besides, in her letters Natalie was overtly gushy, if alternately sarcastic and apologetic, about her sincere love for Clifford. He'd believed she genuinely cared for him then, and even in the light of today's possible reinterpretations, he still believed it.

Clifford pictured the cocoa on the kitchen table. Natalie's mother seemed more concerned than necessary about the effect his absence might have on her daughter. Hardly necessary, unless the worry was about a major health reversal.

"I suppose this Edwin guy was someone you both knew pretty well," Jeremy said, getting it wrong. Edwin had been no close friend of Clifford's, no matter what the fellow might have meant to Natalie. "Seems like a side issue. There's no more mention of him, but she gets back to the good stuff in her next letter, as you'll see."

April 3, 1968

Dear Clifford Olmstead Klovis,

I didn't get a thank-you for my incredible thoughtfulness. Unsure whether they sell Pepto Bismol or anything like it over there, I sprang for the cost of those tablets — plus 80¢ postage! — to get them into your hot little hands. I trust and pray they made it all the way into your queasy stomach. During the break on my visit back home, I was in the drugstore to buy more of my regular meds, and the thought occurred. I never had food poisoning but I figured these couldn't hurt. We have a charge account at the store, but not sure I would have bought them if I knew how expensive it was to mail them. Anyhow...

While I was home, as I had more or less predicted, I experienced the joys of winter's recurrence (for me; it had never left there). A magnificent show, including dirty snow alternating with floods and black ice on the roads. I had lots of time to think about things in general, including school, me, the summer, me, my meds, you, me, and so on. (I tried not to think about Parkhurst, but of course I did.)

Back at school, none of us is getting any work done. Perhaps it's because those lucky ones who spent the break in warmer climes already have highly infectious spring fever and us Eskimos have caught the bug. Things continue to thaw and sprout here, and the male birds are singing their hearts out, so sex is in the air! Our group (mostly kids I've gotten to know since you left, plus Judith) is busy with birthday parties. And if those celebrations don't happen to be spaced regularly enough, we throw in a Merry Unbirthday. You frat boys might use such as an excuse to drink, but our vice is ice cream. The single-sex festivities are not as tame as you might think, though. Some of us (not me) dance on tables. Polly, who is an inch short of six feet and weighs north of 170 collapsed a table in the dining room during her last performance. (The wait staff had already cleared the tables, and they were about to turn off the lights. We were the only stragglers in the place.) Polly also dances on tables and jumps on laps in the S.U., but for some reason the rickety furniture has always held up. Now with the warmer weather, they've put some tables out on the patio of the S.U. So we have the prospect of flamenco al fresco. (I wonder if they make tequila-flavored ice cream?)

"So Judith is in Natalie's new group," Jeremy said. "But she's not the center of attention, or at least not the center of *the group's* attention. This does get more interesting, but your girl digresses first. You must have shared your summer plans with her in your last letter. I know you told me you spent the summer working at a theater not far from Canada. Stunning coincidence, suspicious as hell, but I'll just have to guess at how things turned out. When she talks here about her summer plans, it's clear she hopes to be nearer her campus than to home. I assume you therefore didn't coordinate your plans. Seems like you wanted to be near her, on some level, and she didn't reciprocate. Since she said she was so eager to see you again, that seems odd."

In fact, Clifford hadn't made any deliberate effort to choose the theater's location. He'd applied to summer-stock companies in upstate New York, Vermont, New Hampshire, Massachusetts, and Maine. It was pure coincidence (really?) that his only acceptance was from the Ebbets Theatre Company in Ebbetsville, just five miles from the Bedards' farmhouse. Clifford was sure he told her the name and location of the playhouse. She'd shared no delight over his getting the job, made no offer to see him perform, and expressed no eagerness to see him sooner than their expected reunion at school in the fall.

She remarked on the coincidence not at all, choosing instead to go on at length about her own plans:

> As to my summer plans, my best shot at earning some money is to wait tables at UConn, as I did last year. The student aid office here helps line up those part-time jobs. I don't want to ask Dad for more money. They've done enough already, and I'm sure Suzanne is not applying any economies.
>
> I've told the UConn student employment office that I

absolutely need a single room. I told them — which is true — that because of my condition I need an unusual amount of undisturbed sleep. But my needs are just as much emotional. I want to be a solitary, non-person for three months. It will be essential, restful therapy — because Parkhurst is set to be my roommate again next year. Call me <u>cerebrotonic</u> (cribbed from the last psych lecture, "describing a personality type — introverted, intellectual, and restrained emotionally").

"If 'that Parkhurst girl' put so much stress in her, why the hell does she sign up for another year with the same roommate?" Jeremy asked. "I'm not getting it at all."

Clifford didn't know the reason, and he was just as perplexed why Natalie would suffer Judith voluntarily. Looking back on things, Jeremy's mother-hen theory was the only explanation.

No, it's not the only explanation. I think I see where this is going.

Jeremy announced, "Here's the key, the true confession. I think you'll agree I've been right all along."

Speaking of Judith, I believe now she's given up men entirely. I don't know whether she even had any dates last semester. There was a phase where she was dressing up and flitting off to the S.U., but I don't know if anything came of it. I don't think she was trolling for girls. She's too much of a ten-year-old tomboy to go after such a relationship, aggressive or passive.

Trying to be her friend and living-space companion has been the most upsetting experience of my life so far. More upsetting even than sibling rivalries with Suzanne or the challenges of maintaining my health. The girl is sick, and she's said so. I thought it was just so much phony drama until she unloaded her life story on me the other night when she couldn't sleep (and I needed to). She refuses to get help (afraid, I'm sure). She can't help herself, and her parents are in total denial about unseemly family matters.

Judith is brainy, gorgeous, and her family is wealthy beyond the dreams of avarice. She's stuck in her ten-year-old mindset, and she wants to stay that way. You can be sloppy, irresponsible, zany, and manic. You can prefer the company of girls and not get all hung up on what your tendencies might mean. You can dress up and look pretty when you want, especially if you crave the attention of some father figure. You can ignore your nightmares and tell yourself you're happy and protected because you have a flock of mother hens (including me) trying to protect you.

She lives in a dream world. What will happen in two years when she graduates and has to make her way in the cruel world? I shudder to think.

She says she'll probably kill herself, and I believe her.

"There you have it!" Jeremy exclaimed. "Judith is a lesbian who's still in the closet, and Natalie worries more for her than she does for you. She's devoted to the little snot. She's totally invested emotionally — to the point of needing a summer to restore herself — then intends to walk bravely back into the fire come next semester. I don't know about back then, but a suicide threat these days would get you reported to the dean, if not to the damn police, in a heartbeat." He sighed, then said quietly, "You know, I'm not sure this girl Natalie was ever truly yours, despite her professions of love."

I have to admit, Jeremy may be right. And it's a totally different version of events than I remember.

Considering it all from Jeremy's perspective, Natalie seemed at least confused emotionally — much more confused than Clifford remembered. When Clifford had read her letters the first time, when he was still in Paris, he was an inexperienced young man (and untested lover) whose immature ego assumed this woman was crazy about him. He expected their relationship was his to resume or to end on his return. As to his own roommates, their antics and annoyances might have seemed consequential back in the day, but he'd never stayed in touch with any of them. Living with Judith could hardly be the worst experience of Natalie's young life. Her worries seemed ridiculous. Analyzing those texts now, as Jeremy insisted on doing, pulled those experiences into the adult realm, where love triangles can easily form in various permutations and combinations, and where jealousies have years and even lifetimes to become entangled.

Natalie's medical condition was a confounding complication. Back then, Clifford had made his decision based mostly on what she'd told him about her prognosis. He didn't doubt its reality, but now he wondered whether she'd been using her health as an excuse to avoid intimacy with him. Maybe she didn't yet know whose lover she wanted to be, or in what role.

Jeremy continued reading, saying, "To confuse matters, she adds this bit at the end... "

> Olmstead the Corpse of a Cactus has come back to life. He sat patiently on the windowsill all winter, mostly because I was too lazy to toss him in the trash. In the last two days, he has miraculously broken out in little sprouts (?) buds (?) appendages (?) babies (?) tiny green things (?). My treatment plan for this successful outcome? Tender loving neglect!
>
> I realize I haven't talked of politics in a while, and I fear if I do

at this point I'll go on for pages, in which case this letter will need an extra unaffordable stamp. Suffice it to say, things are getting more and more interesting and complicated, and I do wish I'd been born a year sooner so I could vote this fall.

By the way, I'm thinking of letting my hair grow long. Not as convenient, but maybe sexier?

Hoping you'll Get Clean for Gene,

N. B.

Jeremy said, "I know identifying you with the cactus seems silly, but I think it's her way of saying you're still in the game. You're on the bench with a wounded pitching arm, but she hasn't thrown you off the team. Again, she seems undecided — about a lot of things." Then he added, "Oh, and I did a search on *Get Clean for Gene.* I didn't know it was about Eugene McCarthy's presidential campaign. The idea was to ask grungy hippies to get baths and haircuts so they could show up at the polls as respectable Democrats. It all happened after LBJ's resignation — which took place on *the very day of this letter.* This was all before the Democratic National Convention in August, which disappointed just about everybody by nominating Hubert Horatio Humphrey. You knew the history, but I didn't. There's lots of backstory between these lines."

Yes, after Johnson threw in the towel, Clifford and his classmates thought the war would soon be over. Wishful thinking.

"No more mention of Parkhurst," Jeremy said. "I wonder what happened. Perhaps some falling out? The rest of her letters seem to focus more on you and your situation, more like the kinds of things I'd expect, more chat and less drama. Not much between *those* lines. Ho-hum. From the way she opens this next letter, I suspect you'd sent her a photo of yourself. In a trench coat? I don't think I ever saw that one. And you must have told her you didn't mind her growing her hair long."

May 4, 1968

Dear Cliff,

I admit I'm flattered that you seem to be fantasizing over the image of me with long hair. I hope the result lives up to your expectations. But it's not coming in as nicely as I expected.

Due to her condition, Natalie's hair was starting to thin on top, which could have been a reason for her to decide to let it grow more. Doing so wouldn't improve its thickness. Perhaps it was unconsciously compensating, more like the tendency balding men have to grow beards.

Yes, he'd sent her a snapshot. He couldn't remember who took it. He'd needed a headshot for his submissions to those acting jobs. He posed in the garden of the American Center for Students and Artists. He wore a wool turtleneck with a belted khaki trench coat he'd bought used at a flea market. His hair wasn't long except for his sideburns, which were creeping down toward his chin. Fearing the coat might be riddled with flesh-eating bacteria or bedbugs, he'd had it dry-cleaned. It wasn't a bad fit, and it lent him what he thought was a rakish, literary appearance. But the dry-cleaning had removed what was left of the garment's water-repellent quality. Aside from its romantic cachet, a practical reason for buying the coat was the inclement weather. The chilling April showers in Paris had persisted. In fact, that year, the entire month of May was a continuous, cold drizzle. The nastiness outside did not discourage the student riots, though, which erupted at the Sorbonne's suburban campus in Nanterre on May 2 and soon spread to the main Panthéon campus in Paris, which was just a block from Clifford's residential hotel on rue Vaugirard.

"The riots started about this time," Jeremy said. "I remember you telling me it was going on all around you, but you didn't participate. You weren't unsympathetic, I'm sure. You just didn't want them to jerk your passport."

The riots lasted through all of May and into the third week of June. The American news media, as well as many of Clifford's classmates, assumed the uprising had something to do with anti-Establishment rage brought on by the war in Vietnam. Disapproval of America's role was widespread in France, where popular opinion was disgusted by American stupidity. The arrogant Yanks, lauded as saviors of Europe just a generation ago, should have taken a lesson from the previous French cockups in Indochina and stayed home.

In fact, the origins of the revolt, as Clifford only learned through his readings in later years, had a specific cause almost entirely unrelated to the war, but perhaps not wholly disconnected from the hippie movement worldwide. Around this time, the writings of the years-dead anarchist, philosopher, and sociologist Herbert Marcuse had taken hold in the academic community. A German student leader at Nanterre, Dany Cohn-Bendit (aka Dany the Red), took these ideas to heart and whipped up his fellows into an angry frenzy that went viral. Their fundamental objection was to the French class system, and specifically to the patently restricted career tracks at the Sorbonne. Their perception was, given money and connections, a student from one of the old-line, landowning, aristocratic families could sail into the engineering program, say, and with not much attention to academic performance, eventually slide into a prestigious management job at a company like Peugeot or Dassault upon graduation. Although the French class system has been unarguably rigged since feudal times (despite the brief disruption that inspired Bastille Day), the number of students thus disenfranchised was relatively few. But fueled by the global zeitgeist that began with rock 'n' roll and flowed into electric Kool-Aid acid trips, the mob mentality grew fierce. And when no-nonsense, left-wing French labor unions joined the students in the streets, the aging President Charles De Gaulle became seriously worried the country was facing real revolution. On May 30, De Gaulle went on television to call for a referendum. In effect, he defied the voters to throw him out. Not surprisingly, fearful proles joined the bourgeoisie in giving him their overwhelming endorsement. His response was to surround the city with tanks, and the unrest quieted down.

During this time, Clifford shared a low-rent hotel room with two roommates, a pair of young lovers, Flo and Ted, from Indianapolis who had been high-school classmates of the ill-fated Edwin. Theirs was an odd ménage-à-trois but economically viable. The deal was made barely workable by the chronic absence of the couple, who preferred hanging out at the University of Strasbourg campus, where Flo was an undergraduate. At those times, Ted cut his classes at the Sorbonne, and Clifford had their room in Paris all to himself. On their return, he'd stay out late dining on pommes frites and beer. When he finally hit his pillow in the wee hours, he'd fall fast asleep and not be kept awake by the sloppy sounds of their screwing. (His single bed was separated from their double by a curtain, which gave Flo some modesty but did little else for privacy.)

The full-length windows of their room looked out on the street, rue Vaugirard, which connects the Boulevard Saint Michel and the Sorbonne on one end and the Theatre de l'Odéon and the

Palais de Luxembourg and its gardens on the other. Directly across the street was an elementary school and the Jewish Center for Students and Artists. All during May, rioting would typically begin during the afternoon and carry on into the night. At its peak, students dug paving stones out of the street and threw them at the cops (the *flics*) and overturned cars, setting them on fire. On a few occasions, rioters gained access to the rooftops near the hotel and threw down exploding Molotov cocktails (a bottle full of kerosene with a rag stuffed into the mouth as a fuse) at the police.

The flics would chase the rioters up the street from the Sorbonne and past Clifford's window. One night, the Jewish Center kept its doors open, and students dove in there for refuge. The next night, the flics were back with rifles tipped with teargas canisters. They went down on their knees, weapons at the ready to fire at any lit window. They assumed those places were harboring dissidents. Flo and Ted were out of town at the time, and Clifford was saved from canister shrapnel because his quick-witted concierge ran downstairs and hit the main switch, cutting power to the building.

Because of the riots, the government closed the postal service, which also included telecommunications. Clifford and his fellow students were thus prevented from sending wires home requesting money. Under the circumstances, the American embassy refused to help in any way, lest they be seen as supporting any expat students who were joining the riots.

So Natalie's letter of May 4 arrived much later than expected, and subsequent letters, of which there were three, were also delayed.

I like the trench-coat look, and I'm flashing on early Tyrone

Power. I suppose it's also a French look, but I can't really picture you as T.P. because he didn't walk around with a permanent grin on his face (stab!). But I'm guessing you have more character than he did (unstab).

I mention my plans to grow my hair long because admittedly I wanted to prepare myself for your first sight of me on your return. Lady Godiva kind of thing. Take your breath away. But the date of your return in my mind was always September, start of school. This news about your doing summer stock in my backyard is startling. I just assumed you'd stay over there, bumming around Europe, trolling the museums and the bars, not missing an opportunity.

When I think about it, there's a lot of theater going on in the thawed-out frozen north in the summer. It's where New Yorkers and Bostonians go to cool off, send their kids to summer camp, and generally forget about the oppressive heat and humidity of Northern Atlantic cities in the summer.

I'm surprised you got in, but maybe you lied on your resume? I'll try to come and watch you perform if I can get away from my hash-slinging duties at UConn.

Now that you're coming home (or at least to these shores) I've decided you might have been worth waiting for.

Love,

Natalie

P.S. THIS COULD HAVE TURNED INTO A LOVE LETTER, BUT I DON'T WANT TO FRIGHTEN YOU OFF.

"Fickle? I'll say," Jeremy observed. "From her standpoint, I'm sure she'd say she hasn't changed her tune all along. But we know different, don't we? I sense something going on in the next one."

May 12, 1968

Dear Cliffordski,

I have to confess — and I'm preparing you for the sight of me — I feel like a blimp, and maybe I look like one. They joke about the "freshman fifteen," those extra pounds a newbie puts on. But here I am a lonely sophomore, and the bulk has come on. Paper-writing and exam-taking pressure, yes. But indulging in ice cream instead of booze has also had its effect. Especially for someone in my condition. Amazed I didn't poison myself beyond recovery. The S.U. had mint chocolate chip this week, as if it's an excuse. I may start smoking if I can't find any other way to limit my intake.

Love, love, love,

Fat Nat

P.S. I wrote this on Mother's Day. Didn't you tell me your mother had gotten heavy?

Jeremy's take was, "Indulging in ice cream? I still don't know what her condition was, but it seems like she gave up trying. Again, I'm thinking she was casting a line out to the only ship that would save her — you. The S.S. Parkhurst had already sailed on toward some other paradise.

"The next one is a letter, but postcard length…"

May 14, 1968

Dear Mr. Klovis,

I'm in the throes of a drug reaction, trying to survive on instant oatmeal instead of Rocky Road.

I don't mean to burden you with my personal albatross. You seem like a worthwhile person, someone in whom a person can trust. But for how long?

Confidentially,

N. Bedard

"What kind of reaction?" Jeremy wanted to know. "Insulin? That would explain it. But scarfing down buckets of ice cream would be suicide!"

Natalie's "medical condition," which she had so consistently refused to name, was diabetes. Her condition was sufficiently advanced as to require daily, self-administered injections. She had never taken her clothes off in front of Clifford, mainly because she was ashamed of the scars from the multiple injection sites on her body. One time when they were making out, her sweater rode up from her waist, and he could see finger-length craters in her stomach — injection sites where the drug had caused her baby fat to atrophy.

Natalie's breath had a persistent medicinal smell, which was a side effect of her taking large doses of insulin. A whiff was an exotic mix of a gin-drinker's boozy breath and the ether of anesthesia. Far from being repelled, Clifford found it made her kisses all the more intoxicating. And, needless to say, he was hooked.

She had informed him on several occasions that she did not expect to live very long. This revelation was the deal-breaker, the ultimate ultimatum, in their prospects for intimacy and anything like an adult love relationship. She said premature death was common in patients at her stage. Her hair loss was further evidence she was already on the slippery slope downward.

Before I'd left for Paris, she'd given me the definite impression she didn't want to get intimate for my sake. She didn't want me to fall in love with her because she wasn't going to be around long enough to for us to make a future together.

What Jeremy said next was doubly surprising.

"I read these letters about a month ago. Since then, I poked around the Internet to find out what I could about her. Those references to her medical condition, and even the hints of suicide, made me think she could be dead already. In fact, I was pretty sure of it, but I had to look to be sure. I mean, at your age, how many of your buddies are still around? But the more I looked into it, the more suspicious I became. First of all, there were no obituaries. I'm thinking, okay, everybody these days has some kind of social media presence. But for her — absolutely *zip!* I did some more data drilling and — *presto!* — I find she was married to some high-net-worth building-services contractor, had two kids, one of whom seems to be estranged (lesbian, maybe?), settled in the South. I find an old email address and send an inquiry — it bounces. I see she divorced the guy a few years ago, sold the family home on the lake, moved back to the frozen north, probably in the old family home, which I'm guessing she inherited. Like I say, no social media presence whatever, which is really odd.

"Why does a couple get divorced at your age? I'm telling you, it's probably money. One of them has health challenges, probably her, and it's expensive. Threatens to break the bank. Medicare, insurance, family trust — any of those things can work out better if you're single. So she's alive, but maybe not doing well?"

Clifford's first reaction was anger, so much so he could feel his blood pressure rise and his face flush hot. Jeremy didn't seem to notice.

Years ago, in the nascent days of the Internet, Clifford had taken his own shot at data-drilling for information on Natalie. The tools at his disposal were less evolved than Jeremy's, but Clifford also had the edge on real-life experience and knowledge.

His information came from the two encounters he'd had with her before they'd lost touch.

The first of those was after he'd returned to the States, when he was doing his gig at the summer theater. She came to see him perform exactly once. Coincidentally and ironically enough, it was for his biggest role that summer, Christy in John M. Singe's *Playboy of the Western World*. The leading role required a creditable Irish accent and memorizing more than half of the lines in the script. He was shaky in rehearsal, but he had done all right, after which the cocksure director from New York had exclaimed, "The Ebbets Theater has never heard applause like that!" Clifford's head swelled for a time, but as Ebbetsville receded in the rear-view mirror, he suspected he was no more ready for a career as an actor than the winner of a high-school debate contest is qualified to argue before the Supreme Court.

Natalie hadn't warned him she would be in the audience that night. But on his way out of the theater from the dressing room, there she sat on a bench out front. At first, he hardly recognized her. Long tresses, yes. Her hair had grown out. And so had her waistline and her hips. The freshman fifteen and then some. She was beyond pudgy.

She was wearing a blousy, bright-orange sleeveless top over a pair of knee-length khaki shorts. It was a warm Saturday night, but here she was dressed for, what, a picnic? Shopping at K-Mart?

His heart sank. That much weight doesn't come on in just a month. He felt doubly guilty because not only was he underwhelmed to see her, but also he'd been recently harboring a crush on another member of the cast. (Never mind it was never reciprocated, that summer or ever.)

He had no memory of their greeting. Did they hug? Kiss? If they'd embraced in a passionate kiss, surely he would have remembered.

She told him "You were okay" with a little smile to let him know she was understating with her typical sarcasm. He replied it was all her fault because she was the one who had encouraged him to take up acting.

She said she wasn't sure she'd be able to come to any other performances (which ran Friday through Sunday evenings, with an extra performance, a matinee, on Sundays). She had to work weekends waiting tables at UConn, and this time was an exception because a friend had agreed to sub for her. He said, "Don't worry, you caught my best work. The other parts they gave me are supporting roles."

The theater provided a summer-camp-style dormitory in a rural compound of cabins for the cast and crew. They all shuttled back and forth on a dilapidated staff bus. As Clifford was talking to Natalie, everyone else had boarded the waiting bus. Its doors were still open, and the driver was waiting for him.

Since she hadn't given him any kind of a heads-up, they didn't have plans for the evening. All he knew of the town and its surroundings was what he saw every day from the bus. He didn't even know the way back to the cabins.

When Clifford glanced over anxiously at the bus, Natalie told him to go ahead. She'd have no trouble waiting a short while on the bench. Her father would drive by shortly to pick her up and take her home.

She could have invited him to her house for dinner or proposed they take a stroll to some nearby diner for coffee. But he didn't encourage her, and she didn't offer. How could she be the person who wrote him those eager letters? And why didn't the sight of her after so many months send his heart racing?

Before he walked off, Clifford said, "You said you'd gained weight. I didn't realize. Was it all because of me?" It wasn't the kindest thing to ask under the circumstances, but he had to know how much he'd be blaming himself.

She flushed and shook her head, then mumbled, "My stupid roommate."

At the time, his ego wanted him to believe she was dodging the issue, giving a lame excuse, not wanting to embarrass him. He assumed he was the cause of it all! He thus had justification for his guilt, along with confirmation he might well be some kind of lady-killer, a Tyrone Power, if not an Ernest Hemingway.

But now, because of Jeremy's analysis, Clifford's more mature interpretation of events would be different.

Maybe the real cause of her distress had been her roommate. Or maybe not. And perhaps she was as confused about her feelings for me as I had been about mine for her. How much of a reason not to get involved was her diabetes?

Back then, he was sure her disease was a total show-stopper. The only drug at the time was insulin, and the treatment itself was fraught with risk. But given what had happened since, perhaps the disease was just a bogus reason, a ploy for avoiding a momentous choice she wasn't yet ready to make.

Clifford didn't see Natalie at all when he returned to school in the fall, and they didn't correspond. Their scene outside the theater had been a de facto breakup.

It may have come as a surprise to both of them that they got back together for a weekend in the spring of his junior year. At the same time, Clifford was dating Miriam, a drama student at Sarah Lawrence. They had met when he was in a cohort of male actors loaned to them for a production of *The Crucible*. He had a supporting role as Hathorn, and she ran props. Their one-night stand after rehearsal, his first such experience but not hers, turned into an intimate, steady relationship that lasted two years but then stopped short.

In February, in the dead of winter, Miriam had some other commitment that prevented her coming to spend the weekend with Clifford. Although he'd normally hibernate with a book or a stack of classical music LPs at such times, he took it upon himself, he didn't remember why, to phone Natalie. She didn't sound surprised or angry, nor was she noticeably thrilled. She agreed to take the bus and show up on Saturday morning.

If Clifford worried he was being disloyal to Miriam, he didn't let it stop him. He'd been more than curious about how Natalie was doing. Maybe she was still in a nose-dive and it was all his fault?

The impression she gave on her arrival was as someone transformed. She'd lost most of the heaviness she'd put on a year ago. She was dressed in jeans, which were neither tight nor baggy, with a bulky fisherman's sweater. Her hair was still long, worn in a ponytail.

She now seemed comfortable with herself. It was a notable change.

They spent most of the weekend in his bed in his dorm room, but as before, there was tentative hugging and kissing and nothing further. Clifford wasn't sure how they'd slipped back into this cozy cuddling. He didn't remember making the first move or even steering her into his room. They'd been talking, and then they were in bed. He liked it, and so did she.

Should he have forced himself on her? His personal life story might have been different if he had. But her old boundaries hadn't changed, and he was pretty sure she wanted it that way.

"What I like about you now," she said in a moment of tenderness, "is you're in no big rush."

"We're not going to… you know?"

"Let's not and say we did," she laughed.

"Nothing's changed about, you know, going further?"

"I'm still doomed, if that's what you mean," she said.

"I'm seeing somebody," he said.

"Good for you," she said, without an edge.

After a long moment, he asked, "What are you going to do, I mean, next year, and after that?"

"I'm majoring in speech therapy," she said. "Which is incredible, I love it. But they're telling me there are no jobs. I don't want to live in New York City, much less Beantown, and when you get right down to it, I'm a country girl at heart. Unfortunately, those cows don't need their speech corrected."

"So what can you do?"

"There's a restaurant near the ski resort, Rick's Grotto. I've waited tables there. The menu's classy, it's Rick the chef's gourmet cuisine. High tourist prices, and the tips are good. It doesn't hurt that Rick has a thing for me. I'll probably work there this summer, and if I don't line up something else, that's where you'll find me after we graduate."

They spent the rest of the weekend as friends, like brother and sister, and they parted without much said.

They never communicated again.

The following weekend, when Clifford was escorting Miriam back to his room, his then-roommate Jason passed them on the path, nodded to her, and said, "Hi, Natalie." The two women were about the same height and coloring. And now that Natalie had slimmed down, they were about the same build. In the winter weather, in their parkas, Jason could hardly be blamed for his mistake.

Clifford was sure Miriam heard it, but afterward he didn't mention it, and neither did she. Their relationship ended after senior year, and he didn't see her again, either.

Years later, Clifford's online searches couldn't find anything on Natalie, but he did get a search hit on Rick's Grotto. It was a commemorative website because the restaurant had gone out of business. There was an About page with the history of the place stating that in the later years the popular establishment was operated by world-class chef Rick and his devoted wife, who was unnamed. Clifford naturally assumed this woman was Natalie. The description went on to say that his wife had predeceased Rick. Both of them were buried in unmarked graves on the grounds of the restaurant. The site, it went on to say, has a spectacular view of the White Mountains for miles and miles.

Thus, for years Clifford had assumed Natalie was long-since dead.

"I have one more letter," Jeremy informed him. "I'd like to say it clears everything up, but of course it doesn't."

May 15, 1968

Cliff-o mio,

You should get drunk more often if it means you will compose such heartfelt letters! It took you four marginally readable handwritten pages to tell me you're looking forward to coming home, that you won't be bumming around Europe as I had expected (sorry for you, glad for me), and that those Ebbetsville snobs have assigned you some juicy parts and not just schlepping and scenery painting.

Granted, your picture had a distant resemblance to Tyrone Power, but don't go comparing yourself to Hemingway just because you sat at the plaque marking his place at the Closerie des Lilas. The guy was a shit, pardon my French. An asshole to women, a killer of innocent animals, and a single-handed ruiner of lovely language (my fave, Edith Wharton). Yes, journalism back then needed a healthy dose of plain speaking, but who said the prose novel must be similarly lackluster in its use of language?

When I see you again — and I trust it will be SOON — if you are wearing a tweed jacket with suede-leather elbow patches, I promise I will walk the other way!

Did you know Mart Crowley once did summer theater work in Vermont? If you don't know who Mart Crowley is, you'd better learn before you dare to show your face in these parts.

(We don't much like Vermonters, but we'll take whatever kudos we can get.)

I love you. See? It only took me two pages to say it. My feelings may have nothing to do with you. Maybe I'm in love with the image of gay-blade Tyrone Power or that fart-sniffing oaf Hemingway. Call me a hard-up country girl.

With love, seriously,

Your Natalie

Here, Clifford realized, was the source of his feelings of guilt. It wasn't, as he remembered, that he hadn't ever written back to her. It was clear from this chain of correspondence that he had, and faithfully. He may have even initiated the exchange, and he'd kept up his end, even expressing enthusiasm about her hair and his eagerness to see her again.

What I hadn't done was reply to her last letter. And I had never said I love you *back. In this, my guilt was more than justified.*

But — and this was the new insight from rereading her letters — she may not have been as crazy about him as he'd assumed. They'd both been young, fickle, confused, and inexperienced.

A person should really learn to forgive himself.

Jeremy let the pages fall to his lap and took a long breath before saying, "Hey, better than TV, right? At the end of the day, I have to say I like her. Aggravating, perplexing female, but who wants to be bored? Wish I'd met her. Maybe I even wish you'd stayed with her, although I guess I should be grateful for my own existence. Maybe we'd all have been happier if you'd run away with Nat the Snatch!"

Is Jeremy jerking my chain? Implying he wishes he'd never been born?

Then Clifford's son added, "I'm pretty sure she doesn't have email, but I did find a physical address. The family farmhouse, most likely. Last week I sent her a snail mail. Hope you don't mind."

He twisted the throttle on his wheelchair, and the contraption spun, whirred, and whined. He was almost out the door when he called back, "No reply as of yet!"

The little shit.

Clifford resented Jeremy's teasing, along with the delight he seemed to take in it.

But he was furious with Natalie.

How dare you not die!

12

The night of Jeremy's visit, Clifford drifted off to sleep at his usual time, about an hour after dinner. Someone, an anonymous night-duty nurse, not Myra, had turned on his TV and tuned it to a news channel. He hadn't paid it much attention, but as he lost consciousness, he was aware that the documentary playing on the screen was discussing conspiracy theories about the 9/11 attacks.

In the early morning, hours before dawn, Clifford's eyes popped open. He'd been in a fevered state of REM sleep, dreaming that he was licking Myra's erect, left nipple as she was scolding him for keeping his mouth shut.

As had happened before, Clifford hadn't slept through the night. Before his stroke (a phase of his life he called his *sane period*), he didn't fret much about these bouts of insomnia, having heard that older people don't necessarily need as much sleep. But given his present condition, if his brain function was going to improve at all, it would be through restorative sleep.

There wasn't much to do but lie on his back and stare at the ceiling. At these times, his way of counting sheep was to notice each in-breath and out-breath, as the Buddhist monks taught their novices to do in their meditations. This practice rarely induced in him anything like a trance. But his mind would either flit off into some fantasy or he'd eventually slip back into unconsciousness.

This time, he flashed on the images from the 9/11 documentary, and a new insight occurred: The Insiders spoke to him in riddles and metaphor. There were coded messages, meaningful coincidences, and occasionally voices. Maybe those menacing images had been presented to him for a reason.

As to meaningful coincidences, he recalled some from his sane period. For example, getting dressed to go out in the evening, he might be selecting a necktie. As he lifted the tie he thought he wanted from the rack, another one would slip to the floor. Inevitably, he would consider it a better choice. When he first started noticing these instances, he wondered whether some poltergeist, perhaps his mother's ghost, was making selections for him. Back then, he doubted the existence of ethereal entities, even whether there could be any modes of life other than the physical. In his later years, and especially as, from time to time, he thought about the prospect of his own death, he wondered about planes of existence beyond this one. He began to think of extraterrestrial aliens, ghosts, angels, and secret government operatives as being different names for a single set of entities which exist on some other plane and try — but don't always succeed — to influence events on this one.

He theorized that these entities interact with our world but have limited powers. Physical action here is the provenance of humans. Although the term had different meanings from his in some circles of conspiracy buffs, he called these entities *Insiders.*

What was going on when the other tie hit the floor was not merely an issue of wardrobe selection. Picking it up and deciding to wear it was an acknowledgment of the power and the wisdom being offered from the other side. Deciding to accept the choice and the other tie signaled his *obedience.*

Clifford had only vague notions of who the Insiders were. He suspected no average person, no outsider, did. If you had not been briefed (some would call it *enlightened*), the lore surrounding cults and conspiracies held that they'd have you promptly killed. But perhaps murder was rarely necessary, or even advisable. The Insiders have always understood — from the beginning of time — that truth can't be contained or stopped. Light overcomes darkness immediately, but darkness has no power of its own. Darkness can take over only when there is no light present.

If the truth threatens to betray secrets that the Insiders had wanted to keep close, their solution might not be to try to extinguish the source. Besides being indestructible, truth is universally precious — even, or maybe especially, to Insiders. But truth can be inconvenient at times.

The Insiders' strategy for countering or defusing truth and its consequences would be to create confusion. They'd generate a swarm of conflicting rumors. Each rumor would have an element of truth, which lent credence to the version. In so doing, the version that is the whole truth, and nothing but, would be reduced to the status of rumor. Especially if some of the lies confounding the truth were untestable and therefore unverifiable, the average person would never be sure what to believe.

Consider, for example, the Fermi Paradox. This famous question in exobiology asks, "If intelligent beings exist elsewhere in the universe, why can't we detect them?" In a sleepless, curious moment a few years before Clifford had his stroke, he searched the topic online. As he'd read, there existed no less than twenty-two reasonable-sounding hypotheses why smart aliens either don't exist or can't (or won't) communicate with us. Among these is the Great Filter Hypothesis. This version of the truth holds that the processes required to generate intelligent civilizations are both highly complex and extraordinarily rare. Humans, therefore, exist because of a long chain of highly unlikely accidents. Alien races might have arisen elsewhere but have existed at different times, separated by periods of extinction (relativistic time being a slippery concept here, necessitating further assumptions about transmission modes and distances). Other rumors, perhaps more believable because so easily stated, posit that aliens are either here and undetected (cleverly disguised or hidden) or here and unacknowledged (implying that some humans know about them).

To Clifford, Jeremy's hypotheses about Natalie were similarly multivariate and slippery. The events in Clifford's past could still be interpreted in several ways. Jeremy's version seemed to absolve Clifford of guilty feelings he'd carried around for decades. Perhaps the Insiders had sent Jeremy to deprogram him! For Clifford to move to the next level, toward initiation to Insider status, perhaps he must forgive himself, cleanse himself of guilt.

Is Jeremy, therefore, an Insider himself? Or just an unwitting pawn in their game?

13

I t was another bright, clear morning. Just enough wispy clouds in the robin's-egg blue sky for decoration. Someone had wheeled Clifford out onto the edge of the patio. He'd been too drowsy to know who it was. It couldn't have been Myra. Her intoxicating scent would have startled him awake.

He'd lost track of time. He was pretty sure it was still spring because the ground looked squishy and smelt funky. From his vantage point, he looked out over a duck pond, and beyond a grove of trees he could glimpse the verge of a golf course. High-priced real-estate here, no doubt.

He was not only confused as to time but also as to location. He could remember seeing snow on the ground here, so Jeremy hadn't shipped him off to Florida. There would be seasons. Jeremy must have been the one to make the decision. His son might be making all the decisions these days. Eleanor was a distant memory. He was sure she hadn't visited him. Had she died? Run away with the gardener? Been confined to some rival institution that would challenge his to a bridge tournament?

He couldn't remember whether Jeremy's visit was yesterday or as long as a week ago. Clifford's sharpness and awareness of the present seemed to come and go. Surprising to him, his memory of long-past events was vivid. He could even recall details that he hadn't been aware of noticing as those events were taking place.

Consider the episode with Natalie's family. He remembered the musty, smoky smell of the fireplace in the parlor of their farmhouse. They called it a *parlor* and not their *living room*. He remembered her mother smelled of Evening in Paris, as his grandmother had. It was a cheap scent they sold back in the day at Woolworth's. He wondered if Mrs. Bedard wore it every day, or just for his visit.

A booming voice behind him startled him from his reverie: "Clifford! Hail fellow! Well met!" He turned his head to see the towering figure of Rev. Immanuel Thurston, the tall, ebony-skinned chieftain who had pastored the church his parents attended sixty years ago. These days, the fellow would be pushing a hundred, and this handsome manifestation didn't look more than forty. So — this must be another dead man, a phantasm come to chat.

Clifford smiled and offered his hand. "Reverend?"

"It's Manny, please!" the fellow exclaimed. "Don't you remember the old days, circumstances not dissimilar to those in which you find yourself this very day?"

Succinct, he never was. Yes, this wasn't the first time Clifford had been confined to an institution. After his Parisian education, after his stint in summer stock, he'd visited his family doctor for a physical. One purpose was to get a letter of medical fitness he could submit with his application to the graduate program in drama at Juilliard. The doctor told him his vitals were all okay, but he noticed on the chest X-ray a small spot, about the size of a dime, in the left apex of his lung.

The doctor reassured him that his was a minimal case of tuberculosis, readily treatable with a regimen of pills. Complicating Clifford's situation, state health law back then required TB patients to be confined to a sanitarium for about two months. Sputum samples would be taken, and the duration was necessary because it took that long to grow a culture (or not) to determine whether the patient's cough could infect others.

There went the plans for Juilliard. But Clifford's condition did exempt him from the Vietnam draft. So in this significant respect, far from threatening his life, contracting TB may have saved it.

On a day-to-day basis, Clifford's stay in the sanitarium seemed to him like doing time in a minimum-security prison. He shared a semiprivate room with, but kept his distance from, a young man who had a chronic cough. Clifford hoped his own case was noninfectious, but it would take weeks to prove he was harmless and earn his release.

He dressed every morning, had his provided cafeteria-style meals, submitted to a daily injection of Streptomycin in the butt, took a handful of meds, played chess with a fellow down the hall in the afternoons, and read a stack of books. Most days after chess, he watched the afternoon movie on a portable TV his mother had sent him. (Neither of his parents ever visited. The hospital had probably told them they'd better not until they had the verdict on his infectiousness.)

He started to write a novel about his experiences there, but he eventually tore up the manuscript in disgust.

All these thoughts came flooding back because Reverend Thurston had been his only regular visitor. Since Clifford did not attend his parents' church regularly, he hardly knew its pastor. But Manny showed up at the sanitarium at 3 p.m. every Wednesday. They'd chat as they strolled around the grounds.

A few years later when he lived in the West Village, Clifford dated a social worker named Ursula. On hearing his story about being in the sanitarium and his likening it to prison, Ursula asked him whether he felt he was being punished. Clifford agreed he had a sense of unexplained guilt about it all. But since he was informed of his military exemption more than a year later, it shouldn't have been a reason for him to feel guilty during his confinement.

For decades afterward, Clifford carried this vague sense that he'd offended Fate in some way, that his stay in the sanitarium was payment for a karmic debt he owed.

It wasn't until Eleanor had talked him into attending one of those self-help weekends that he got an inkling, not of what he had done, but how his very presence on Earth was a cosmic offense. The focus of this seminar, which involved about a hundred paying participants, was to overcome the presumed effects of each person's individual *life sentence*. The seminar's therapeutic approach was based on a premise developed by the Santa Cruz school of psychiatry: A common experience in human development occurs at an early age when the child goes from feeling nurtured and loved to feeling separated and even alienated from its parents. This is a normal step in defining the individual personality and sense of self. But this step comes at a huge price. The child judges the separation to be punishment for its own bad behavior or lack of worth. As a result, the subconscious mind passes *sentence,* an assessment of guilt, along with a lifelong prescription for suffering and compensatory behavior. Mental health, in the seminar's therapeutic plan, is achievable only when the mind can identify the personal sentence it passed on itself long ago. Healing can take place when a person understands that his sentence — the fundamental reason for the person's unhappiness — is simply a childish mind's naïve and unjust condemnation of itself.

When he and Eleanor took the seminar, Clifford thought these notions simplistic, even downright silly. But for months afterward, his subconscious mind must have been fretting about the question. One morning, he awoke and knew he had the answer. He remembered when he was a small boy, his father told him about his tour in the Navy during World War II. Franklin had served in the Pacific as an engineering officer on an LST — a massive tub of a troop carrier. The crew called it a *Large, Slow Target.* Clifford must have asked his father about the experience because he was fascinated with his father's war souvenirs — which included shiny items from his uniform — gold buttons, medals, and battle ribbons. He remembered his father saying his war experience was long periods of boredom separated by moments of pure terror. But the most revealing thing he said to his little boy was: "You would have never been born if it hadn't been for the A-bomb." The devastation of Hiroshima stopped the war. The dogged Japanese enemy finally surrendered. Had President Truman not decided to use the horrific weapon, Franklin and his crew would have necessarily had to invade Japan. The War Department estimated the invasion would have cost the lives of about two million American soldiers.

Perhaps Franklin carried his own sense of survivor's guilt. But his intention in telling the boy about this probably was to instill gratitude. He was trying to tell Clifford that he was one exceptionally lucky young man. He was special, one of God's elect.

But as the boy grew older, he learned in school that hundreds of thousands of Japanese — including children like himself — perished in the two nuclear blasts that ended the war. Far from making him feel special, the child's notions of guilt multiplied when he realized his puny, little life could never be worth the loss of so many other children.

His sentence, therefore, was not the mundane verdict the therapy had suggested to some others: *I always do the wrong thing,* or *I'm not worthy of love.*

No, Clifford's sentence must have been: *I don't deserve to live!*

"SHALL WE TAKE A WALK?" the phantasm of Reverend Thurston suggested. He gestured toward the trail that led around the pond, skirting the golf course.

Clifford looked around to make sure no one was watching, and the pastor helped him up out of his wheelchair. He didn't know how long it had been since he'd stood on his own. He was wearing sweatpants, a T-shirt and cardigan, and running shoes. He was ready, and they set off. Clifford walked haltingly at first, but he managed on his own.

They walked in silence until they were on the far side of the pond. There the path veered off into a forest, where they wouldn't be seen or heard.

As they entered the grove of trees, Clifford turned to him to ask, "So, Manny, do you think God is all that there is?"

"I confess I never heard anyone put it that way," he said. "There are so many nasty things and events in this world, I don't like to think those are aspects of the Almighty."

"But how could it be otherwise?" Clifford wanted to know.

"Well, let's see," Thurston mused. "Lucifer was an angel, created of God. Then Lucifer got big for his britches and fell from grace. Changed his name to Satan, and he gets the blame for everything bad. Following your line of reasoning, it's fair to say everything that exists *came from* God. But is a thing, once created, separate? Does it have its own existence apart from God? You got yourself a whopper of a question there."

"I don't see how Creator and creation are any different. And, if that's true, then maybe God is no more or no less than the sum total of creation!"

"An intriguing and baffling concept, is it not?" Manny teased and laughed. "We're made of stardust that took millennia and generations of stars to produce. The molecules of our bodies are borrowed for a ridiculously short time, recycled endlessly from one generation to the next. I read somewhere that every breath we take has at least one molecule once breathed by Julius Caesar. Maybe it's not literally true, but you get the idea."

Clifford studied the pastor's elegant appearance. He was wearing a cream-colored suit with a brilliant purple necktie. "You, you're not the least bit molecular these days, are you?"

Manny laughed again. "I live in your fevered brain, my boy. Nevertheless, I'm delighted to be here. I always enjoyed your company."

"And I yours," Clifford said. Then he asked, "Are you nowhere else? Now that you've passed on, do you have any existence outside my mortal brain?"

He shook his head. "I have no idea. The person who is speaking to you is an animated image you have manifested. I have no consciousness of my own. You could say I'm a part of you in the way you're saying God is inherent in everything. I am real to you now, but there's no *me* here to think my thoughts. You, my friend, at this moment, are the thinker of my thoughts. But, in a way, those thoughts are no less mine. Do you see?"

THAT AFTERNOON, Clifford woke with an oppressive, groggy feeling in his head. He was on his back in the bed in his room. He got a whiff of mint and opened his eyes to see Myra hovering over him. Dr. Christensen stood behind her. Moments after regaining consciousness, he had the distinct impression he'd been drugged.

"What did I tell you about trying to get up?" she whispered, and her sweet breath was the balm he craved.

The doctor addressed him loudly, "Mr. Klovis, do you know where you are?"

Clifford didn't answer. Myra glared at him. He didn't know whether she wanted him to answer or was sending him a silent message to shut the fuck up.

"You were given a sedative, Mr. Klovis," the doctor continued. "You stood up suddenly out of your wheelchair, and you fell. Very, very dangerous. Fortunately, you weren't injured. I don't know how much you understand of what I'm saying, but if you try it again, we'll have to sedate you as a matter of routine."

And he left the room.

"You old, stubborn motherfucker," Myra fumed. And she followed him out.

God might be all that there is, Clifford thought. *But no way is this quack Christensen in any way related!*

14

The human being is a marvelous, a wondrous, creation. Alone among species, except perhaps for the cockroach, people are endlessly adaptable. If we survive long enough to launch settlers to Mars or some good-sized asteroid, some of them will no doubt survive, despite seemingly insurmountable challenges. Cockroaches can eat the wiring in old TV sets, and we will eat shit or each other if it becomes necessary. The Donner Party discovered this, as did Napoleon's army, the Germans at Stalingrad, and Rwandans who thought their life mission was to hack their neighbors to pieces with machetes.

Clifford wasn't sure he had the right stuff. He was serving his sentence, after all. But he knew he was deserving at some level, as a human who pondered the nature of existence, as a person who wondered, as we all eventually do, what would happen to him when he died.

One thing he was sure of. The dead, if they have any consciousness at all, do not experience regret. Regret is an emotion. Emotion in a human being is a complex process of mental activity and bodily sensation. It is a feeling in the gut, registered in the brain. This is why it's difficult to imagine eternal souls or angels or astral beings having individual personalities. The personality in a human is a swirling mixture of emotional and mental states, mind interacting with body. After the body ceases to function, after it is little more than a residue, the process can't continue. There is some question about the persistence of the mental states, about consciousness, if indeed those are the same.

There is a notion by which the instance of a human personality could be eternal. That is, rather than the soul being an aspect of the human, the human being is a temporary manifestation of the soul, which possesses continual individuality. Maybe a quirky or a cranky soul creates a quirky or cranky human, perhaps one lifetime after another.

Such mentation can be exhausting, but what else did Clifford have to do?

I DO NOT DESERVE to live, he thought.

No one should have to carry those thoughts around with them. Nazi experimenter on human subjects Joseph Mengele may never have experienced such thoughts on his worst days. How could Clifford condemn himself so?

Eleanor had been critical of him. She had set the bar high. But it was only because she expected more, demanded more, needed more. He'd risen to the occasion. And he didn't regret a moment of their life together.

As for being the father of Jeremy, Clifford considered himself an abject failure. No wonder his son resented him. Clifford's philosophy as a parent had been "benign neglect." He'd be there when his son asked for affection or money, but not necessarily at other times. Clifford believed this fatherly role would encourage his offspring to self-reliance. Despite his infirmity, Jeremy had turned out to be self-actualizing and independent, with an attitude bordering on arrogance. Mission accomplished!

Clifford loved Jeremy deeply. He had no doubt of that, nor did he make any apology for it. But he also resented his son hugely. Mostly for the parts of himself he could see had been inherited, whether by genetics or conditioning.

If I don't deserve to live, if I should never have existed, what about Jeremy?

∾

THE PROSPECT of getting shot up continually with tranquilizers or sedatives unnerved Clifford. Myra had warned him, but he hadn't realized how serious the threat was. He'd thoroughly enjoyed his chinwag with Thurston, even though it had cost him dearly. Judging from his caregivers' version of events, from the moment Clifford stood up, his walk with the pastor in the forest was pure fantasy.

Clifford's challenge was to live fully what remained of his life, both real and imagined, and he'd have to deal with the consequences.

He hadn't really intended to be so philosophical. His life to this point hadn't been what you'd call meditative. If such had been his intention, he could have saved time and been a monk.

Do those guys ever figure out what's going on? Maybe eventually they are just satisfied to get free food, clothing, and a reason to get up in the morning.

One thing Thurston's visit had impressed on him: It doesn't matter what you believe. As the German philosopher Wittgenstein stated with such aggravating simplicity, *The world is whatever is the case.*

CLIFFORD KNEW and understood that his lust for Myra was never to be gratified. Were he younger and more capable, this would have been a disappointment. But as things stood, lust was a gift. It was another reason to get up in the morning. It was a life force, which could be respected for itself, if not for its gratification. Her scent sent him into a swoon.

Thank you, God!

15

It was time he had it out with Eleanor. He'd hoped she'd visit him, as Jeremy had. Jeremy's side of the conversation had seemed very real. But Jesus, when he was posing as Christiansen, had been telepathic, possibly but not necessarily imaginary. The historical personages who had visited Clifford were surely projections from his own mind. But when Eleanor suddenly appeared in his room, he could not be sure whether her presence was physical. He didn't know whether she was alive or dead, here or there (wherever *there* might be). In any case, the conversation might have been the same.

"I never imagined you'd go and have a stroke," she complained.

"It's not like I planned it," he said.

"Do you even know where I am now?" she asked.

"No fucking clue," he said.

"I'm working with orphans in Africa," she said. He noted a tone of self-righteousness in her voice. But he judged it was forgivable.

She had a right to be proud of what she was doing, and she didn't need to be defensive about it, especially around him.

"Are you spending my money?"

"*Our* money?"

"Who is underwriting your mission is all I'm asking," he said.

"You. And the Pan African Beneficent Alliance," she said.

"Oh," he said. "David Rockefeller or David Koch?"

"Don't be snarky," she said. "Who cares where the funding comes from if it's doing good?"

"Point taken," he said. "How are you personally? Are you getting three squares a day?"

"I get by," she said. "Seems like you're managing, as well."

"I do all right," he replied. "I have the hots for the day-duty nurse."

"It's good to have a goal," she said, and her presence either evaporated or he fell off to sleep.

IN THE MONTHS just preceding his stroke, he and Eleanor had occupied the same house. They weren't drifting apart because, in effect, they were already sailing in parallel. But there was no rancor, no fundamental disagreements. They were both sailing in the same direction, away from hurtful past experiences and toward the respective days when each would depart the planet.

They both fretted about Jeremy, but worry is not the equivalent of love, nor even of benign neglect. In his outward behavior, their son had rejected them both, each for different reasons. Emotionally, he was his mother's child, but he resented his dependence. And he resented his father for not being man enough to challenge his mother when, in his view, she was being unfair to him. Jeremy had begun to express these feelings when he was in high school, where he was an above-average student who could have excelled if he'd been willing to work at his studies. But as it was, he passed his exams after barely skimming the textbook, and his essays were just glib enough to earn him passing grades. Since his lack of study made him thin on background, his written assignments were almost devoid of facts. But his teachers must have been sufficiently impressed with his vocabulary and logic. Perhaps they weren't fooled, but what other kid in their class was turning in work that read like an intelligent, if vapid, editorial in a major newspaper? After all, facts can be ferreted out in a wink online. The power of persuasion is a rare talent.

All through Jeremy's teenage years, the kid was increasingly aloof. His parents judged his rebelliousness as more or less normal, possibly even evidence of a healthy ego. Everyone these days seems to know what it takes to get ahead in a society that demands competitiveness, if not fair dealing.

But Jeremy became embittered after his automobile accident. It was prom night of his senior year. His friend Hal was driving, and their dates Cindy and Louise were also in the car. It was a single-car mishap with no one at fault. Hal's Toyota Corolla hit a patch of ice on a rural highway, went over the guardrail, and rolled over twice before coming to rest in a ditch. They were all wearing their seatbelts, and all of them survived. But the torque of the tumbling fractured Jeremy's spine, severing his spinal cord in the lower lumbar region. He'd be paralyzed for life (or until medical science discovers how to induce nerve cells to knit back together).

From the standpoint of Jeremy's self-discipline and his career path, his disability had a transformative effect. Confined to his wheelchair, he learned to like, even to prefer, his own company. It's a trait shared by writers, programmers, and theoretical physicists. Jeremy's analytical mind fastened on math. Applying his skill for threading his way through complex, logical processes, he found his métier. Now he was working as a programmer while he finished his doctorate in mathematics. Jeremy's colleagues were encouraging him to teach eventually, but, in his father's opinion, the young man might well be happier as a research fellow, living happily in a closet somewhere, only to emerge decades later with the solution to some baffling, fundamental problem.

Clifford's brief chat with Eleanor clarified one thing — in her absence, the family responsibilities, including the details of Clifford's care, must have fallen to Jeremy. Clifford wondered whether his brainy son could muster the patience to deal with such mundane chores. But no one was threatening to throw his father out of the place, so Jeremy must be taking care of business.

It upset Clifford at first when Jeremy told him about cleaning out the family home. Granted, Jeremy had explained, quite logically, that Clifford probably wouldn't be going back there. Jeremy must have decided that Eleanor wouldn't be coming back either.

ONE MIGHT THINK Jeremy's spinal injury would have been the end of his sexual performance ability, but far from it. The accident had severed his spine between the L3 and L4 locations of the lower back. The result was a loss of sensation and control in both legs below the knee. After the accident, he was as surprised as anyone that he still got erections, at both inspired and uninspired times. His doctor explained there are two kinds of arousal, which occur in both sexes. The first type is *psychogenic*, which results from conscious thought, whether from stimulating sights and sounds and smells or from fantasies. The nerve connections to the groin form a reflex arc, starting at the T11 vertebra in the middle of the back, carrying signals to and from the penis or vagina, and connecting at the L2, which is two vertebrae above Jeremy's lesion. Thus, his psychogenic pathway was undamaged and fully functional. The other type of response is *reflexogenic*, which is automatic and involuntary, typically in response to touch, whether from a lover's caress or inadvertently brushing against an object. The nerve connections are in the S2-S4 sacral region of the pelvis. This location is several inches below the site of Jeremy's injury. But the autonomic nerve response occurs not in the brain but in the spinal cord. Consequently, reflexogenic erections can actually increase after such an injury because the brain can no longer inhibit them.

Jeremy was embarrassed to find he was getting spontaneous boners all the time.

So, he'd be aroused, which could trigger mental stimulation as well, and then he'd be frustrated because he didn't know what to do about it. A possibility would be finding a woman who was similarly disabled. But the prospect did not appeal to him. Jeremy was saddened to admit he was not as able to forgive imperfection as the other person would have to be to live with him.

As with any healthy male, masturbation was both an option and a routine necessity, but Jeremy craved more tenderness than the life of a self-abusive monk.

Computer geek that he was, he eventually sought emotional connections via the Internet. He joined dating and matchmaking sites, using his actual handsome headshot and personal profile tidbits but avoiding mention of his impaired mobility. It intrigued and titillated him to pursue these relationships to the point where a meetup would have been suggested by one or the other participants. But he stopped short there. He told himself he had no intention of following through. Sooner or later, he resolved to actually make a date. But he never did.

Along the way, he maintained a lot of superficial friendships on social media. On Facebook, as has happened to so many people, his childhood friends, including forgotten acquaintances, were eager to reconnect. Surprisingly, bullies from his grade-school playground turned out to be thoughtful adults who professed to remember him fondly. Most of these people didn't know about Jeremy's infirmity, and he saw no advantage in advertising it. Granted, he found some of their political opinions downright offensive, but these days he could hold his own, at least when the slugfest was intellectual.

He played online chess and Holdem Poker and got so good at it he thought he could psych out a player who was bluffing even without physical tells or eye contact.

In moments of reflection, Jeremy understood that his injury and the limitations it imposed had put him on the sidelines. Then, one morning when he was in a blue funk, it occurred to him that he'd been in this passive role all his life — even before he'd had a physical reason not to participate.

It went back to those bullies in the schoolyard. As a boy, Jeremy had been frail. He judged himself uncoordinated and untalented at sports. In team sports and playground games, he would not assert himself, and he was typically the last one picked when it was necessary to choose up sides. Why was it that the bullies were always captains of the teams?

It came as a revelation, then, on that blue morning: His injury had given him a perfect and seemingly permanent excuse not to participate fully in life.

He resolved to do better.

16

Clifford's lust for Myra was not diminished because he had zero chance with her. Oh, he was handsome enough for a man of his age. Dress him up in a gray-flannel suit with a crisp, white shirt and yellow tie — and he could pass for some charismatic CEO. Just don't ask him to give a speech at someone's retirement dinner. The communication challenge was at the heart of the matter. Despite what makers of cologne and romance novelists who write about animal magnetism might want you to believe, seduction — and even basic attraction — can be all about language. A homely man who can make a woman laugh will almost always have an edge on a lame-speaking hunk, at least after initial impressions have faded into the background.

So, the fact that Clifford couldn't or wouldn't speak was indeed a barrier to his success in gratifying his desire. True, he and Myra shared a bond of secrecy. Alone of all the staff, she suspected that he had lucid thoughts — and probably rich, interior monologues — going on inside his damaged brain.

But why does she pay me any attention at all? Is it some watery, calf-

eyed look in my eyes? Does she like me because she can sense my grati-
tude for her ministrations? Surely no one on the floor, or even every
marginally attractive man of whatever age, receives the same loving
touch as she massages them, if she touches them that way at all.

Could their connection be telepathic — or dare he hope it could
become so? He'd had stimulating conversations with characters
in his life story, alive and dead, in recent days. Why couldn't he
converse in the same way with her? She'd already whispered
confidentially to him that his acting out might bring on over-
medication, and now the doctor was threatening to follow
through. She might have sensed Clifford understood her then,
but she showed no sign of being able to hear his thoughts. And,
actually, because of the unfortunate episode with Reverend
Thurston, perhaps Myra assumed Clifford *hadn't understood* her
warning. In Clifford's version of events, the pastor offered to
walk with him, and he got up out of his wheelchair and
followed. But according to Dr. Christensen, Clifford had tried to
stand up, passed out, and fell over. Were there witnesses? Did
Myra see it?

Maybe she thinks I defied her warning, thinks I betrayed her trust.
Or worse, maybe she decided she's been wrong about me all along.
Perhaps now to her I'm just another zombie.

He pictured a late winter evening in the comfortable, book-lined
living room of a well-appointed Tudor house. Casting the only
light, the cozy fire on the hearth caressed the room with a flicker-
ing, golden glow. Directly in front of the fireplace and close
enough to be enveloped in its warmth, stood a red-velvet-
covered, overstuffed easy chair. Naked but for a short, filmy
teddy that barely covered her hips, Myra gave him a smile more
radiant than the flames, took him by the hand, and bent herself
obediently over the arm of the chair. He untied the sash on his

plush bathrobe and let it fall open as his dogged soldier came to full, urgent attention. He entered her from behind and, after a few decisive thrusts, leaned his full weight on her and rocked and rocked, cushioned by the warm, supple flesh of her gorgeous, pear-shaped ass, as she was cradled softly by the thick, luxurious padding of the chair arm.

He kept it up diligently and ardently, longer than he ever had, as she gasped repeatedly. She shuddered and cried out, and he exploded. Perspiring now, they both sank to the floor, exchanged a knowing look, then began to giggle like school kids.

He said he'd fetch the brandy.

His fantasy was notably lacking in intimate conversation or the details of foreplay. But given that his attention span for lustful thoughts these days was far shorter than his fanciful physical staying power, Clifford couldn't be blamed for making his own movie and cutting to the chase.

Like Eleanor said, it's good to have a goal.

WHEN MYRA ENTERED his room again, he was wide awake, lying on his back, his head propped up just enough to see the TV, which was placed high on the wall. He was watching, but not necessarily following, a baseball game. During his sane period, it had been his favorite sport, partly because it provided random periods of boredom during which companions could converse or refreshments could be replenished. You had to keep your eye continually on basketball or ice hockey, and the breaks were scheduled. He couldn't abide football, especially after he learned about all those old pros with brain damage. He wished he'd learned the annoyingly complicated rules of cricket, but where would he have seen them play?

As she stood by the bed and lifted his wrist to take his pulse, she fumed, "So what happened out there? You get some itch in your shorts? Panties in a twist?"

He tried in vain to put an innocent look on his face.

"You gotta mind me better, or I'll punish you good."

She performed the other routine metrics in silence, including fever strip and blood pressure.

When she was about to go, she bent over him, inches from his nose, and said quietly, "If they want to pump you full of the sleepy-time shit, I don't have to give it to you. It's a fine line. A judgment call could get me written up or worse. But I could always say we heard your son would be coming by. Now, they pay attention when the relatives come, especially the ones who pay the bills. Your people see you bright as a new penny, they're not inclined to argue about things. They figure what can be done is being done, you're as good as you're going to get. All they can do is hope you're comfortable. So if there's a flush in your cheeks and you don't mess your pants, you'll be fine, at least on those days."

He wanted to give her an eager, affirmative response. He managed an eye twitch, which he hoped she'd take as a secretive, knowing reply.

She rested a hand gently on his chest, and added, "Not to be mean, but this is the last warning you're going to get from me. No point risking my job for somebody who doesn't appreciate the effort. But preventing what they try to do to some nice people is kind of a righteous cause of mine. I know you can keep a secret. I just hope you're smart enough to take advantage of my generosity — and my lack of respect for authority."

And she left.

So our conspiracy is still afoot, and now I'm thrilled to know she has skin in the game!

17

The year was either 1990 or 1991. Clifford couldn't quite remember. He stood in the gift shop of the RMS Queen Mary fingering trinkets aimlessly as Eleanor shopped. They didn't have any grandchildren, but the progeny of their nieces and nephews was numerous. Eleanor kept meticulous track of their birthdays, impending graduations, and even sporting achievements. Although in Clifford's opinion any kid would prefer a check or a gift certificate, Eleanor insisted that the obligatory monetary gift be accompanied by a suitable greeting card along with something, however small, "to remember us by."

The bins on the table in front of Clifford held keychains and fobs, pencil sharpeners, paperweights, drink coasters, and miniature replicas of the gray-lady steamship. The souvenirs were festooned with images of the ship, some with its royal insignia, along with the Union Jack. Some items also bore the Stars and Stripes with the label *Long Beach, California* in recognition of the decommissioned vessel's current mooring place.

The Queen Mary had been repurposed as a floating hotel and

conference center. On a trip to L.A. to check in on Jeremy, Clifford and Eleanor had enjoyed a late afternoon lunch in the elegant restaurant on the poop deck, in full view of the array of colossal conveyors and immense container ships in the South Bay shipyards. Jeremy hadn't wanted to come, even though these days he seemed perfectly mobile and as comfortable as could be expected in his electric wheelchair.

Something to remember us by? Okay, they'll think we're not only cheap but also clueless and vain. We send a key fob to a kid who has no keys, who has no concept of why anyone would want to visit this boat, the memento made in China by people who never saw any ship, much less this one. And the children who labor mightily in dismal factories to churn out this crap? What must they think of us, who have so much money we can waste it on tiny trinkets that aren't even toys?

Eleanor had found a scarf and a necklace — for herself. A pretty young sales clerk held up a mirror as his wife tried on a pair of matching earrings and studied the lines in her face.

At that moment, Clifford had a sudden flash of certainty:

This was the pharmacy. I came here for seasick pills.

He also knew that next door had been a tailor shop. What better use of a gentleman's time on a long sea voyage but to make repeated trips there for a bespoke suit? It took fully two weeks to complete the leisurely and lordly process of selecting the buttery worsted cloth, discussing the cut so as to minimize this ugly bit and build up that one, submitting to intimate measurements including bum and crotch, fitting and adjusting the work in progress with its draft stitching and chalk marks, admiring the transforming impression of the final product, then outfitting with accessories, including shirts and collars and stays, ties and cravats, stickpin, studs, cufflinks, keychain and watch fob, spats, and perhaps a new pair of wingtips or half-boots from the cobbler down the hall. All this bother so on arrival he could be glimpsed by anyone who mattered, dressed to the bloody nines with a coat, vest, and two pairs of pants, along with a crisp haircut and mustache trim to top it off. Oh, and he must find a suitable top hat that didn't make him look like a huckster or a circus clown.

No other place else on the boat had looked familiar to Clifford or triggered any memories. Moments after this reverie, as Eleanor concluded her purchases and signaled for them to go, he wrote it all off as a vivid fantasy, as one might get an image of living like a pharaoh on viewing antiquities in a museum.

THE BRIEF EPISODE on the Queen Mary hadn't been Clifford's only inkling of another lifetime. Over the years, impressions had come, as the one on the boat had, in flashes. When he thought about them at all, he rationalized the images or sensations as snippets from old movies he'd forgotten or products of the over-active imagination of someone who lingers over the descriptive prose in novels.

During his student days in Paris, on spring break, Clifford and classmate Jason Ettinger took a trip to London. They hitchhiked north through Lille, to Amsterdam, then into Belgium. In Bruges they boarded a cheap Channel-jumper flight to Lympne Airport, which had been an RAF airstrip during the war.

As the tires of the old DC-3 squealed onto the tarmac at Lympne, Clifford caught sight of the lush, emerald-colored grass bordering the taxiway, verging on a thicket of pine trees. The day was gray and chilly and damp, which is more or less typical of the British Isles most days of the year.

I'm home, he thought.

YEARS LATER, Clifford's career direction shifted from the commercial world of advertising to the rarefied scholarship of ancient history. Soon after he'd accepted his teaching post at UCLA, he received an invitation to speak at the University of Norwich in East Anglia. He managed to append three days of vacation to the mostly reimbursed trip. In London, he met up with almost-was girlfriend Priscilla Northcut, who'd been a Brit diplomatic brat living with her family near the Bois de Boulogne when he'd attended the Sorbonne.

Priscilla had long tresses of chestnut hair with a perennially pouty look lent her by a slight underbite and full lips. Her ample figure was mounted on a long pair of fashion-model legs. Why they'd never been more than pals was a mystery to Clifford. Then as now, she was friendly and chatty, but also pragmatic and somewhat cold. She lived the life of the mind, followed a macrobiotic diet, and practiced Zen meditation at every dawn. She'd never been married and had never spoken to him of her exes. Clifford wondered whether she was a lesbian, but she never gave him any indications one way or the other. She acted delighted to see him again and seemed to enjoy his company. She was the manager of customer relations at a major bank, and the one passion she betrayed was shopping for designer shoes with matching handbags.

She took him to the British Museum, where they shared a gee-whiz moment beholding the Rosetta Stone and marveling at both the ingenuity of scholarship and the certainty that the race has lost more significant written records than have been preserved. They spent an afternoon at the Tate, where the guts spilling out of the ugly humans in Francis Bacon paintings were so disgusting they decided to leave early in favor of cream tea. That night, they took in a show on the West End, a revival of *Billy*.

On their last Platonic day together, Priscilla suggested they drive out to Windsor Castle to take the tour. They couldn't avoid witnessing the Changing of the Guard. The Round Tower was not open to the public, and Clifford wondered whether anyone had ever bothered to scrub the blood off its walls. The Queen was not in residence at the time, so they were allowed to tour the State Apartments. Amid the overstuffed opulence, they saw Queen Mary's Doll's House, complete with its collection of miniature crown jewels.

The part of the tour Clifford remembered vividly was St. George's Chapel. Besides housing the tombs of sovereigns, including Henry VIII, the chapel is renowned for being the home of the Most Noble Order of the Garter, the highest order of chivalry, into which only a few of England's nobility may be inducted. Here is one of the venues where the monarch also confers honors such as the Order of the British Empire on military heroes, dignitaries, and celebrities. Not coincidentally, St. George is the patron saint of soldiers.

Their small tour group was escorted down the plush red carpet of the nave aisle as Clifford and Priscilla walked with them toward the altar. Clifford imagined throngs of dignitaries in the stalls on either side who would be looking down on him as he advanced in some solemn procession.

Until that moment, Clifford thought the expressions *spine-*

chilling and *blood running cold* were just colorful figures of speech. But suddenly the back of his neck felt ice-cold. As he drew closer to the place where investitures were made, the tips of his fingers went numb. Along with those sensations came a growing feeling of dread.

And with a stab of pain in his stomach, he felt an overwhelming sense of *shame*.

He whispered to Priscilla he was in distress, and they hurried out of the church. Within minutes when they were in the car on their way back to London, all his symptoms had disappeared.

THE MOST OMINOUS of these intimations — beyond the episodes of Queen Mary and St. George — occurred some years later, just before Clifford became engaged to Tessa. They'd been living together in his apartment on Christopher Street in the West Village for a month. They'd only known each other for three months, having met in a singles bar. In those early days, they were unsure about where their relationship was going, or whether they even had a relationship. She'd recently been through a nasty divorce from Milton Dunham, a fellow who was the stereotype of the sleazy traveling salesman. According to her, he was physically abusive to her when he was home and then totally unresponsive when he was absent, often for months at a time. On brief visits a year apart, he'd fathered her two children, Timothy, age four when Clifford met her, and Sarah, who had just turned three. She'd filed for divorce when she found out he had another family in another state.

Tessa was understandably distraught because her children were not with her. After the divorce and before she'd met Clifford,

Milton's girlfriend had assisted him in abducting the children on their second day of preschool. The girlfriend had arrived at the school unannounced. She told the staff she needed to take the children to the health clinic for their mandatory vaccinations, which were supposed to have been done before their admission. Unbelievably, whoever was in charge was more worried about the kids getting their shots than who would be taking them. No one thought to question the woman's identity, and so Timothy and Sarah disappeared along with their captors.

Even as she was getting involved with Clifford, Tessa remained sure she'd track Milton down and take back custody of her children. This was in the days before the federal Uniform Child Custody Act, which, if it had been in force at the time, would have carried criminal charges of kidnapping. As it was, the abduction was a civil dispute between divorced parties, made more complicated by differences between state laws.

In the early stages of my relationship with Tessa, I admit I was indifferent about whether she would ever get her children back. I could see the strain on her, and I feared an emotional breakdown would make it unbearable for us to remain together. But, realistically, I doubted she had the resources — or the persistent will — to prevail over a man who was both secretive and ruthless. I also admit it was her fervent and persistent passion — perhaps redirected from her frustration and anguish — that attracted me and kept me at her side.

Tessa had a star-shaped birthmark on the back of her neck. It was the size and color of a dried puddle of red wine. When she lay on her side facing away from Clifford in bed and her hair was pinned up, he could see the blemish protruding above the neckline of her pajamas. So, after she woke, he asked her about it. She said Tim had a similar one lower on his spine, and Sarah had one on her chest. She informed him she had a recurring dream about the three of them being chased by men on horseback. She dove into a dry waterhole for cover and dragged the children in after her. When a horse skidded to a halt at the edge of the pit, looming directly above them, its rider raised his rifle and shot the three of them at point-blank range.

It was a horrific story, but Clifford never regarded it as anything more than a fantasy. Yes, she and the children had similar birthmarks — not an unlikely consequence of shared genetics — and she'd come up with a rationalization for how and why her clan carried this trait. Tessa had said her ancestors were from Oklahoma. Clifford guessed hers was a Wild West story her subconscious had fabricated, and those raiders were Cheyenne, Arapaho, or Apache.

Not until much later — after Tessa had left him and he was married to Eleanor — did Clifford begin to suspect Tessa's story had anything to do with his memories of a former life as a British gentleman.

18

I *f I was some stuffy British guy in a former life, what the hell did he do that carried over into mine? And, no matter what it was, what difference would knowing the story make to me now?*

The following version of events may have been embedded somewhere in Clifford's subconscious. Or it may have been the plot line of some book or movie. Or it may exist in some etheric record in a library that can only be read by spiritual beings. Significant portions of it — that is, significant to Clifford — never showed up in any history book.

BRIGADE BRIGADIER ARTHUR MONTAGUE RATTIGAN studied the map of Afghanistan spread out in front of him on the desk in his command tent. The year was 1880, the month was August, and the ongoing crisis was the Second Anglo-Afghan war. For the second time this century, the British Army, supported by its loyal Indian sepoys, was trying to prevent Russian incursion into the region. A sizable Russian presence would threaten the stability of the British Raj in India. But neither the rulers of Afghanistan nor its unruly tribesmen wanted the imperial army there.

Rattigan's brigade was the remnant of a seven-thousand-man force that had made its encampments as far north as Kabul. In a series of major battles and minor skirmishes over the last two years, the fortunes of the Afghans and the British occupiers had reversed numerous times. The most recent setback for the British, less than a month ago, was the defeat of imperial forces under General Burrows at Maiwand. The victors were led by Ayub Khan, the son of the late Amir, who claimed he was his father's rightful successor, destined to rule the country and expel the invaders. The Russians were content to await the outcome.

What was left of Burrows' army retreated south to Kandahar. Ayub's forces followed them and inflicted more heavy losses. The British high command then decided that all their forces in the Kabul region should abandon their stations and proceed with all haste to Kandahar — there to reinforce Burrows, regroup, and be resupplied. If the tide of the conflict didn't turn, this would probably be the British Army's last stand of the war (which in fact it was).

It was late in the month, and the brigade Rattigan commanded would be among the last to leave the area. Decamping would be especially challenging for them because they would be burdened with both heavy armaments and chattels. As to weapons, besides scores of crates of rifles and ammunition, their deployment included a dozen seven-pound mountain guns and several Armstrong forty-pound breech-loaded cannon (the poundage referring to the size of the projectile). Mule teams would haul the rifles and mountain guns, and the elephants would pull the cannon. Leading these impudent and recalcitrant beasts with their iron burdens would be ponderous at the best of times. Rattigan feared there was no alternative. They had their orders. Leaving powerful weapons of war behind for the Afghans to capture was not an option.

The logistical category of chattels included equipment and supplies in the mess tents, forty-plus head of cattle and swine, and a crucial personal worry for Rattigan — his wife and two young children. Last year, after he had already been on post and away from home for eighteen months, Megan begged him in a series of weepy letters to allow her to join him in the field. Doing so was a privilege granted only to senior base commanders. Even in those cases, the army command did all it could to discourage it. But his wife was as willful as she was sorrowful, and eventually he'd allowed her wishes to prevail. No sooner had she and the children joined him than she judged life in the compound to be insupportable, even though she'd brought all the comforts of home, including copper cookware, Irish linens, down comforters, crystal glasses, a silver service, and fine bone china.

Much of the latter items could be abandoned. Let the Afghans have their tea — but not a single round of ammunition!

Rattigan was making a list of expendable items when Lt. Vijay Kumar, his Indian second-in-command, entered and requested permission to speak.

"I've come upon some potentially worrisome intelligence, sir," the officer said.

"Lieutenant, I assure you, we have all the worry we can handle at present," Rattigan quipped back. He had meant it as gallows humor, but Vijay either didn't get the joke or didn't want to break decorum.

"I have reason to believe an attack on the compound is being planned — within days, if not hours, from now."

"Your vigilance is commendable, Kumar, but I assure you there's not a contingent of Ayub's force anywhere within striking distance. I'm still getting reliable scouting reports. By now they are all well south of us, intent on running Burrows into the sea."

"Not the Afghan army, per se, sir. Tribesmen. A ragtag bunch, left-behinds, but whipped up and loyal to the Amir, and wanting no less than our heads. They will be armed and on horseback."

"How do you know?"

He gestured toward a scuffling sound outside the tent. "If you will permit me? It's not pretty."

"Proceed," Rattigan replied.

At Kumar's signal, two sepoys entered, dragging a frail old Afghan between them. The fellow's face was bloodied, his nose twisted and no doubt broken. There was blood also on his crumpled hands, which he held prayerfully in front of his dirty robe. His bent fingers may have also been broken or disjointed.

"I recognize this fellow, Bahlul," Rattigan said, wishing to God he had not been presented with this spectacle of suffering. He knew torture occurred as a matter of routine, but the protocol was he needn't be a party to it.

"Bahlul is one of our paid informers, sir," Kumar replied. "This evening he brought us the story and demanded his usual payment. With ordinary rumors, we would simply pay and weigh his version against the many others we receive. But in this case, the urgency and the magnitude of his news demanded our due diligence. So we were obligated to take other means to test his veracity."

"How many attackers?" Rattigan demanded as he stared down the sniveling fellow.

"More than a hundred," Bahlul replied, spitting blood.

Rattigan immediately wanted to know, "And when are they coming?"

"At daybreak," Bahlul said. "Day after tomorrow."

"Why wait?" Rattigan asked.

"Men and boys must be summoned from tribes all over. They need time to gather guns and horses. The boys will be on foot, carrying grenades and rocks and bottles."

The British soldiers in what was left of Rattigan's battalion numbered just sixteen now, having dwindled, due to sickness and malnutrition or as casualties of conflict, from a force several times as large. He commanded thirty-three more sepoys and their three Indian officers. They had four mule teams, six elephants, and sixteen large guns.

Staying and fighting would end in a rout. Even as unskilled as the Afghans were likely to be, no stratagem or superior military skills would prevail against a relentless force three times the battalion's size. Not only would his brigade and his family be decimated — but also their artillery would inevitably end up in the hands of the enemy.

Whatever Rattigan decided to do next, he could not allow any rumors of his plans to betray to the spies in the hills that he knew an attack was coming. Deception was his only tool, and he must act as if the British were as arrogant and foolish as the Afghans presumed they were.

19

Clifford's plans for his life did a turnabout when he fell in love with Tessa, or what he thought at the time to be love. Her soft, reflective side touched him, and he began to want what she wanted more than he wanted whatever it was he'd thought he wanted for himself. Fundamentally, he wanted to see her happy. He wanted the black cloud that followed her around to be swept away. He wanted her to laugh without caution or shame.

So he paid for a private investigator to find the children, then he hired a family-practice law firm to handle the paperwork. He went through the savings he'd accrued in his years of bachelorhood in a month. The court had no trouble ruling against Dunham in the fellow's absence. Once Tessa had custody officially, she and Clifford were married in a small ceremony in the dining room of a hotel in Midtown. Tim was ring bearer and Sarah was flower girl. His parents flew in to attend, still bewildered by his life choices, but his mother said confidentially she thought he was brave and doing a fine thing to take responsibility for those children. Tessa's widower father Hank was there, arriving from points unknown, having sobered up for the occasion. Their two best friends, a young couple who lived in their apartment building, were best man and maid of honor. The officiant was the pastor from a church that operated a soup kitchen in the Village, a congregation where Clifford had told himself he meant to join.

Ten years later, after the family had moved to Cleveland and then to Los Angeles, teenage Tim died in a freak sports accident. Tessa suffered an emotional breakdown that lasted two years, then she ran away with the maître d' of their favorite restaurant, leaving Clifford to care for fourteen-year-old Sarah. He was struggling financially at the time, as they pretty much always had since their marriage, and he would become all the more stressed when soon afterward he began his career transition from marketing to academia.

Sarah had been a shy and withdrawn child even before her brother's accident. She had Tessa's softness without her cleverness. Whereas the trauma of the kidnapping had made Tim a hyperactive risk-taker, Sarah cowered in his protective shadow and rarely made any decisions for herself. After her brother's death, she was numb and listless, and she never quite understood where he'd gone or why. Clifford and Tessa tried family therapy, going to a practitioner who took their case as charity work and didn't charge much. But Tessa's grief overwhelmed it all, and Sarah's issues retreated with her into the background. After Tessa left, Sarah had another bout of wondering how and why Tim was gone, but by this time she must have felt she deserved, or had somehow caused, all the hurtful events in her life.

During the time Clifford was a single parent, he had Sarah in private school and hired a cadre of college-age babysitters in the afternoons. He was giving serious consideration to quitting his

ad-biz job, but he couldn't live without a paycheck when having
to deal with attorney's fees for the divorce and teen care for
Sarah. His own emotions weren't exactly stable during this time,
either. He was about to ask his mother to come and live in for a
while to care for Sarah. But then Tessa showed up at his door
with her boyfriend and demanded custody of her child, as if Clifford, like Dunham, had meanly spirited the girl away.

Although Clifford feared Tessa wasn't yet ready for the responsibility, he didn't have much choice. Sarah was legally hers, and
letting the child go avoided the nasty alternative of inviting his
own mother back into his life on a daily basis. So he helped
Sarah pack her limited wardrobe, gave her a kiss, and promised
life would just get better and better for her from now on. Several
months later, after Tessa had refused to let him visit and then
moved with no forwarding address, he filed for divorce.

Having disposed of both his wife and his daughter — albeit not
voluntarily — Clifford went through with his plans to jump
from advertising to historical scholarship. He got by on a gradu-
ate-school internship with stipend at UCLA, combined with that
chunk of money he'd wheedled from his father. Franklin judged
that a professorship would someday be a more stable — and
more respectable — job for Clifford than the rollercoaster of
media hucksterism.

Two years later, after he'd taken the position at UCLA and
received the invitation to speak from East Anglia, he thought
Fate might be setting him up with the comely — and practical
— Priscilla Northcut. Her forthrightness might be just the thing
for him. But after her pleasant but sisterly companionship in
London, he crossed her off his list, which had no other names.

By now, he had most of his debts paid. He was living frugally
and even beginning to put a little money aside. His course load

and proctoring responsibilities didn't demand that he devote all day every day to work, but shifting gears from the commercial to the academic world was a jolting cultural adjustment. People in the world of money count success in terms of salary increases, bonuses, job titles, and office-space square footage (with potted plants as bonuses). But lacking large financial incentives (except for rarely successful book publications), professors measure success in seemly petty ego points and peer-awarded bumps in reputation. Steady income, yes. Getting rich, no. Clifford didn't offer to repay Franklin, who must not have expected it. University staff could take evening extension classes at a discount, so Clifford enrolled in an eight-week course in personal investment management. His goal was to make the most of what little he was managing to save. The content of the course, which met twice a week in a drab, windowless basement, was borderline useless. The instructor was a broker who specialized in annuities, and he had a self-serving agenda. But sitting opposite him in class was Eleanor Demarco, who turned out to have Priscilla's practicality (hence, her desire to manage her own money better) and Tessa's passionate volatility. On the last night of class, someone said, "Let's all go for coffee!"

CLIFFORD's grand epiphany about his former life came unbidden in September of 2001. He'd been married to Eleanor for eleven years, and their son Jeremy had just turned ten. Clifford was now an assistant professor at UCLA, and he'd published his first book, *The Death of Hypatia and the End of Fate.*

Eleanor was going through one of her recurring spiritual-discovery phases. She was reading everything she could find on Chinese acupuncture, wheatgrass application and diets, meditative visualization, and other alternative healing modalities. She was captivated by a series of books by Dr. Eliza Grossman, a clinical psychologist who had also studied with a similarly cross-cultural guru named Bobbyji in India and had taken for herself the name Lakshmi.

Eleanor told Clifford she wanted to help cancer patients who'd received terminal diagnoses to find alternative treatments. She wanted to go to Maui, where Lakshmi occasionally mentored a small group in her home. Lakshmi's students included both patients and practitioners.

Jeremy had just started a new school year in fifth grade. He liked his school and his teacher, and he already had plans for his big science-fair project. When his parents informed him they were planning a three-week vacation to Hawaii, Jeremy was happy to hear he could camp out for the duration at his geek-buddy Harvey's house. Among other attractions, Harvey had been gifted with a full-blown chemistry set and a high-powered microscope. As well, under wraps in his garage, Harvey harbored another toy that neither the Klovises nor Harvey's parents knew about. Over the summer the boys had recovered an old cathode-ray-tube TV from a trash heap. They'd already taken turns generating electrostatic discharges — three-inch-long lightning-like sparks — using the TV's high-voltage power supply. Occasionally they'd shocked themselves, first unintentionally, then with glee. Their parents must have never noticed the burn marks on the tips of their fingers.

LAKSHMI HAD HER LONG, graying hair pinned up on the back of her head, one stray lock falling down. She was dressed in a simple housecoat, as if she'd thrown it on after just coming from the beach. Were it not for her yoga pose as she sat cross-legged on the plush carpeted floor of her living room, she appeared to be what she had been before her studies in India — a highly educated New Jersey housewife who exuded kind generosity. The skin of her face was sallow, as if she rarely greeted the sun, and the bags under her eyes gave her a mournful, commiserating look, as if she'd seen more grief than she could bear.

On either side of her sat four other students, all middle-aged, all white and presumably middle-class. Eleanor had understood they'd arrived separately from the mainland the previous day. But, from the openness in their eyes and their passive expressions, you'd think they'd been sitting with their mentor for years. Eleanor had also said they were all somehow dealing with cancer.

A note taped to the front door, which had been left ajar, advised them to enter quietly without knocking.

"Welcome to my home," Lakshmi said with a weak smile as she gestured for them to join them in their poses.

Eleanor sat right down, but Clifford said, "I'll just be dropping Eleanor off."

"No reason to hurry away," Lakshmi said. "Please. Sit."

"But I haven't paid for the conference," Clifford said, unsure whether he had the right term for whatever type of session this would be.

The teacher's appraising gaze scanned him quickly from head to toe. He wondered whether he was being diagnosed.

"No matter," she said. "Something has brought you here." She glanced at the others, as if for approval, which of course she didn't need. "We are a small group. No reason you can't stay and participate, if you wish." Then she added after she'd closed both her eyes momentarily, as if consulting an inner voice, "I'm sure what you experience here will be far more valuable to yourself than whatever else you had planned."

I'd been considering hanging out at the bowling alley, so leaving now, in my mind, amounted to lying to my higher self that bowling was somehow more important than self-awareness. I hoped the good doctor wouldn't be presenting me with a bill at the end of the week, but I thought it would be insensitive to ask. At the time, I was also a younger, healthy male, and maybe she just liked my looks.

He sat and gave the room his own appraising glance. Lakshmi's townhouse was decorated as Mrs. Grossman's might have been, with careworn but not antique furniture in tones of avocado and mauve, as well as engravings of nineteenth-century whaling scenes, which at one time were staple wall décor in the hotels of Hawaii. His impression was that either she'd rented the place furnished or perhaps she'd borrowed someone else's for the duration of the seminar. He was sure none of the participants would have approved of killing whales, even though back when these drawings were made, whale oil lit the parlors of many a house.

The morning's work was taken up with introductions, followed by descriptions of each participant's personal challenges, along with their expectations for the weeklong session. Isaac, who preferred to be called Zok, was from Brooklyn but had recently retired to Haifa. His doctor back in the States had told him for years he could safely ignore his prostate cancer, but then on his last checkup its growth was significant enough for consideration of more aggressive treatment. Zok wanted to stop worrying so he could enjoy whatever time he had left. He stopped short of saying he wanted to be healed. Perhaps he thought it wasn't possible or was too much to ask.

April was from Scottsdale and wore a knitted cap to cover her bald head. She'd just completed a course of chemotherapy and didn't yet know whether it had arrested her disease.

Lucille was from Dallas. Her mother had recently lost her battle with breast cancer, and Lucille had been told she'd inherited the gene. She wanted to improve her chances, maybe even avoid having a tumor at all.

Magda was from Budapest. Her accent was so thick it was difficult to understand her English. She had a lump in her gut and wanted it gone.

Eleanor didn't pretend to be ill or worried about her own health. She stated that she'd been fascinated by Lakshmi's books and her therapeutic techniques. Eleanor wanted to experience them first-hand because she was considering studying to be a nurse practitioner with a concentration in hospice care.

Clifford shrugged and said as politely as he could that he was there to support Eleanor.

Through all the case histories, Lakshmi said not a word. She nodded in assent or appreciation from time to time. Clifford wondered whether this whole week mightn't be one long talk-therapy session, the kind where the shrink just sits back and lets the clients talk themselves into or out of whatever mindset they needed to be out of or into.

After they'd talked through the basics, their mentor encouraged them to go deeper, to express whatever fears they had at the core of their experience. *Cough it all up,* she seemed to say.

Zok was the most forthcoming and the first to speak. "I know I'm not going to live forever. And I've had a good life. I don't have any family left. Grandchildren would have been a blessing, but who's counting? I have extended family — friends I grew up with in Brooklyn — in Haifa. From my old shul. So, I'm comfortable there, accepted. They have children, and their children have children. So there are a lot of kids around. I play some chess, I babysit the children whenever anyone asks. I go to services. It's a peaceful, happy life. I don't need this *tsores* that followed me across the ocean. I'm a good man. I know this is not a punishment, so I wonder why it's happening. I don't know how many days I have left, God willing. But I just don't want to be miserable at the end."

Who of us does? But so many end that way, and who really cares? Medical science is all about extending life and relieving pain. What you're talking about, Zok, my friend, is icing on the cake.

Lakshmi finally spoke. "There is not a physical condition of the body that consciousness cannot heal. After all, we are not humans having a spiritual experience. We are eternal spiritual beings having a temporary human experience."

I'd heard this before.

She went on, "The body is simply a manifestation of spirit. We are what we wish to be, what we are destined to be, what we must be to learn whatever we have come here to learn. Whatever our state, be it fat or thin, tall or short, healthy or afflicted, it is, at some level, what we have *willed* to be. The spirit can never be hurt, harmed, or endangered. Therefore, at the level of the timeless, of the eternal, there is no disease. There is also no pain. But, understand, for the eternal soul there is also no joy, as we know it. No pleasure, no earthly sensations. To laugh, to taste food, you must have a body. Do you see? We endure the trials and the difficulties of this world because we lust for the human experience, for the sights and the sensations and the feelings. These are blessings."

So, the sufferer somehow brought the disease on himself? Blame the victim! Sure, for the oppressors, whether priests or potentates, it's the oldest trick in the book.

Clifford was caught off-guard when Lakshmi turned her full attention on him.

Has she read my *thoughts?*

"Mr. Klovis, tell us," she said. "Are there histories of disease in your family?"

He had to think for a moment. "Well, the only cancer I'm aware of, my grandfather had it in the throat. He was a chain smoker. Picked up the habit in the war, they say. My grandmother made him smoke in the bathroom when it was too cold for him to go outside. As I kid, I remember their whole house, the bedding, the carpets, reeked of smoke. Luckies or Camels, I don't remember which."

"Do you smoke?" she asked.

"No, never," he said, then added, "Okay. Some weed, years ago."

"And other conditions? Other than cancer?"

"I got TB," he admitted. "Slight case, but it kept me out of the army and the war."

"All right," she said. "What else?"

"Stroke," Clifford said. "I guess that's the big one, for us. My father, and also his mother, my grandmother. Minor episodes, grand mal seizures. His killed him right away. She wasn't too aware of her last few years on Earth."

"So do you worry you'll have a stroke?"

"Sure," Clifford mumbled. "Sure, I do."

"Do you know what Ram Dass said about stroke?"

"No," he said. "No, I don't."

She turned to the others to give the background. "As many of you no doubt know, Ram Dass, or Dr. Richard Alpert, began his practice much as I did — as a clinical psychologist. And, like me, his curiosity and his spiritual path took him to India, where he studied esoteric practices, including Hinduism and transcendental meditation. When he was in his eighties, he suffered a significant stroke — here in Hawaii, as a matter of fact. After his stroke, he depended a lot on caregivers for his physical comfort, but he claimed the ensuing years were among the richest in his life." She turned to Clifford and said, "Ram Dass said, 'I don't wish you the stroke. But I wish you the *wisdom* from the stroke.'"

"Meaning," Clifford asked her, "he had a lot of time to reflect?"

"I suppose so," she said, "although I haven't had the experience, so I really don't know."

By then, it was time for lunch. Lakshmi got up and brought a tray of sliced fruit from the kitchen. Everyone ate off the tray with their hands, and the only other refreshment was a pitcher of tepid water.

When they'd finished, there was nothing on the tray but a few watermelon seeds. Lakshmi passed around a damp towel for them to wipe their hands, and lunch was over.

"Now, I'm going to take a nap for a half-hour," she announced. She gestured to a pair of sliding glass doors by the couch. "I invite you to meditate on my patio, or nap also. If you have errands, now would be a suitable time. We will be continuing our work until about four, after which we will adjourn until morning."

Her seminar did not include lodging, so they were all staying in local hotels. Her townhouse was in an apartment complex just off the main highway, so it wasn't exactly a retreat. And, judging from lunch, Clifford was hoping they wouldn't be expected to stay for dinner.

Low-budget, get to know your local guru-shrink.

When the others had left the room, including Lakshmi, Eleanor was still seated. She caught his eye. "Well, what do you think? Do you want to stick with it?"

"I don't see why not," he said. "I mean, no blinding rays of light, as yet. But how can it hurt?"

"Okay," Eleanor said. "I think it's going to get interesting."

"In the academic sense or the Chinese?" Clifford quipped.

Just then, Lakshmi stepped quietly back into the room. It was just the three of them.

In a low voice, she said, "Now, if you two want to make love on the couch, feel free. It would give such positive energy to my house. Who knows? You might even conceive a child! And wouldn't that be wonderful?" And she turned and walked back to her bedroom.

The Klovises shared a look. There was no way.

Is there a video camera hidden somewhere? Would the others stumble in on us? Is the doctor wanting a three-way?

Another time, when they were on vacation in the Bahamas, Clifford and Eleanor had done it, naked on a deserted beach, caressed by the surf and somewhat irritated by the sand. Neither of them was feeling sufficiently adventurous now.

LAKSHMI'S THERAPEUTIC approach was mostly guided meditation, along with interviews about personal routines such as sleep habits, exercise, and diet. There were also discussions of close relationships, recent traumas, and milestone events. Even as unschooled as Clifford was in the field, nothing the doctor-guru said or did seemed unique or innovative. He had to admit though, that her powers of concentration and her compassion made each participant, including him, think he had her full attention. It was as if she would pull each of them through the process simply by the force of her own caring and will. And she informed them that, the year after she'd returned from India, she had cured herself of breast cancer.

On their last day with Lakshmi, she encouraged each of them to summarize their impressions and sensations during the sessions, along with sharing how their attitudes and expectations might have changed.

As Clifford had predicted on the first day, no one reported experiencing stunning enlightenment. But he didn't feel as though any of them had been cheated, either. They'd paid for Lakshmi's healing attentions, which they'd received individually and as a group, in generous helpings.

As a last exercise, Lakshmi proposed a group-hypnosis session during which they'd explore past lives.

She explained, "Some of my clients have told me they suspect they are fated to be sick because they have to burn some karma from a past life. I don't hold with this. Some of my colleagues in the field of psychiatry refer to all this past-life talk as *The Big So-What!* So what if you used to be Marie Antoinette? (No one is ever a common beggar or a thief!) If you can't remember much of that life, how can knowing you've lived before inform your decisions and actions now? And if you're destined to forget this life and its lessons as you enter the next one, isn't it kind of a pointless process?"

As with her other techniques, Lakshmi's past-life regression was straightforward. It was a counting backward from earliest-remembered childhood memories.

Clifford was thinking *so-what* when he felt the same ice-cold chill he'd experienced so many years ago at Windsor Castle. And the experience washed back over him.

Under the dome of St. George's before a hushed crowd, the man they called Rattigan stood ramrod straight in front of the aged queen. Her platform was just high enough to make her taller than he was. She therefore had to bend down slightly to pin the investiture on the chest of his red dress uniform. There alongside his battle ribbons she fastened the Victoria Cross. Beneath the lion symbolizing the sovereign and the image of the crown, its inscription read, *For Valor.*

He had told himself he wouldn't, that under any circumstance he shouldn't, that a soldier mustn't — but tears rolled down his cheeks. Her Majesty and her entourage no doubt thought they were tears of pride and patriotism.

He alone knew — and he could never confess to anyone — they were tears of shame.

RATTIGAN'S PLAN of action had gone strictly by the book —
ignoring the cruel reality that among the expendables in the
abandoned compound were his wife and children. Before dawn,
he led his brigade off to the north, opposite the direction in
which the enemy would expect him to retreat. They trekked
away from the compound, out of the line of fire and the
watchful eyes of the enemy's scouts, as if staging for a valiant but
useless onslaught elsewhere. They left the heavy guns behind in
the compound. They took the elephants with them but then sent
them off in another direction with their mahouts. The Afghans
would covet the cannon but would have difficulty moving them
without these animals. And they'd try only after they'd abandoned their pursuit of the British. On their northward journey,
Rattigan's men cached the rifles and the lighter guns in a cave.
Having done so, they were ready to turn south and make haste
on horseback to Kandahar.

After Kumar's visit and his fateful news, Rattigan had spent a
sleepless night in his command tent. He sent word to Megan he
was preparing for a dawn raid and wouldn't be returning home
until the foray was over. He couldn't bear to face her, and he
feared the sight of his children would melt his heart and his
resolve. He tried to tell himself it was all her fault for insisting on
joining him. He briefly considered feigning illness and staying
behind, defending them to the last. Or, he could wound himself
and claim an accident while cleaning his gun, in which case he'd
be an even more incapacitated defender. Or he could shoot them
as they slept, then blow his own head off, a rash act that seemed
both cowardly and unnecessary. None of those options would
change the result.

Most of his men had families too. Where would be the justice in sacrificing all his soldiers just to spare his own dear ones?

He decided his plan would not succeed without his leadership. Saving his own skin in the process was an unavoidable consequence, another military necessity.

After the brigade had set off, the enemy struck at the point of maximum vulnerability and maximum gain. The compound, its minimal guard detail, and its innocents were overrun and decimated. Before they rode off in search of the brigade, the attackers set fire to everything.

The two sepoys who tortured Bahlul had slit the old man's throat soon after leaving Rattigan's tent. Kumar had ordered it. They had no brig in which to confine the fellow, and setting him loose manacled would have resulted in a slow, cruel death. Decidedly, lest the man survive his wounds long enough to warn the enemy, he had to be eliminated. In his orders for the decampment, Rattigan had ordered Bahlul's torturers to stay behind with the minimal guard detail at the compound. They perished in the attack. They didn't know the plan for retreat, so even if they had survived and were tortured themselves, Rattigan's plan would stay secret. Kumar had been calculating and clever to the last.

So only the fiercely loyal Kumar knew of Rattigan's strategic decision. And the Indian was the only one in the brigade besides Rattigan who knew they'd had advance warning of an attack. To all the world, and especially to the high command and the military historians, it would forever look as though Rattigan had learned of the surprise attack on the compound after he'd led his brigade off on another routine mission. Then, despite the news he'd suffered a horrible personal sacrifice, his superiors would judge he'd orchestrated a valiant retreat that had spared his fighting force.

Twenty-nine of Rattigan's men made it back to Kandahar, including Kumar. Rattigan later worried the man would betray him, but the fellow succumbed to a fever just as the rest of the British army was shipping out for home.

Arthur Rattigan did not remarry. He took a furnished bachelor flat in Chelsea and lived off his military pension, which was more than ample for his needs. He played whist and chess at his club, and he occasionally accepted invitations to deliver after-dinner speeches about his adventures in far-off lands to church groups and ladies' aid societies.

His health was robust, and he lived to age ninety-three. His last voyage across the Atlantic was by first-class accommodation on RMS Queen Mary when he responded to a cousin's invitation to visit Boston. However, he never laid eyes on his relative because he suffered a fatal heart attack after a sumptuous dinner at the Waldorf Astoria the day of his arrival in New York.

His body was shipped back to England, where he was buried, not in his dress uniform, but in the bespoke worsted-wool suit he'd had tailored during his crossing.

Eleanor thought Clifford's past-life story was pure fantasy and told him so. Neither the other participants nor Lakshmi expressed opinions. That night, he tried to write it down. After he thought he'd captured all the details, with many edits and crossings-out, he realized it read like the script of a bad B movie.

The next morning was September 11, which would be the beginning of kick-back time he and Eleanor had planned for after the seminar. They woke at 4:30 a.m. Clifford drove their rental car west along the shore to the Wailea peninsula, where they met a tour guide and a small group of fellow enthusiasts. The water was calm and shallow there, perfect for launching kayaks. Eleanor wanted to see dolphins.

They went a half-mile out and paddled around for a couple of hours. Then the tour guide in the lead boat motioned for them all to circle back. By now, it was almost seven Hawaii time and the sun was up. When the other kayaks had drawn near, the guide stood up and announced that the World Trade Center had been attacked. He must have had the news before they'd set out, but, whether out of sensitivity or fear of demands for refunds, he'd delayed telling them.

Later in the day, they learned that the dolphins hadn't come because, per DEFCON protocols, the U.S. Navy had turned on its network of "underwater toys."

20

D ata drilling was Jeremy's favorite thing. Within his own lifetime, it had become possible to query the collected wisdom of the human race in seconds — on any subject. What was Sandy Koufax's batting average in 1952? What is the average annual rainfall in South Sudan? How do you add metal links to an expansion watchband? What makes the holes in Swiss cheese? Why did the ancient Mayan civilization disappear so suddenly?

During his day job, Jeremy developed and then fine-tuned algorithms for conducting searches of online databases. He'd built on a scheme known as *binary trees*. When a search engine finds a new piece of information, it stores the path to it as a sequence of directions through the networked information maze of cyberspace. Choice of direction at each junction, or node, is binary — left or right, one or zero. The path to the South Sudan rainfall result might involve a billion such choices: left-right-right-left-right-left-left-left, and so on. Before anyone ever searched for the information, finding the path to it took a while. But once the path was stored (as when a Web crawler hunted down a new keyword), traversing it again to receive the result typically took less than a billionth of a second. But in Jeremy's world, even those billionths can add up and snarl the works. His persistent goal was to make searches shorter and therefore more efficient. Doing so would make it feasible to search ever-larger and more complex databases — and collections of databases.

Jeremy's specialty as a programmer was the *balanced binary tree.* With all those left-right branchings, search trees tended over time to become lopsided, having many more nodes on one side than the other. But in a network of branches that is roughly symmetrical — having as many choices on one side as on the other — the time required to traverse any branch is a short as it can be. The tree at that point is said to be *balanced,* or *tuned.* Jeremy had found ingenious ways to rebalance binary trees in the background — performing his balancing act between searches, invisibly. His job was like a mechanic's on an old Jaguar sports car — the kind with manual rather than hydraulic valve lifters. The newer hydraulic lifters were forgiving, but sloppy. The mechanical type were precise, but fussy. Due to wear, weather, and changing oil viscosity, the valve timings kept going out of adjustment, requiring an expensive visit to the shop every few weeks. And in the days before electronic diagnostic equipment, the veteran mechanic had to develop an ear — like a piano tuner's — for the sweet spot when the engine was humming at its peak performance.

Jeremy thought of his job as a quest for the sweet spot. His goal was an elusive thing of beauty, all the rarer and more wonderful because few people — not even his colleagues, and certainly not their system users — would ever notice his invisible magic.

His algorithms existed in a world of mathematical abstraction. When he was tinkering with the internals of search engines, he cared not at all for the content of the searches that would benefit from his labors. His programming must work flawlessly, regardless of the user's keywords or the matching data retrieved.

But in his off-hours, Jeremy's quests were all about subject matter. No particular topic intrigued him the most. He was not a battlefield reenactment buff or a model-railroad enthusiast. No, he was the Don Quixote of data questers. He loved questions with elusive answers, chases up blind alleys, and cold cases from ancient history for which written records were almost nonexistent.

His father's past-life story about being an officer in the British Army was such a case. Even after Clifford's revelation in Lakshmi's seminar, he didn't know what his name was back then. He didn't even know which countries he was fighting in or for. He did assume he'd been decorated somehow because of the feeling of déjà vu he'd experienced on his visit to the chapel at Windsor Castle. And perhaps the most significant memory was his feelings — at the deepest level — not of pride, but of guilt. He alone knew he deserved to be horsewhipped or maybe hanged instead of applauded by royalty and members of Parliament as he stood on the red carpet.

Despite the scarcity of facts and lack of any plausible means of verification, Clifford had told the story many times. Jeremy had heard his father relate several such anecdotes from his life experiences, which tended to grow more colorful with each retelling. Clifford would launch into those tales at cocktail parties and in front of dinner guests and bridge partners — in fact, to anyone he could hold captive long enough to listen. What's more, knowing his audience might have heard the story before deterred Clifford not at all. Jeremy had read somewhere that traits common to storytellers were repetition and embellishment.

According to his biographers, Abraham Lincoln would pull you aside and talk your ear off with a tale you'd already heard from him, if you gave him half a chance.

So Jeffery had heard the cowardly soldier yarn countless times over the years. Like his mother, when he first heard it, Jeremy thought the plot sounded like a fantasy. He thought it might be from pulp fiction of yesteryear — something from the yarns about faraway places intended to titillate schoolboys by H. Ryder Haggard or Edgar Rice Burroughs.

In fact, when Jeremy started drilling into it, his initial objective was to find the fictional story or movie from which his father had unwittingly plagiarized the tale. Finding it would give Jeremy double satisfaction — inducing the source from minimal evidence, as well as showing his father to be a suckered believer in New Age hokum.

His father believed the story. It was not a deliberate concoction. Jeremy knew because, along with old letters and various ephemera, he'd also found Clifford's journals. There were note-books from college courses, trip logs of vacations, and diaries filled with musings and self-reflection. But Clifford was far from a diligent diarist. The journals were all in nicely bound, saddle-stitched books. But, except for the course notebooks, the journals were mostly empty. It was as though Clifford would buy a new book to mark the beginning of some new venture, record his thoughts for a week or two, then abandon the effort.

But there was enough of the past-life experience for Jeremy to understand that his father was deeply curious, if not troubled, by those events. In particular, he'd jotted down his thoughts about the Hawaii trip during each evening of Lakshmi's seminar.

Starting with the assumption that the basis of Clifford's fantasy was some work of fiction, Jeremy compiled lists of likely sources in both books and movies (and many of the movies had also been books). His short list included *Gunga Din, King of the Khyber Rifles,* and *The Five Feathers.* He did full-text searches of both plot summaries and the narratives themselves. Although he found similarities, including several descriptions of surprise raids on encampments by tribal forces, there were no stark parallels.

He then turned his attention to historical records. He remained open to the fictional possibilities, especially since he suspected, even hoped, that Clifford had mistaken a forgotten made-up story for real events.

The incidents on the Queen Mary and at Windsor Castle were milestones in time. But the Queen Mary clue was initially an ill-fitting piece of the puzzle. There had been three ships by that name. His Majesty's Ship Queen Mary was the last battleship built before World War I. It was commissioned in 1912 and was sunk in the Battle of Jutland in 1916. Most of the crew, numbering 1,266 sailors, went to the bottom. Although it would be plausible for an older British officer to have been aboard, Clifford's memory of a pharmacy — and of the tailor shop — suggested an ocean liner instead of a naval cruiser.

The first passenger ship bearing the name, the Royal Mail Ship Queen Mary, didn't begin transoceanic service until 1936. It was decommissioned in 1967. The old gal was the ship his parents had visited in Long Beach.

The third ship, the Royal Mail Ship Queen Mary II, is a modern luxury liner, still in service. Not a possibility.

To have been on the first passenger ship — while also being a veteran of some war in the nineteenth century — the fellow would need to have been elderly and on one of the early voyages.

Although British forces were deployed east as far as India in World War I, the overrunning of the encampment by tribesmen on horseback suggested some earlier conflict. The First Anglo-Afghan war began in 1839 and ended in 1842. That war was too early. The second went from 1878 to 1880. If the soldiers in Clifford's story were involved in the disastrous retreats near the end of the campaign, the math about the commander's age just might fit neatly into the puzzle.

To be a senior officer, and yet young enough to have made it onto the ocean liner at an advanced age, he'd have to have been in his thirties in 1880.

The investiture at Windsor Castle was another pin on the timeline. The Order of the British Empire didn't exist until King George V created the title in 1917. That year would have been late for honoring a veteran of the second war with the Afghans. Before then, Queen Victoria bestowed the Victoria Cross, which was a rarer honor given for bravery under fire. The commander's being honored near or after the end of the Afghan campaign would suggest a ceremony sometime in the 1890s. Although the Queen sometimes held such ceremonies at Buckingham Palace, the chapel at Windsor, named for its patron saint who is usually depicted slaying a dragon while in full armor, would have been the most appropriate venue for a military ceremony.

Military forces all over the world keep meticulous and often detailed records. Today's genealogical databases are replete with them. Because World War I chewed up soldiers like so much sausage, the list of knighthoods with the OBE is extensive, with thousands of names. Posthumous awards generally weren't given, but the policy was changed after the end of the war, which made the lists even longer. However, Jeremy didn't have any trouble finding listings of recipients of the Victoria Cross for the Second

Anglo-Afghan War. There were sixteen of those men. But none of them were officers who had been acknowledged for their command decisions. Almost all of them were of lower rank, and the main reason given for the decoration was their having gone back to rescue a wounded mate while outnumbered by the enemy and under fire.

As well, none of the VC recipients had lived long enough to have been a passenger even on the maiden voyage of the RMS Queen Mary. Most of them died before the turn of the century, many of them as casualties of later conflicts. One made it to 1925, and the last of them died in 1931.

The lateness of the Queen Mary voyage, whenever it was, had made Jeremy focus on the late stages of the Afghan war. He had to tie the strand of one episode to the end of the other, with the date of the investiture somewhere in-between. But no single set of facts met the case. Furthermore, none of the VC recipients' stories were remotely like the one Clifford told. And if all his remembered events didn't fit together on a single lifeline, the unraveling made a tightly knitted solution impossible.

Perhaps the ocean voyage, the investiture, and the war experience were all parts of different lifetimes. If the person who remembered the pharmacy on the Queen Mary was not the same as the soldier, the timeframe for the Afghan war could have been anytime during the first or second campaigns — and would span the entire nineteenth century. Also with those decades, the British were involved in many more foreign conflicts — not only in Afghanistan, but also in India, the Middle East, and Africa. The universe of possibilities was just too big.

Perhaps records of the war incident had been expunged. Or, more likely, the British high command didn't consider the incident sufficiently unusual for commendation. The VC commendations apparently were given not only to thank the heroes but also to pump up esprit de corps and thereby motivate heroic actions by ordinary soldiers in the future. Officers were expected to be clever, resourceful, and daring. They were not necessarily expected to put the welfare of the men under their command above the lives of noncombatants, especially British subjects, and certainly not of their loved ones.

There may have been no record of the command decision. For all anyone knew, the decimation of the compound, had it happened, was a surprise attack. Perhaps Clifford's recollection of receiving the VC wasn't accurate. Perhaps his former self attended someone else's investiture in the chapel and projected his guilt feelings on the event.

Jeremy had come to a dead end. If the Queen Mary and Afghan events were experiences within the same lifetime, he surmised that the likely wartime era was around the defeat of British forces at Maiwand.

21

On Clifford's television, Neil deGrasse Tyson was talking about the size of the universe. The accompanying animated illustration started with a micro view at the atomic level, then spiraled out — *there was the spiral again!* — expanding the view over and over until the entire known universe, a network of filaments containing more than two trillion galaxies, fit on the small screen.

Appalling to Clifford, the immensity of the universe was beyond words. Not just for him, for any breathing human. Certain mathematical notations can express its unimaginable size, but it's a useless abstraction unless all you want to do is more math. He remembered some of his science lessons from the 1950s. At the time, students learned about the solar system. And lots of people understood that most of the stars in the sky were other suns. But no one had the data to calculate — much less imagine — the size of the universe as it has become known based on deep-space observations in the first two decades of the twenty-first century. And now that new telescopes and sensing arrays were being stationed a million miles from Earth — how much bigger, in our calculations if not in our minds, could it all get?

Clifford recalled reading about how Tyson and some of his sci-geek buddies in theoretical physics had been toying for years with the notion that reality is somehow an artificial construct — a colossal computer game. James Gates at the University of Maryland remarked that the underlying math of some aspects of physics bears a strong resemblance to rigorously structured computer programming. Max Tegmark and Nick Bostrum speculated that perhaps our world is a simulation created by some advanced beings for their own amusement. Others guessed that the purpose instead is a study of history, as future scholars recreate the lives of their ancestors, in effect time-traveling back to relive pivotal eras in the emergence of civilization and technology. In this scenario, some of us exist here and now — and some are tourists from the future. Clifford's generation saw the advent of the computer, the global extension of consciousness called the Internet, and space travel. The generation before him invented the airplane, widespread electrification, and the atom bomb. Perhaps other researchers from tomorrow are dropping in on the innovative humans who discovered the wheel and the longbow.

Such theories would neatly solve the Fermi Paradox. We haven't been contacted by alien beings because we live in a tightly bounded reality they've created. The rules of the game don't permit contact — or, haven't yet.

Clifford thought he knew, as perhaps few of his fellow humans had yet appreciated, that these beings were the Insiders. Whether they were God's hierarchy of angels or the master race of the universe was a distinction without a difference. Clifford had suspected for a long time that the Earth was some kind of laboratory, the development of its creatures an experiment. But if

Darwinian evolution were as haphazard as the scientific consensus would have us believe, why do all living creatures share the same coding scheme based on DNA? Human technologists are just beginning to experiment with self-replicating robots, and they don't need to copy DNA to get the job done. Computer viruses are already as tenacious and successful as biological ones, but their codes don't look at all like DNA. In a random universe, surely the evolutionary process would have followed more than one scheme. And yet, with the DNA that fashions us all, tweak it one way and you get a cockroach, make a few changes and you get Leonardo da Vinci.

And at that moment, while Tyson ran a clip of Carl Sagan talking about "billions upon billions of stars," Clifford had an epiphany. This one was almost as thought-provoking as his obsessive curiosity about the spiral:

If the Insiders have created our reality, we are its co-creators.

For example, those theoretical physicists postulated there's something called the *Higgs boson.* They built a massive, highly complex machine to detect it. And after a few years of trial and error — they found the little critter.

But perhaps the Higgs boson didn't exist until someone looked for it!

Consider Heisenberg's Uncertainty Principle. And Schrödinger's Cat. The act of observation always affects the result of the experiment. Maybe molecules didn't exist until the Greek philosopher Democritus decreed they must. Maybe the stars were just pinpricks in velvet until humans devised instruments to study them more closely.

And — here was the stunner — if it's all an illusion, perhaps the immensity of the universe is a fiction, created to impart humility and awe in a race of lab rats who might otherwise think themselves gods.

Then, too, the notion of space-time is slippery. The radiation from star systems takes so long to reach us that those stars probably don't still exist. Although we have the proof it took successive generations of stars to produce the complex molecules in our bodies, it's just a presumption that star systems continue to evolve indefinitely. Way out there, there might be no *there* there. (And yet the astrophysicists assure us that the 14-billion-year-old universe is relatively young — and expanding!)

Yes, Clifford didn't fear the Insiders, but he was suspicious of their messages, and even more wary of their intentions. He suspected they were benign, but then his own little life had not seen much strife, compared to the sufferings of millions of his fellow humans.

Perhaps I've just been lucky.

A young man stood by Clifford's bed. He had not heard the fellow come in. The lad looked to be about twenty and was wearing a British public-school rep tie with an ill-fitting blazer.

"And you would be…?"

"Stephen Hawking, Mr. Klovis. I believe you have some questions."

"You look a lot like Eddie Redmayne," Clifford said.

The late theoretical physicist grinned sheepishly like the schoolboy he was pretending to be and admitted, "In some ways I liked his version of myself better." He shrugged, "I'm just a manifestation of your consciousness, after all."

Indeed, the apparition was an ideal version of Hawking, much as he must have looked when he attended Oxford as an undergrad-uate, before the onset of the motor neuron disease that crippled him so horribly in his adulthood.

"Questions?" Clifford asked.

"Sure," Hawking said. "Fire away."

Clifford didn't know where to start. Then he remembered one of those chicken-and-egg problems from his college philosophy course — the presumably unanswerable question that had dogged Leibnitz, Heidegger, and Wittgenstein: "Okay, why is there something rather than nothing?"

"Who says there's something? You were just thinking it's all some kind of simulation."

"Is it?"

"Our current version of the English language does not yet have the words to describe what 'it' is. You know, like those Greenlan-ders have so many different words for *snow?*"

"I had this argument with my dad. It irked him when I told him God is all that there is."

"That's a good one," Hawking said. "I suppose you could say *consciousness* is all that there is. If you want to call it God, it makes no odds in the scheme of things."

"Well, if consciousness is all that there is, are we all in a dream?"

"Not necessarily. The statement works no matter how you define reality. Reality is what consciousness perceives. It's the some-thing, and it's obviously not nothing. But you ask *why* it exists? Asking why implies there was a time when it didn't exist. If consciousness has always existed, there doesn't have to be a reason for its creation because it had no beginning and will have no end."

"Do *you* still have questions?"

"I'm still curious why time can't flow backward. I mean, the answer is entropy, but then there's the question why entropy is necessary. It gets silly and circular when you say, well, entropy exists to force time to flow forward. Maybe I'll come back as a dolphin to figure that one out. Bigger brain capacity, you see. And lots of free time!"

"I do have a question," Clifford said. "It's personal, though, and I wouldn't want to offend."

"To have emotions requires a physical body. Nerves in the stomach lining, feelings in your gut. I don't have the ability to take offense. So, go ahead. I'm all yours, so to speak."

"How did you get your nurse to fall in love with you? I mean, here you were in a wheelchair, all twisted up, and she falls for you?"

He shrugged. "It's no big mystery. We spent a lot of time together. As a caregiver, she cared whether I was happy. And I showed my gratitude by making her laugh."

Clifford wondered again whether he stood a chance with Myra. Maybe he'd have to come up with some jokes and break his vow of silence. He did value his autonomy more than he needed to satisfy his lust — but only slightly more.

Not long before he died, Hawking had speculated about possible future contact with space aliens. He predicted that contact could be disastrous for humans. He feared that a superior race would have about as much consideration for us as the Spanish conquistadores had for indigenous tribes.

"So what about the Insiders?" Clifford wanted to know. If anyone knew anything, this guy should. Not only must he have thought a lot about alien contact, but he'd undoubtedly also been bound by the Official Secrets Act when he was alive because of the sensitivity of any fundamental research in physics. So he might know a lot about the people who run the Deep State or the aliens who are posing as humans and waiting for the right time to take over the planet.

"Insiders? As in agents of the secret government? Stock market manipulators?"

"You know, aliens from outer space who might do us harm."

"I wouldn't worry about them," Hawking said with that sly grin of his. "I was kind of wrong about that."

"How do you mean?"

"The ones who seeded this planet are long gone. Maybe they lost interest? If there are any left, they don't know why they're here."

"There are some?"

"I'm not saying there are, and I'm not saying there aren't. I don't know of any. Just because I'm dead doesn't mean I'm all-knowing."

"But how could there *not* be? And what about the Fermi Paradox?"

"Civilizations don't last very long, in the scheme of things. The vastness of the universe makes any communication improbable because the different civilizations exist at widely separated times and distances."

Clifford let the remark sink in, then he said, "That's a disappointing answer."

Hawking shrugged. "No, it's beautiful. We're more like flowers than we are like rocks."

Clifford didn't want the great scientist to leave. But what more was there to ask?

"They preserved Einstein's brain," Clifford remembered. "Surely they didn't toss yours away."

"They have my head in a freezer," Hawking told him. "Someday maybe I'll wake up at a country club on Mars and chat with Walt Disney and Howard Hughes. I want to have a serious discussion with those guys about invention and playfulness." Then he added, "I like your notion of spirals, by the way. If they'd called waves *corkscrews* from the outset, humans might have developed *n*-dimensional math a lot sooner. But, at the end of the day, our understanding of the universe might not be different. Mathematics is not reality. It's a language to describe what we observe. Cheery-bye!"

Hawking gave him a wink and then dematerialized, as if beamed back up to the bridge of the Starship Enterprise.

22

J eremy generally dreaded airline flights when he had to travel on business. But when it came time to pay another visit to Willoway Manor, he actually looked forward to the trip. Even though there might be nothing he could do to improve his father's prognosis, he would be doing a son's duty. He would be checking on the treatment plan and the list of medications — including any reported side effects. He would cross-examine and harangue the attending physicians and care-givers — not to alienate them, but at least enough to command their due diligence. And he would be paying the bills.

He was in charge of the finances now, and he flew First Class. He rationalized the option because he needed a wheelchair with an attendant on the jetway. The attendant would lift him from the chair and carry him through the hatch and into his seat. Booking a seat close to the front of the plane avoided the inconveniences of being carried down the aisle like a big, floppy piece of luggage.

Far from being embarrassed by this procedure, Jeremy regarded it as royal treatment. He'd grown used to the typical reactions of the other passengers. Most would look, then glance away, then stare back to study him when they thought he might not be looking at them.

Jeremy figured their behavior would be no different if he were George Clooney or Elon Musk (ignoring the fact that neither of those celebrities probably flew commercial anymore).

Ever since he'd first required such assistance, he preferred the attendants to be women. But as he grew older and bulkier, the job required a larger and more muscular person. And perhaps because their work was more strenuous, the bigger folks didn't smell as nice. When he was lifted by a strapping guy — Jeremy imagined them to be dedicated weightlifters — the fellow's touch and stance were surer. Jeremy was not as afraid he could get dropped.

Life was so much easier when you trusted your caregivers. This aspect of Jeremy's logistical challenges made him appreciate how much Clifford's day-to-day comfort and wellbeing depended on the dedication of a small army of professionals.

Another thing delighted him about flying First. They took your coat and hung it up. Jeremy always traveled in a sport coat. He liked having concealed pockets for his pens and his glasses so he didn't advertise his geekdom. And whenever he went Back East, he insisted on carrying an overcoat, or at least a convertible rain-coat. To his mind, Southern Californians who didn't sufficiently fear the rigors of cold weather (rainy, snowy, or goddamn slushy) were just plain foolish.

This time, besides graciously accepting his navy blazer and gray Harris-tweed overcoat, the flight attendant efficiently found a way to store what Jeremy had come to call his *sticks*.

WHEN JEREMY ARRIVED at Willoway Manor, Myra was waiting for him behind the automatic glass doors. As his taxi pulled up, she brought a wheelchair out, and with the driver's help she hoisted Jeremy into it. Getting lifted up by Wonder Woman was much to be preferred to being manhandled by a mere mortal weightlifter. This chair was not electric, and he also decided he'd rather she do the driving.

"Good to see you, Jeremy," she said.

"Likewise, Myra," he said.

"Whatcha got there?" she asked, indicating the long, zippered oilskin bag in his lap.

"A surprise," he said cryptically. "How's he doing, by the way?"

"No change," she said and smiled. "Just as stubborn as yesterday."

She wheeled him into Clifford's room, where, having just cleaned his breakfast plate, the patient was sitting up in his elevated bed.

"Look who's here!" Myra announced, then said to Clifford, "We'll get you cleaned up and into some clothes soon enough. Not gonna let you loll around in your stinky peejays all day."

Just inside the doorway, Jeremy raised his hand and said to her, "Put the brake on, if you would." And she did.

He then unzipped the bag and removed a pair of bentwood canes. Grabbing a cane in either hand, he directed her, "Now lift me from behind by the shoulders." And she did.

As he shifted his weight to the canes, Jeremy stood up. He flashed Clifford a wry smile.

"Hi, Dad."

Clifford stared at him.

Jeremy!

Myra muttered, "Ohmigod" and moved to Jeremy's side. She reached out to cradle him by the waist, but he tossed his head to wave her off.

With slow determination, Jeremy took a dozen halting steps to the guest chair opposite the bed, turned, and let himself fall into it, panting and grinning with the exertion.

Catching his breath, he announced, "Stem cell therapy. UC Norris. Not approved yet. Got myself on the clinical trial. Not half bad, huh?"

Myra's gaze was fixed on Jeremy as she choked back a sob. Jeremy was studying Clifford's face as a tear ran down his father's right cheek.

"He's crying! Myra! *Do you see that?* My father is crying!"

She glanced over at Clifford and said, "I'll note it in his chart. But don't make too much of it. You're the one with the medical miracle." Indicating the wheelchair, she asked Jeremy, "Are you gonna need this for later?"

"Not ready to run the marathon," he said. "So leave it parked."

Myra nodded and said, "I'll get someone to clear his breakfast tray," and she left.

After she was out of earshot, Jeremy asked Clifford, "What's up with her? Are you pinching asses too?"

Don't I wish, Clifford thought. *But two wishes in one day? That's too much to expect. Wow! Just wow!*

Clifford was thrilled for his son, sure. But stirring at this moment was a conflicting swirl of emotions. He was all the more amazed because he'd never suspected — he'd never dared hope — that Jeremy would ever walk again.

Those types of spinal injuries just don't heal.

What's more — and this is where Clifford felt not just embarrassment but abject shame — he'd never given any thought to, much less taken any responsibility for, the prospect of his son's healing. He'd prayed often enough for a miracle for himself — knowing full well that miracles were unlikely if not impossible in his own case. But he hadn't prayed for Jeremy, not even for the boy's life to get better, much less to be able to walk.

And what about my conversation with Jesus — er, Christensen? I only asked for myself. Maybe the answer would have been different if I'd asked instead for Jeremy.

So the tear was as much for Clifford's shame as for his joy. Now he realized anything might be possible. Jeremy was walking, and Clifford was crying. But he feared he didn't deserve the same good fortune.

Jeremy didn't suspect any of this, and he continued in an optimistic mood.

"I wanted to report on my research," he said. "Not just weepy letters from old girlfriends. I found your journal entries about your past-life experience."

I wrote it down? That's embarrassing. What else did you find?

"I have your journals locked away," he hastened to add. "I mean, as to the letters, it seemed logical to destroy them. But I couldn't decide about those books. It's not like I'm getting phone calls from people who want to write your life story. I don't know, maybe I will someday?"

Jeremy proceeded to share the steps along the crumb trail of his investigations. He made it sound to Clifford as though he was building up to a big revelation, an astounding discovery, even proof that those past-life recollections had a solid basis in reality. Sadness and then sorrow welled up as Clifford imagined the slaughter of the British officer's wife and her children — even though he couldn't picture them and could hardly know their names. But the pain he'd lived through with Tessa and Timothy and Sarah in this life was all too real, pain he assumed was brought on by the cowardly actions of his former self. And those emotions brought more tears, which Jeremy couldn't help but see as he studied his father's face for any hint of recognition.

It puzzled Jeremy that Myra discounted his father's tears. They seemed proof he was present and reacting appropriately to stimuli.

It was the sign Jeremy had hoped for. He wanted — he craved — his father's forgiveness. He wasn't sure why.

"But I hit a wall," Jeremy concluded. "It seemed for a while there that all the pieces could fit together. But the military records didn't bear it out, and your guy couldn't have possibly received the Victoria Cross — unless someone way back when literally tore pages out of the official record."

Jeremy sighed. "I was left with the thought that your story was fanciful, and most probably the plot of some book — which you've long since forgotten you read — and it's so obscure I missed it."

Jeremy was looking down at his hands, which were folded in his lap. He looked back up, and there were now tears running down his own face. "But I've decided I don't want it to be fiction. We were never big on church. You never pushed it, neither did Mom. But I knew you had your beliefs. They were silly to me. You know, children, at some point, mock their parents. It's part of developing an independent personality, or so they say.

"What I got from you mainly, what I took away, was a belief in science. Maybe you passed it on because it was the best part of granddad and you didn't value your own career choices as much. You were certainly disapproving of his religion, and I'm glad you didn't push *that* on me.

"I was drawn to mathematics because, in that world, all the pieces have to fit. If it doesn't work, you throw it away, you ignore it, it must be extraneous data. My faith in — you might even call it my worship of — mathematics instilled no belief in the divine. I was a de facto agnostic — but I wasn't vehement about it, didn't give it a lot of thought. The purposelessness of the universe was a basic assumption, as fundamental as the law of gravity.

"But, oddly enough, not being able to carry my investigation into your story any further hasn't discouraged me from believing your recollections could be true. I've come to realize how selective the historical record must be, how entangled are the fates of individuals and the consequences of events. To make any sense of it all, historians need to generalize and simplify. But human experience is so much messier than they suppose. You know, truth is stranger than fiction — that idea.

"Most of all, my hopes have changed. From wanting your stories to be rooted in fantasy, I was shocked to find I *want* the notion of reincarnation to be real.

"No one knows how much longer either of us has. I mean, you

could outlive me. I could get hit by a truck." Then he muttered, "Although it seems like my karma in that regard has already been burned. Poor joke, I guess.

"I don't want to be morbid, but I might not see you again. What I'm saying is, for your sake — and for mine — I want there to be more. Maybe the lesson of all my data drilling is we don't get to know what more there is. Even if I'd nailed the guy, it might not be proof of anything.

"But what I do know is this — it matters that we *want* it."

Clifford didn't know what to say, even if he could.

"Oh," Jeremy said, in afterthought. "I got no reply from Natalie. I thought maybe I might have at least had a letter from one of her kids. Ruth Gold Beckwith still paints and owns a gallery in Austin, Texas. She has a son who is nineteen years older than I am. I also got this weird email from a woman named Gina Maslow — Gina for Aubergine, can you imagine?

"You see, I did this DNA test a couple of years back. You know, they do matching on those, and you get a notice of other subscribers who might be relatives. Well, this Gina says her test shows we're related — maybe even *closely* related. Her mother's name was Celeste Adelle Purdy, who is not around anymore to answer questions. Gina has no clue who her father was, and apparently her mother wasn't all that sure, and she never married. I've got a fair amount of genealogical data on both yours and Mom's sides, but I can't find a connection."

Clifford's confused mental circuits were on overload. There were apparently so many realities besides his own in which he must have played leading roles.

Whoa. Ruth? Celeste!

As Myra wheeled Jeremy from his father's room, she bent down to whisper in his ear, "I think I figure in there somewhere."

This threw him until he realized she must have been eavesdropping.

"How?" he asked, hoping for some new information.

"I have no idea," she said.

"Do you believe in this stuff? Reincarnation? Karma?"

"I don't know," she said. "I'd like to. But nobody ever lost a buck telling people what they want to hear." Then she asked him, "How much do you think your father understands?"

"A lot, I think," Jeremy said. "It's like you and the karma thing. I'd like to believe it. Is there a reason he's special to you? I want to believe he understands it all. When I was growing up, we didn't talk much, and even then it was mostly him lecturing me. I never really knew him as a person, not until I found his letters and his journals. So those are talking to me now, and I'm answering back to him."

"I don't know it for a fact," she said. "But I suspect, if he can think, he's spending his time trying to put it all together. *He* might just be getting to know himself as a person now."

23

How to get Myra to care deeply for him — the problem burned in Clifford's brain more than the structure of the universe or the nature of consciousness. More than the meaning of spirals or the elegance of math. Those questions were mind games for geeks. Admittedly, he was one. Or had been. But who would pay attention to him now, even if he could or would speak? Other more accomplished theorists would get Nobel prizes for puzzling it all out someday.

He thought the spiral thing was important. Hawking said the notion of the corkscrew *could* have made a difference way back when. But mathematics must have evolved well enough, having progressed according to a different point of view from the one Clifford was suggesting. After all, this math got astronauts to and from the tiny International Space Station with regularity.

Hawking surely had it right about women, though. Make the lady laugh. You didn't need to be a Nobel winner to figure that one out. But — break his vow of silence? Language would be essential, fundamental, to any successful plan. Fart sounds and burps might amuse but wouldn't get him the quality of attention he craved.

The question was now unavoidable — could Clifford speak if he wanted to?

He had told himself he'd been withholding speech. It took a Herculean strength of will to resist the diagnostic prodding and poking, to remain passive and unresponsive to all those cleverly devised stimuli.

Have I outwitted their tests or simply failed them?

Dr. Zahra Gilani waltzed into Clifford's room surrounded by an entourage of sober-faced interns. Her beautiful face was heavily made-up with eyeliner and rose-tinted shadow. Her abundant, raven hair was styled full and long in a smart, sumptuous wave. She wore a brightly colored Hermes scarf and dangling earrings, as if to defy the drabness of her lab coat. Her skin was the same cappuccino color as Myra's, and if the woman hadn't proven to be so officious and rude, Clifford would have fallen in love all over again. Her gaggle of young interns appeared to be of various Asian races, with one round-faced female African who was trying her best not to smile.

Here is the future, Clifford thought. *After a few more generations, the complexion of the human race will be a uniform mocha color with almond eyes. The official language will be English, but a streamlined lexicon in which all idiosyncrasies of spelling and pronunciation have been removed. Will those be improvements?*

The click-click of the doctor's designer high heels on the polished floor added to her efficient, haughty air. She had been lecturing loudly nonstop since she was within earshot in the hallway:

"As you know, dementia is not a disease but a matrix of symptoms with various causation. For example, Mr. Klovis here has not spoken a word since his admission two months ago. One might suspect the onset of Alzheimer's, but that is decidedly not the case with him. Mr. Klovis suffered a stroke in the frontal lobe and prior to the event presented no evidence of pathology. However, in numerous forms of dementia, including Alzheimer's, loss of speech is typically a precursor of a cascading series of progressive disabilities. As of now, Mr. Klovis can feed himself, and he can go to the toilet on his own. But he can't fill out his daily menu selections in the morning. So that's not only loss of speech but also indicative of impairment of verbal skills, perhaps of the ability to conceptualize."

A tall young man who might have been Malaysian raised his hand meekly. Receiving a curt nod from Dr. Gilani, he asked with an apologetic wince, "Do you think he understands what you're saying?"

She replied, "An excellent question, Dr. Yii." The senior doctor didn't seem at all embarrassed by the possibility she might have inflicted an indignity on the patient. "In many cases, a speechless patient may retain the ability to understand conversation. A simple test is whether the person can respond to yes-or-no questions." She turned abruptly toward Clifford and asked him, "Isn't that right, Mr. Klovis?"

Clifford stared at her impassively.

"He doesn't respond to questions, you see. A pinprick in his arm, and he will flinch. But if you ask him whether it hurts, or whether an ice cube is cold or hot, you won't get an answer."

"But," Yii persisted, "if he can walk to the restroom, surely he can pick up a pencil."

"He might be able to grasp it," Gilani said. "But he won't know what to do with it."

She hasn't seen my spirals!

Yii offered, "Is there a lack of motivation? Maybe antidepressants would help?"

"Is he depressed?" Gilani asked with rhetorical vehemence. "How do you diagnose? How do you assess *affect* — listlessness? That's not much to go on. There are side effects, including some adverse ones in some patients with mental impairment. Some clinicians might take a scientific, wild-ass guess, administer a drug, and see what happens. Such an approach would not be sound medical practice, *doctor.*"

Raising an inquisitive but half-hearted wrist, an Asian woman asked, "What about brain activity? What do his scans show?"

"Glad you could join us, Dr. Kihara. A perfectly logical line of inquiry. There are basically two issues here. One is cost-benefit. Is the expense of an MRI series justified? We're not a research institution. Put bluntly, what practical difference would it make to his care whether he can understand us — especially since the communication would seem to be only one-way. The second issue is, if we do scans to highlight region-specific activity, what will we learn? Anybody?"

"You could see whether there's activity in verbal regions in response to questions," Yii offered.

"Yes," Gilani replied with a smirk. "But how do we interpret any activity we see? Is it coherent thought or a meaningless jumble or just noise? We don't yet have the technology to know. What you're asking for is a mind-reading machine." She focused directly on Yii and said, "Teams are working on it. If you make it through your residency here, go for it if you want to waste your time." Turning on her heel, she announced, "We're done here."

The chocolate-skinned intern gave Clifford a commiserating smile. As she followed the others out, she called after them, "Do any of the speechless patients express themselves at all?"

Clifford could hear Gilani's laugh in the hallway as she shot back, "Believe it or not, some of them *sing!*"

Singing? Singing!

Clifford had never thought of himself as a singer.

Perhaps having a stroke makes you better at it?

Here could be a way to captivate Myra. As with his other undisclosed capabilities, his crooning to her could remain their secret.

How delicious!

He hummed to himself quietly, as the leader of an a capella group might set the pitch before the others join in song. Clifford's vocal cords were working — responding to what sounded to his partially trained ear as middle C!

Hot damn! But what to sing?

Despite all those times he'd played The Band's songs on lonely weekends, he couldn't remember a word. True, he'd logged all those hours with Miriam listening to the Beatles, but he couldn't recall more than a phrase. To him, it was never about the lyrics. (And when you're stoned, the words might not mean the same as when you're sober.) He figured humming Schumann to Myra could amaze her, but she might think his achievement a mere parlor trick rather than an expression of love.

He could probably manage the national anthem or *America the Beautiful.* Not the stuff of sentiment unless you were huddling in some foxhole together getting shelled.

He *did* remember some of the hymns they sang in church when he was a boy. Everyone in the congregation sang — most of them at full volume, whether or not they could carry a tune. Many of the lyrics were dreary — all about sin and suffering. But others were pure expressions of joy.

His memory took a side trip just then. In Southern Baptist churches, typically once a year, they'd hold a weeklong series of meetings called a *revival.* Besides a lot of singing, group prayer, and the occasional inspirational shouting, there would be a guest speaker — an evangelist who had a soul-winning rep, recruited from the wide world (and paid handsomely) to pump up the locals with a big, fresh dose of the Holy Spirit.

Back then — or perhaps ever — the world's soul-winningest revival speaker was the Reverend Billy Graham. Even when he was a young man, the crowd-drawing power of his superstardom exceeded the capacity of the largest churches in any city. His revival tours would fill sprawling auditoriums, converted warehouses, exhibition halls, and even ballparks — requiring gargantuan public-address systems to reach each and every eager standee at the back of the enormous throng of worshippers, as well as repentant backsliders and salvation seekers.

When Clifford was barely preschool age, his parents took him along to see and hear the great Billy Graham.

Graham's retinue included a bass-baritone — George Beverly Shea — whose thunderous voice, amplified by megawatts, could shake the rafters, make hearts bleed, and suck the tears out of dry eyes. The guy had the build of a stevedore and the pock-marked, pulverized face of a prize-fighter. Belting out a song from the podium in a sky-blue suit, he exuded humility and conviction. If this big Irishman feared God, there was no place for anyone else to hide.

Shea's signature song was *How Great Thou Art,* and Clifford remembered most of it. But even though he regarded Myra as downright spectacular, he feared the message of the song wasn't suitable. (She might mistake the lyrics for his admiration of her, which would be true enough, but hardly appropriate to the song.) The lyrics of another of the recurring favorites of Shea's fans were just as lofty, but the message was more intimate. *Out of the Ivory Palaces* had a haunting waltz melody. And it was a love song, albeit a profound expression of love for Jesus.

Very quietly, in tones low enough he was sure no one could hear, Clifford sang:

> *Out of the Ivory Palaces*
> *Into a world of woe*
> *Only His great redeeming love*
> *Made my Savior go.*

The words didn't make sense in the present context. They expressed more emotionally than they meant logically.

Ivory palaces? Surely God wouldn't build a heaven out of elephant carcasses!

World of woe? Well, yes, there is plenty of woe here to go around, but there is also coffee, wine, Italian cooking, and Sunday-afternoon sex on cold winter days with a log on the fire.

The rest of the chorus had the same theme as *Jesus Loves Me,* but the combination of the waltz melody and the longing between the lines was magical.

Clifford had long since decided that fundamentalist Christianity was naïve, sometimes willfully ignorant, and often bigoted. Nevertheless, in this moment, the song brought a tear. Hearing himself sing — and forming words with his lips — was momentous enough. But the emotion coming up was a vein of molten gold buried deep in his past.

He was a little boy in short pants, holding hands with both of his parents, looking up at them with trust and awe, hearing the sweetness of his mother's voice singing along — and watching in amazement as tears streamed down his father's face.

He thought:

If you believe something fervently, does it matter whether other people think it's true?

Is faith not beautiful or valuable or precious if it's based on fantasy?

Is love not love if it's abandoned or betrayed?

His mother had become an embittered wreck. His father had turned into a humorless cynic — doubly hypocritical because he continued to parrot the punitive teachings of his church long after he'd ceased to practice them.

And, as for Clifford, he thought his stroke had walled him off from ever experiencing love again.

I won't sing to Myra right away. I need to consider the consequences carefully first.

And I need to rehearse!

ABOUT THE AUTHOR

Gerald Everett Jones is a freelance writer who lives in Santa Monica, California. *Clifford's Spiral* is his ninth novel. He is a member of the Writers Guild of America, the Dramatists Guild, Women's National Book Association, and Film Independent (FIND), as well as a director of the Independent Writers of Southern California (IWOSC). He holds a Bachelor of Arts with Honors from the College of Letters, Wesleyan University, where he studied under novelists Peter Boynton *(Stone Island)*, F.D. Reeve *(The Red Machines)*, and Jerzy Kosinski *(The Painted Bird, Being There)*.

He is the host of the GetPublished! Radio Show (getpublishedradio.com), and his book reviews are published on the Web by *Splash Magazines Worldwide* (splashmagazines.com).

Photo by Gabriella Muttone Photography, Hollywood

ALSO BY GERALD EVERETT JONES

Fiction

Preacher Finds a Corpse: An Evan Wycliff Mystery (#1)

The Misadventures of Rollo Hemphill (#1 - 3)

My Inflatable Friend

Rubber Babes

Farnsworth's Revenge

Mr. Ballpoint

Christmas Karma

Choke Hold: An Eli Wolff Thriller

Bonfire of the Vanderbilts / *Bonfire of the Vanderbilts: Scholar's Edition*

Stories and Essay

Boychik Lit

Nonfiction

White-Collar Migrant Worker: Finding Your Way in the Gig Economy (series)

How to Lie with Charts

The Death of Hypatia and the End of Fate

The Light in His Soul: Lessons from My Brother's Schizophrenia (with Rebecca Schaper)

Searching for Jonah: Clues in Hebrew and Assyrian History by Don E. Jones (Afterword)